STAR TREK®
NERO

STORY
ROBERTO ORCI & ALEX KURTZMAN

WRITERS
MIKE JOHNSON & TIM JONES

ARTIST
DAVID MESSINA

COLORIST
GIOVANNA NIRO

LETTERER
NEIL UYETAKE

ORIGINAL SERIES EDITOR
SCOTT DUNBIER

COLLECTION EDITORS
JUSTIN EISINGER & MARIAH HUEHNER

COLLECTION DESIGNER
NEIL UYETAKE

IDW Publishing
Operations:
Ted Adams, Chief Executive Officer
Greg Goldstein, Chief Operating Officer
Matthew Ruzicka, CPA, Chief Financial Officer
Alan Payne, VP of Sales
Lorelei Bunjes, Dir. of Digital Services
AnnaMaria White, Marketing & PR Manager
Marci Hubbard, Executive Assistant
Alonzo Simon, Shipping Manager
Angela Loggins, Staff Accountant

Editorial:
Chris Ryall, Publisher/Editor-in-Chief
Scott Dunbier, Editor, Special Projects
Andy Schmidt, Senior Editor
Bob Schreck, Senior Editor
Justin Eisinger, Editor
Kris Oprisko, Editor/Foreign Lic.
Denton J. Tipton, Editor
Tom Waltz, Editor
Mariah Huehner, Associate Editor
Carlos Guzman, Editorial Assistant

Design:
Robbie Robbins, EVP/Sr. Graphic Artist
Neil Uyetake, Art Director
Chris Mowry, Graphic Artist
Amauri Osorio, Graphic Artist
Gilberto Lazcano, Production Assistant
Shawn Lee, Production Assistant

STAR TREK created by Gene Roddenberry
Special thanks to Risa Kessler and John Van Citters at CBS Consumer Products, David Baronoff and JJ Abrams at Bad Robot, and Rick Sternbach for their invaluable assistance.

www.IDWPUBLISHING.com
ISBN: 978-1-60010-603-3   13 12 11 10   1 2 3 4

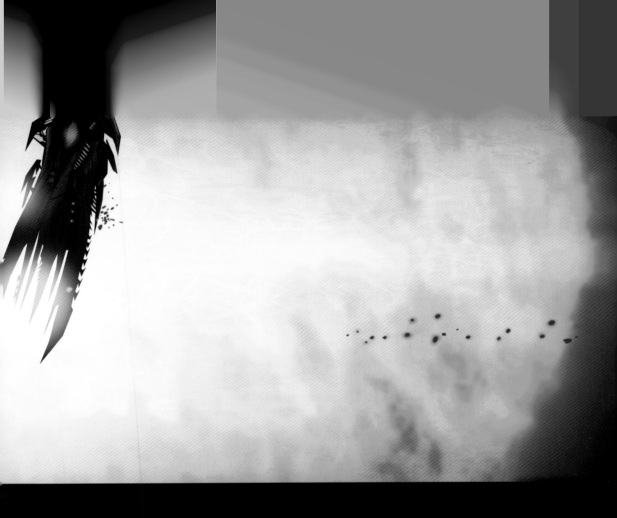

STAR TREK®

NERO

CHAPTER ONE

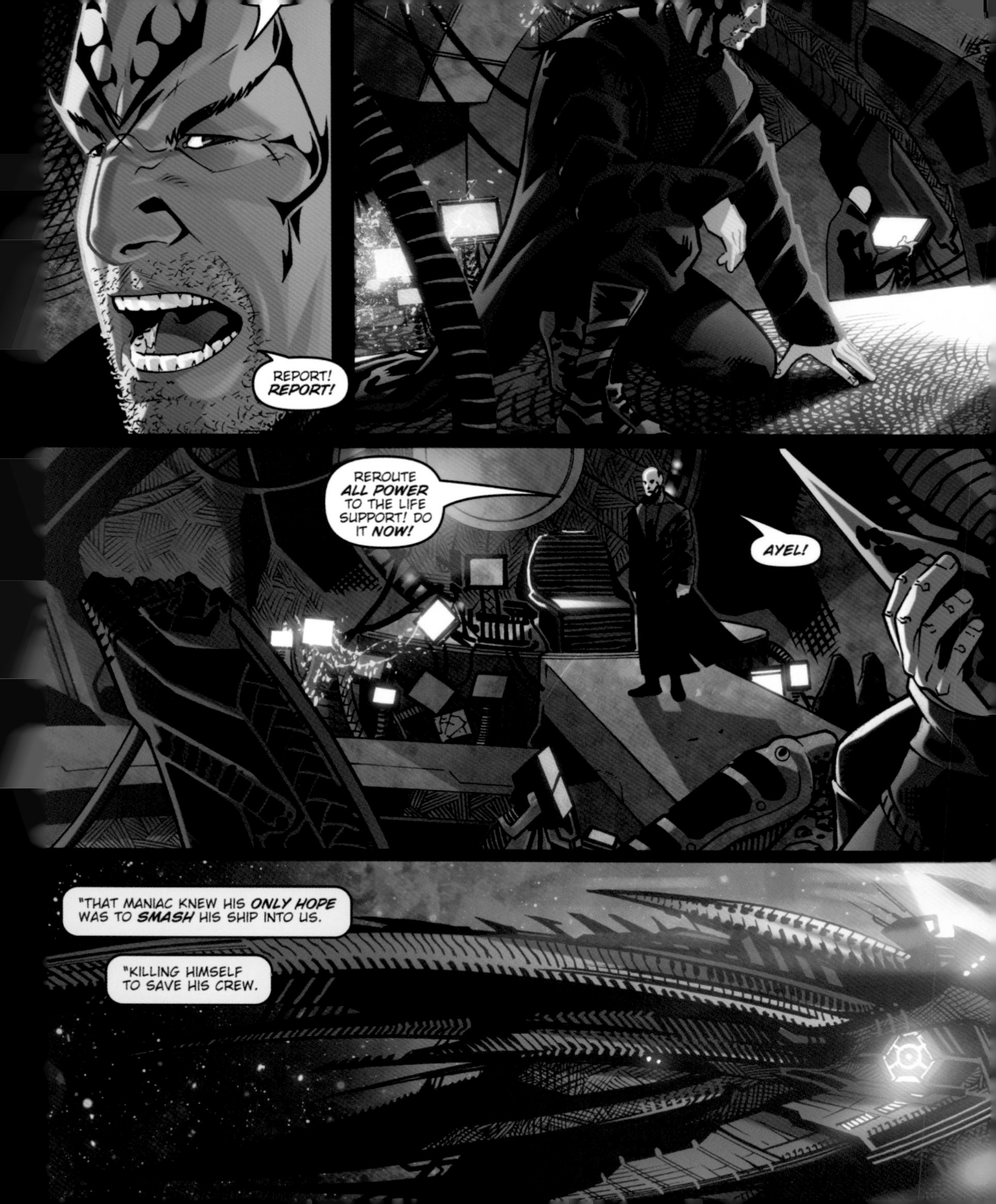
REPORT! REPORT!
REROUTE ALL POWER TO THE LIFE SUPPORT! DO IT NOW!
AYEL!
"THAT MANIAC KNEW HIS ONLY HOPE WAS TO SMASH HIS SHIP INTO US.
"KILLING HIMSELF TO SAVE HIS CREW.

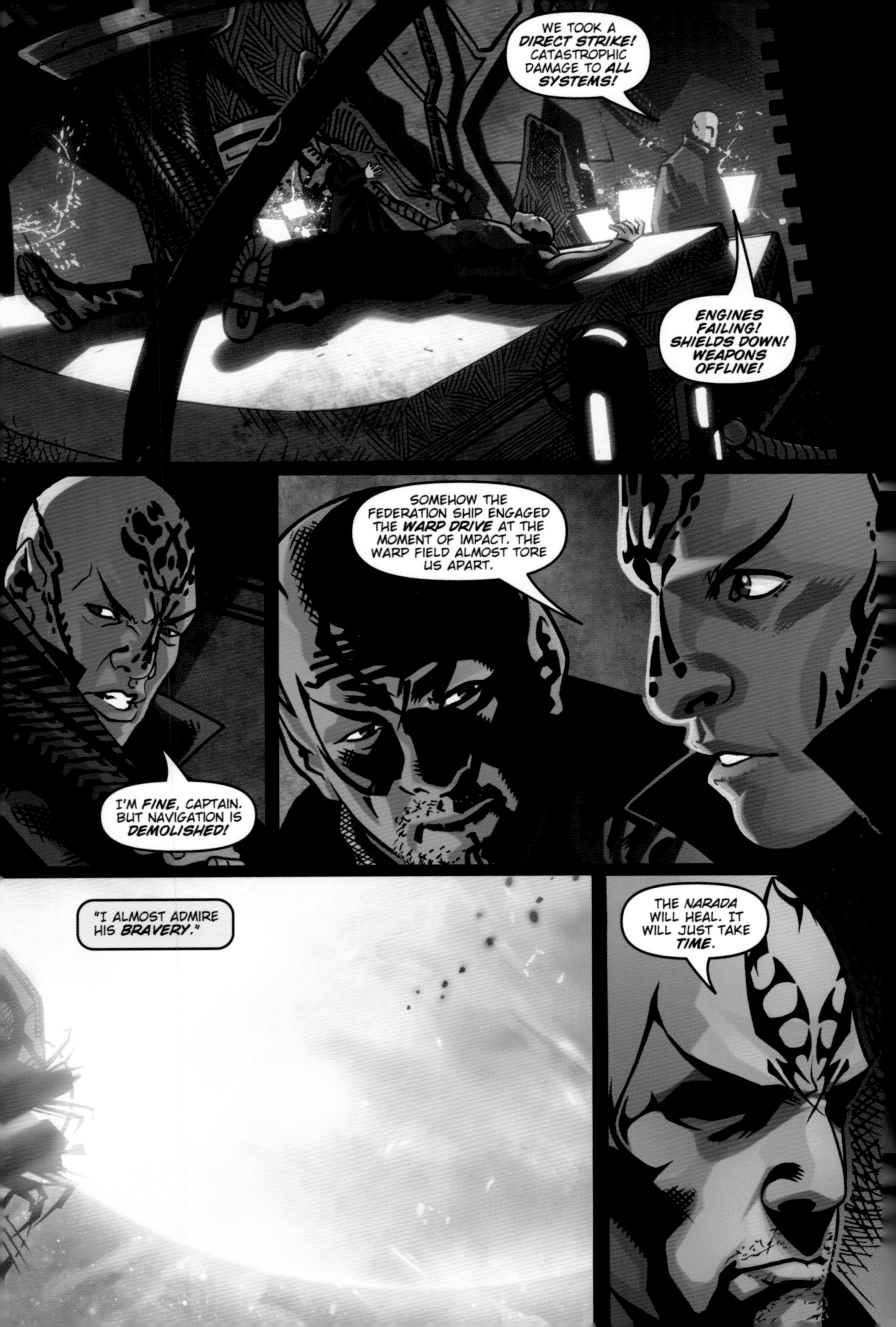
WE TOOK A DIRECT STRIKE! CATASTROPHIC DAMAGE TO ALL SYSTEMS!
ENGINES FAILING! SHIELDS DOWN! WEAPONS OFFLINE!
I'M FINE, CAPTAIN. BUT NAVIGATION IS DEMOLISHED!
SOMEHOW THE FEDERATION SHIP ENGAGED THE WARP DRIVE AT THE MOMENT OF IMPACT. THE WARP FIELD ALMOST TORE US APART.
"I ALMOST ADMIRE HIS BRAVERY."
THE NARADA WILL HEAL. IT WILL JUST TAKE TIME.

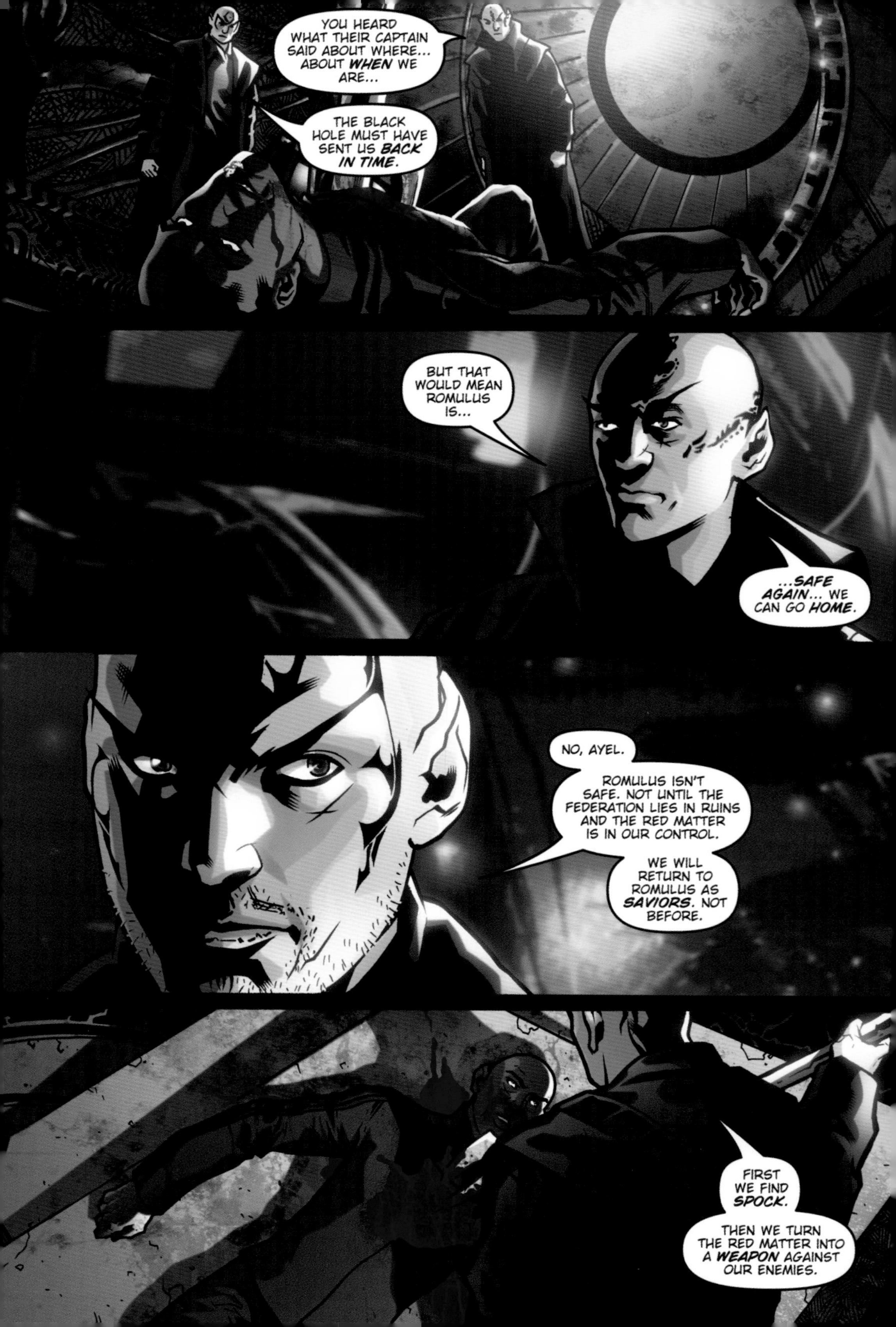

YOU HEARD WHAT THEIR CAPTAIN SAID ABOUT WHERE... ABOUT *WHEN* WE ARE...
THE BLACK HOLE MUST HAVE SENT US *BACK IN TIME*.
BUT THAT WOULD MEAN ROMULUS IS...
...*SAFE AGAIN*... WE CAN GO *HOME*.
NO, AYEL.
ROMULUS ISN'T SAFE. NOT UNTIL THE FEDERATION LIES IN RUINS AND THE RED MATTER IS IN OUR CONTROL.
WE WILL RETURN TO ROMULUS AS *SAVIORS*. NOT BEFORE.
FIRST WE FIND *SPOCK*.
THEN WE TURN THE RED MATTER INTO A *WEAPON* AGAINST OUR ENEMIES.

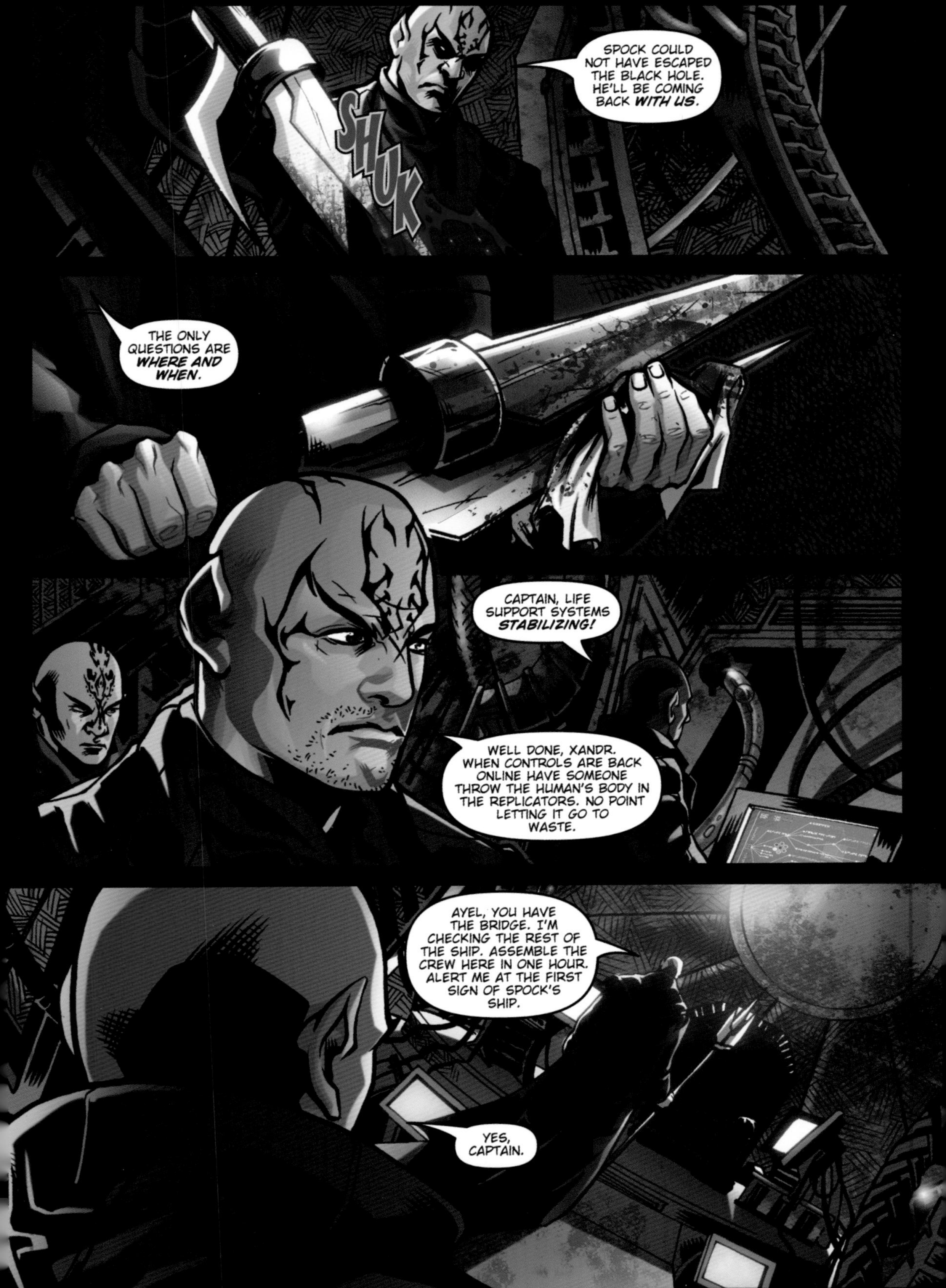
SPOCK COULD NOT HAVE ESCAPED THE BLACK HOLE. HE'LL BE COMING BACK ***WITH US***.
SHUK
THE ONLY QUESTIONS ARE ***WHERE AND WHEN***.
CAPTAIN, LIFE SUPPORT SYSTEMS ***STABILIZING!***
WELL DONE, XANDR. WHEN CONTROLS ARE BACK ONLINE HAVE SOMEONE THROW THE HUMAN'S BODY IN THE REPLICATORS. NO POINT LETTING IT GO TO WASTE.
AYEL, YOU HAVE THE BRIDGE. I'M CHECKING THE REST OF THE SHIP. ASSEMBLE THE CREW HERE IN ONE HOUR. ALERT ME AT THE FIRST SIGN OF SPOCK'S SHIP.
YES, CAPTAIN.

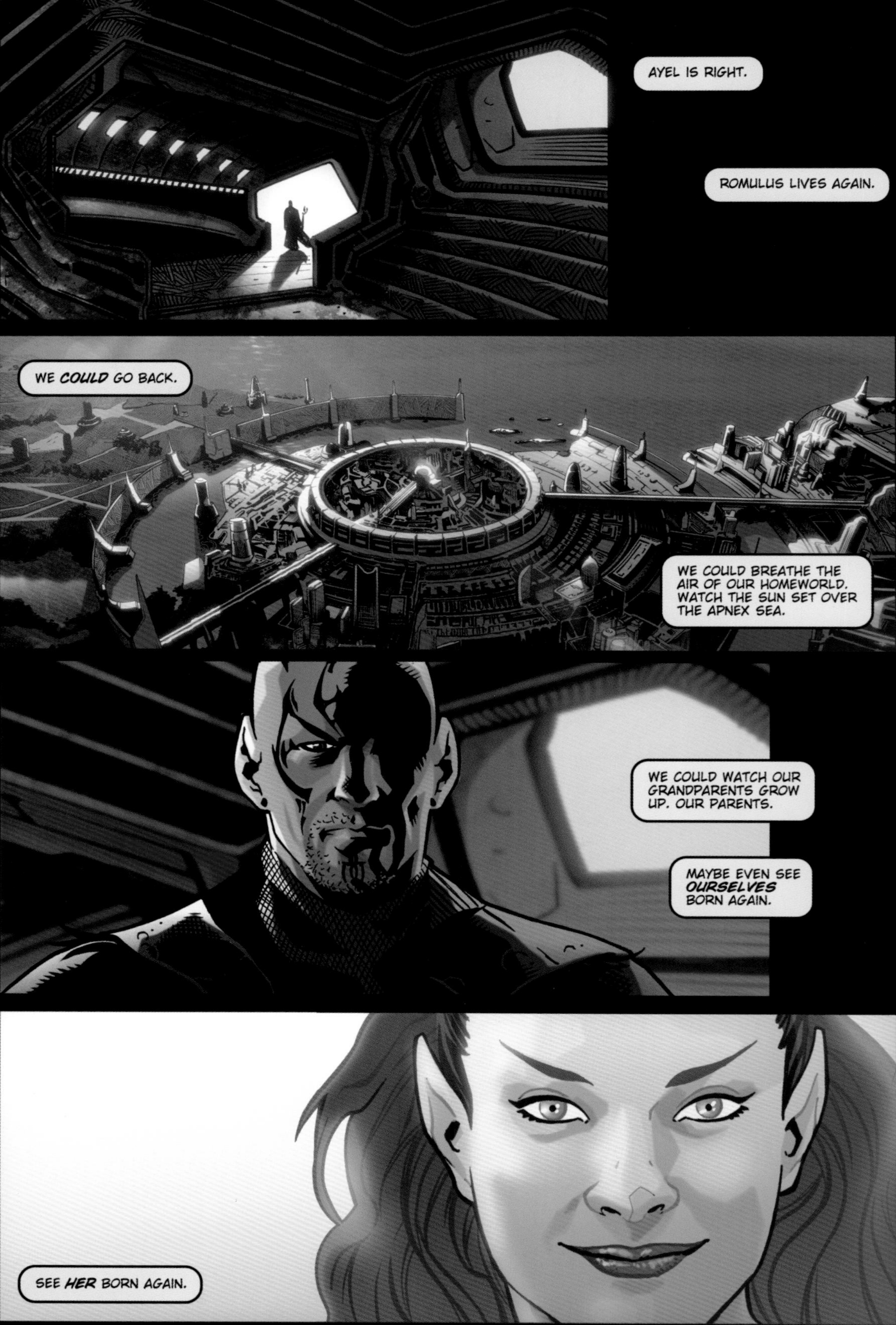
AYEL IS RIGHT.
ROMULUS LIVES AGAIN.
WE COULD GO BACK.
WE COULD BREATHE THE AIR OF OUR HOMEWORLD. WATCH THE SUN SET OVER THE APNEX SEA.
WE COULD WATCH OUR GRANDPARENTS GROW UP. OUR PARENTS.
MAYBE EVEN SEE OURSELVES BORN AGAIN.
SEE HER BORN AGAIN.

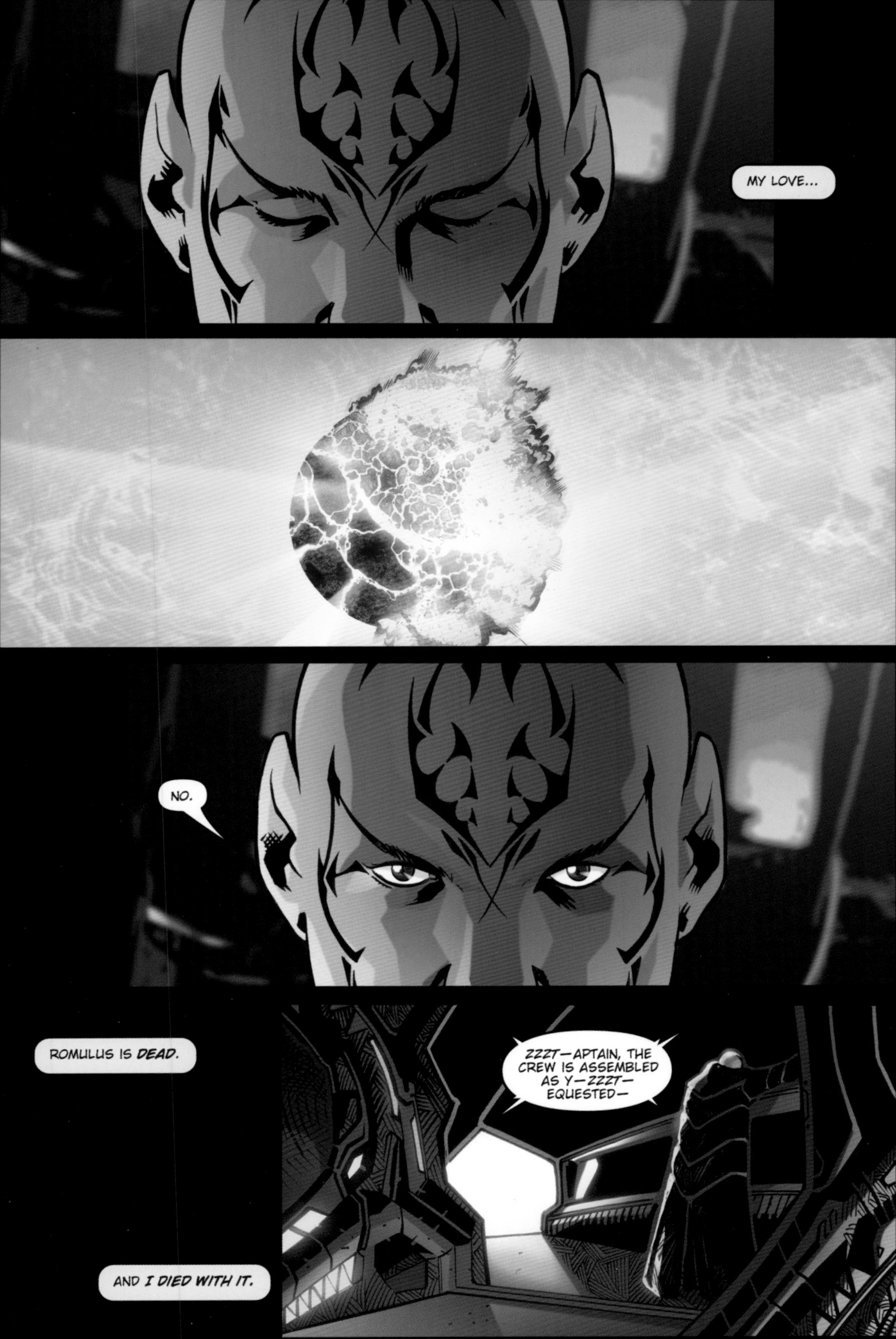
MY LOVE...
NO.
ROMULUS IS DEAD.
ZZZT—APTAIN, THE CREW IS ASSEMBLED AS Y—ZZZT—EQUESTED—
AND I DIED WITH IT.

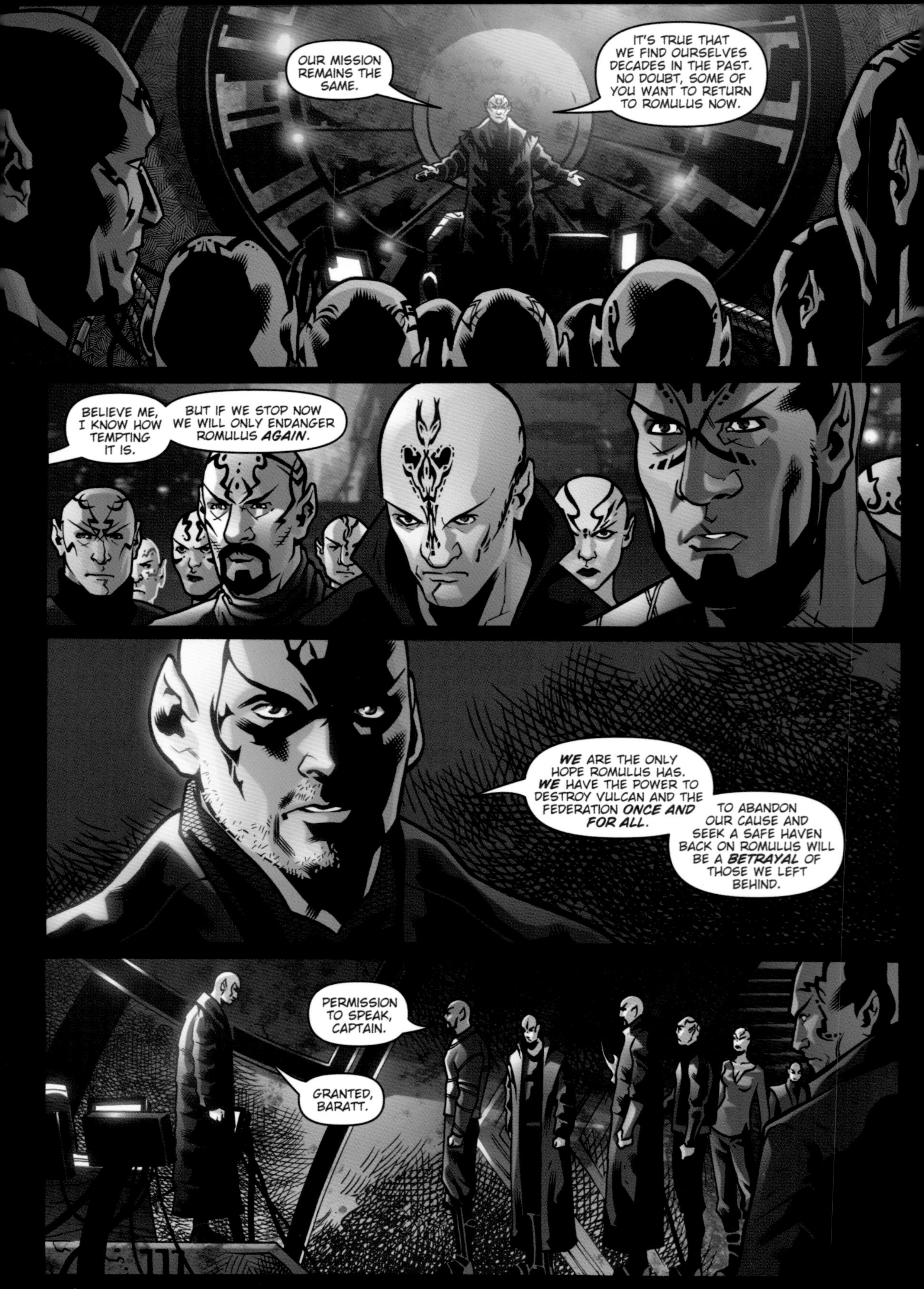
OUR MISSION REMAINS THE SAME.
IT'S TRUE THAT WE FIND OURSELVES DECADES IN THE PAST. NO DOUBT, SOME OF YOU WANT TO RETURN TO ROMULUS NOW.
BELIEVE ME, I KNOW HOW TEMPTING IT IS.
BUT IF WE STOP NOW WE WILL ONLY ENDANGER ROMULUS AGAIN.
WE ARE THE ONLY HOPE ROMULUS HAS. WE HAVE THE POWER TO DESTROY VULCAN AND THE FEDERATION ONCE AND FOR ALL.
TO ABANDON OUR CAUSE AND SEEK A SAFE HAVEN BACK ON ROMULUS WILL BE A BETRAYAL OF THOSE WE LEFT BEHIND.
PERMISSION TO SPEAK, CAPTAIN.
GRANTED, BARATT.

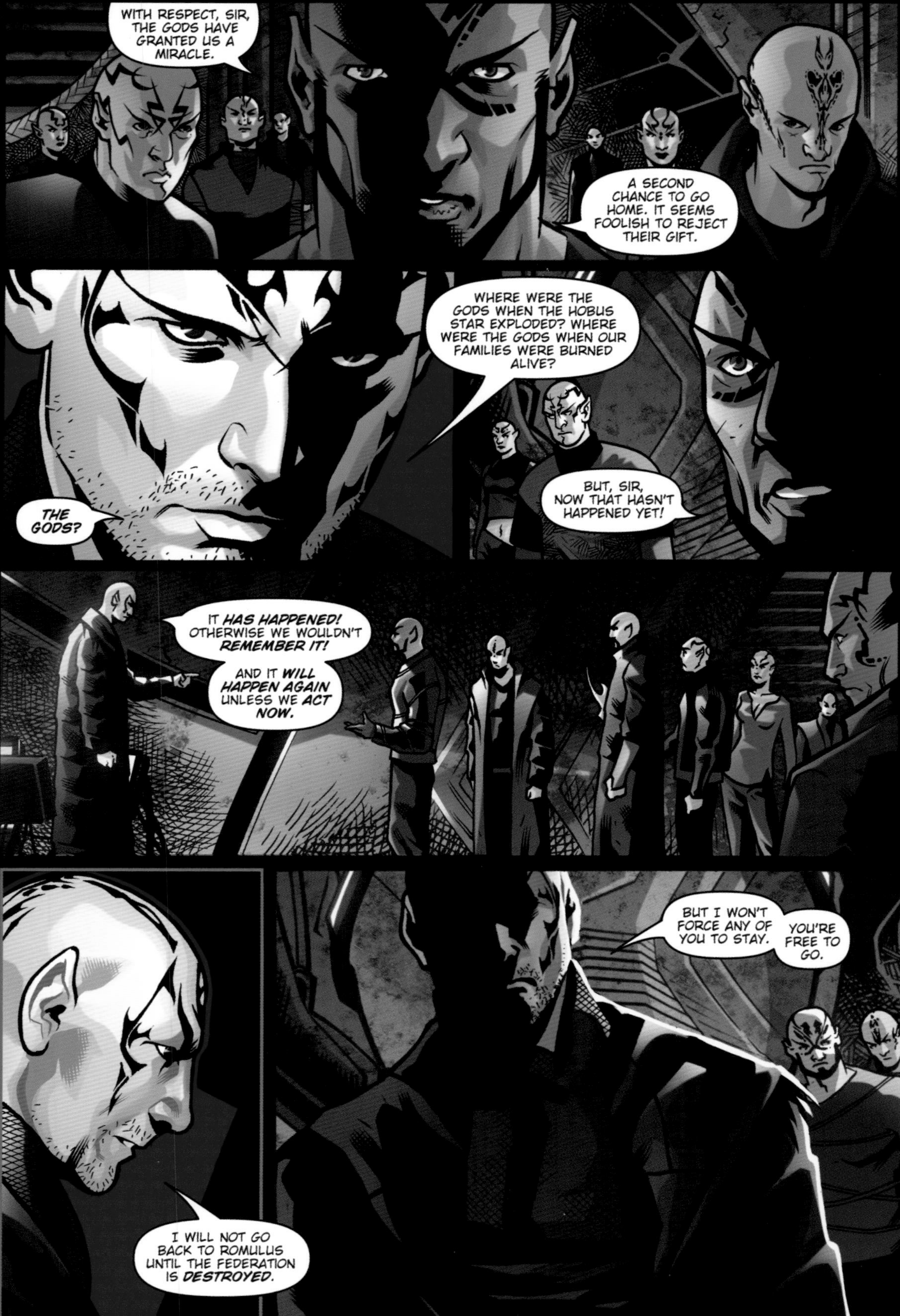
WITH RESPECT, SIR, THE GODS HAVE GRANTED US A MIRACLE.
A SECOND CHANCE TO GO HOME. IT SEEMS FOOLISH TO REJECT THEIR GIFT.
THE GODS?
WHERE WERE THE GODS WHEN THE HOBUS STAR EXPLODED? WHERE WERE THE GODS WHEN OUR FAMILIES WERE BURNED ALIVE?
BUT, SIR, NOW THAT HASN'T HAPPENED YET!
IT HAS HAPPENED! OTHERWISE WE WOULDN'T REMEMBER IT!
AND IT WILL HAPPEN AGAIN UNLESS WE ACT NOW.
BUT I WON'T FORCE ANY OF YOU TO STAY.
YOU'RE FREE TO GO.
I WILL NOT GO BACK TO ROMULUS UNTIL THE FEDERATION IS DESTROYED.

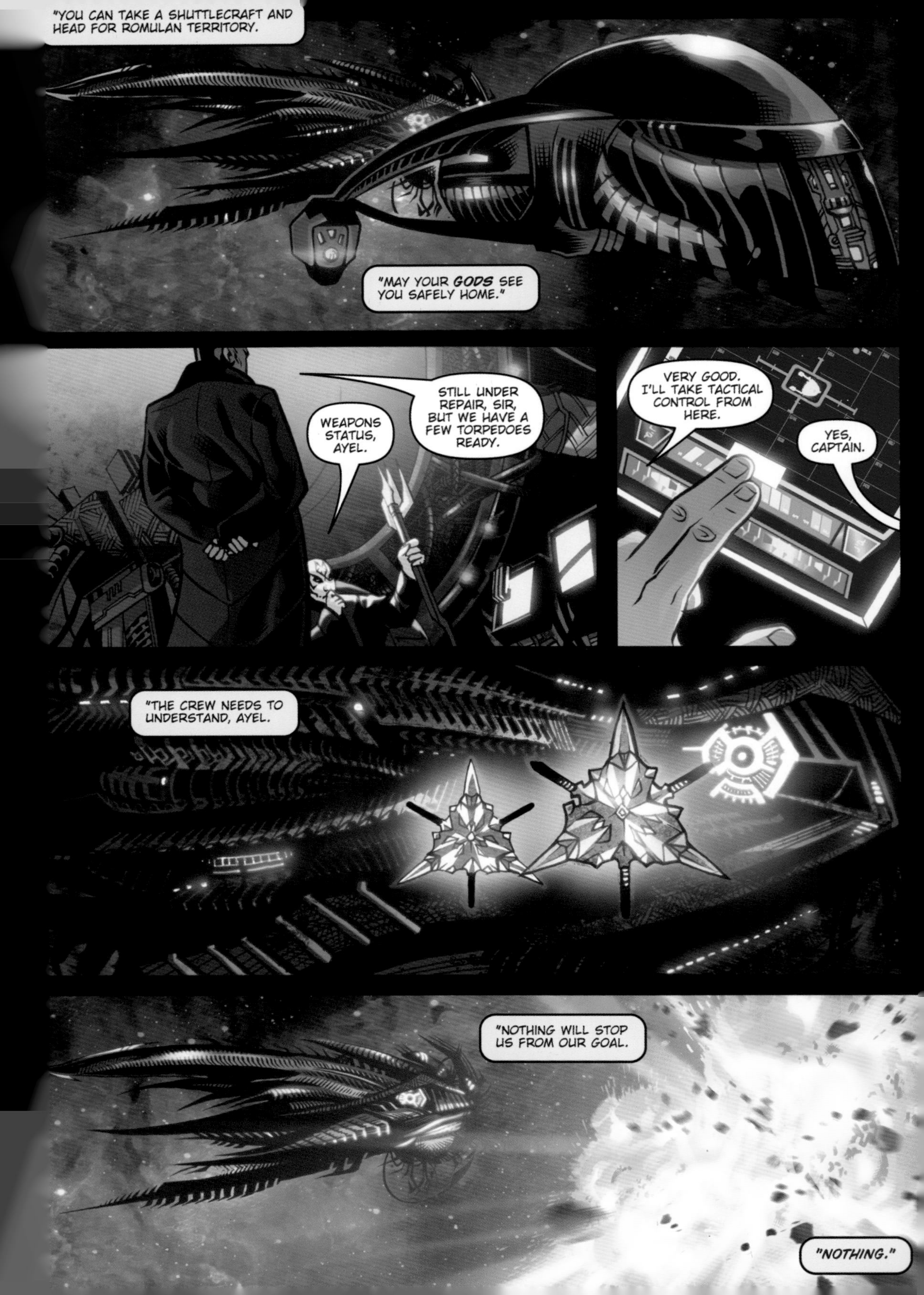
"YOU CAN TAKE A SHUTTLECRAFT AND HEAD FOR ROMULAN TERRITORY.
"MAY YOUR GODS SEE YOU SAFELY HOME."
WEAPONS STATUS, AYEL.
STILL UNDER REPAIR, SIR, BUT WE HAVE A FEW TORPEDOES READY.
VERY GOOD. I'LL TAKE TACTICAL CONTROL FROM HERE.
YES, CAPTAIN.
"THE CREW NEEDS TO UNDERSTAND, AYEL.
"NOTHING WILL STOP US FROM OUR GOAL.
"NOTHING."

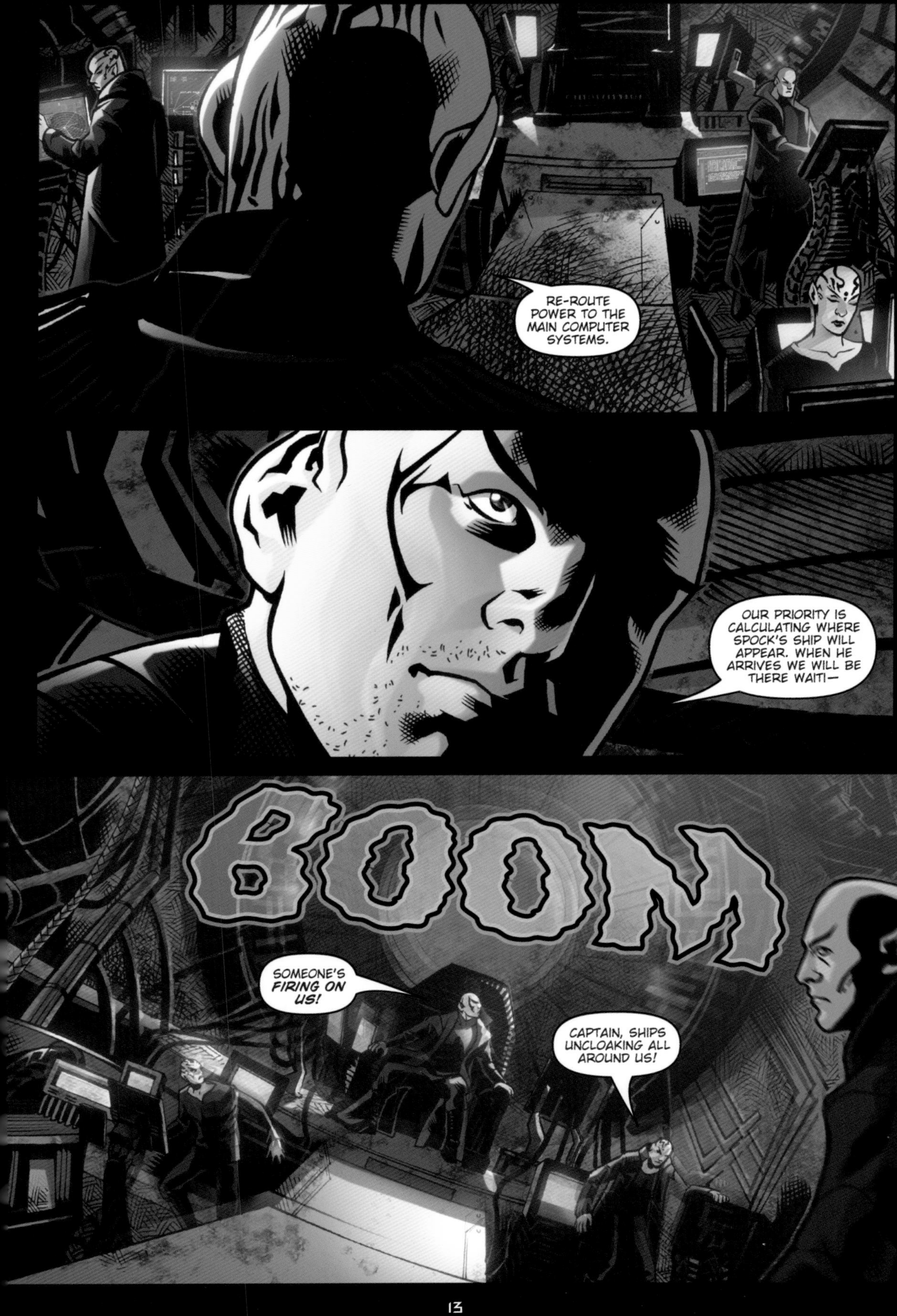
RE-ROUTE POWER TO THE MAIN COMPUTER SYSTEMS.
OUR PRIORITY IS CALCULATING WHERE SPOCK'S SHIP WILL APPEAR. WHEN HE ARRIVES WE WILL BE THERE WAIT!—
BOOM
SOMEONE'S *FIRING ON US!*
CAPTAIN, SHIPS UNCLOAKING ALL AROUND US!

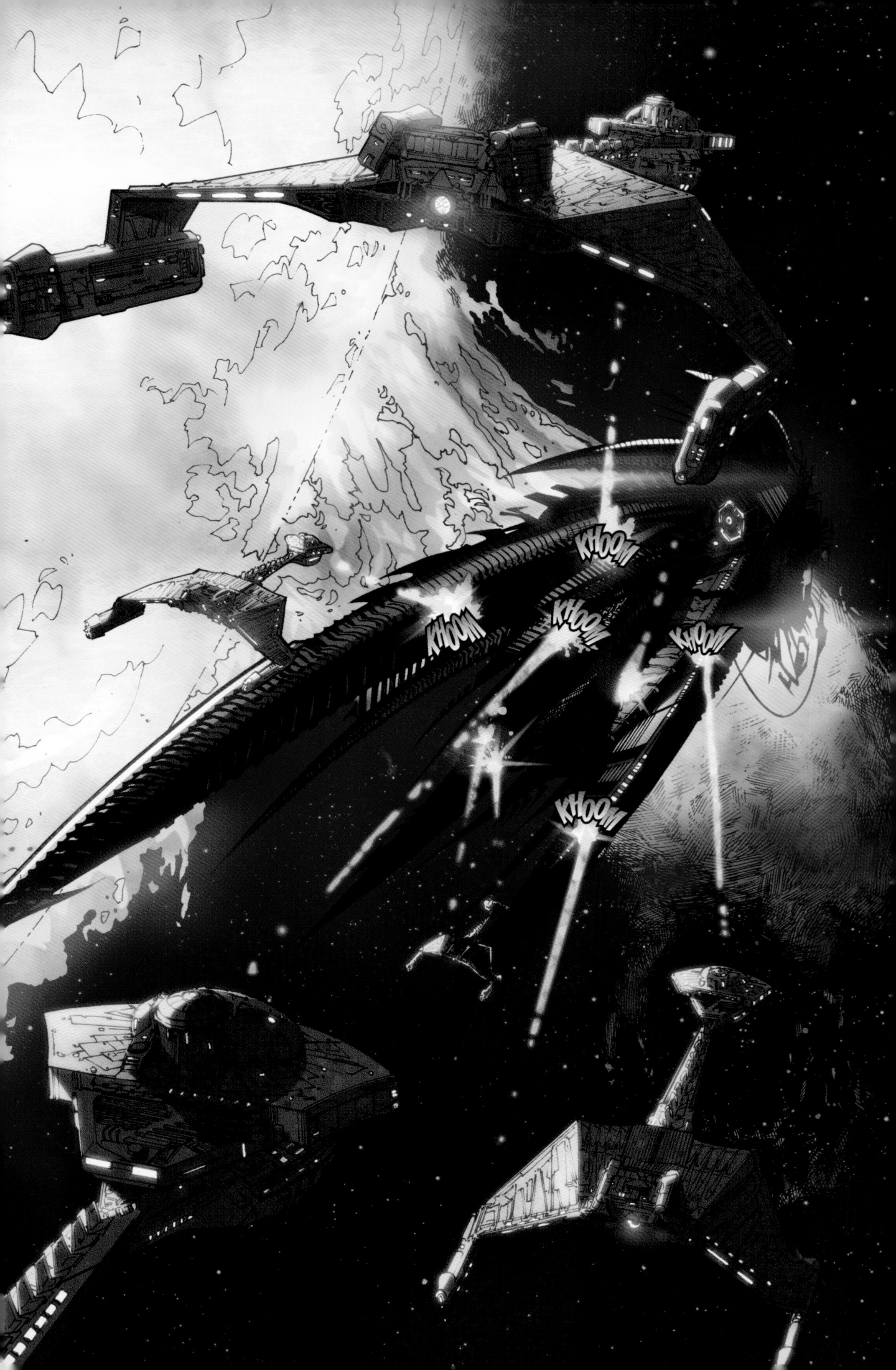

KHOOM
KHOOM
KHOOM
KHOOM
KHOOM

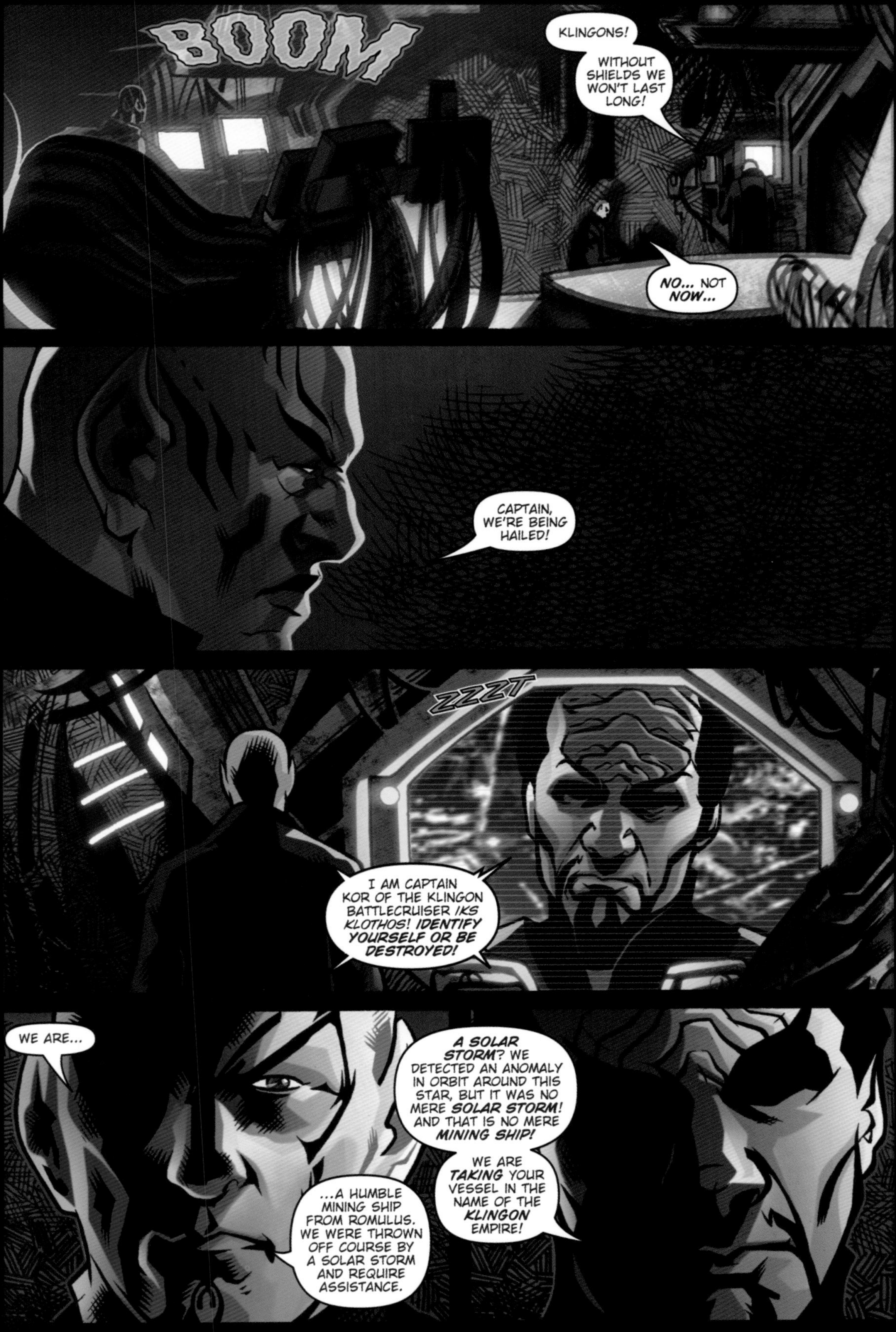
BOOM
KLINGONS!
WITHOUT SHIELDS WE WON'T LAST LONG!
NO... NOT NOW...
CAPTAIN, WE'RE BEING HAILED!
ZZZT
I AM CAPTAIN KOR OF THE KLINGON BATTLECRUISER IKS KLOTHOS! IDENTIFY YOURSELF OR BE DESTROYED!
WE ARE...
...A HUMBLE MINING SHIP FROM ROMULUS. WE WERE THROWN OFF COURSE BY A SOLAR STORM AND REQUIRE ASSISTANCE.
A SOLAR STORM? WE DETECTED AN ANOMALY IN ORBIT AROUND THIS STAR, BUT IT WAS NO MERE SOLAR STORM! AND THAT IS NO MERE MINING SHIP!
WE ARE TAKING YOUR VESSEL IN THE NAME OF THE KLINGON EMPIRE!

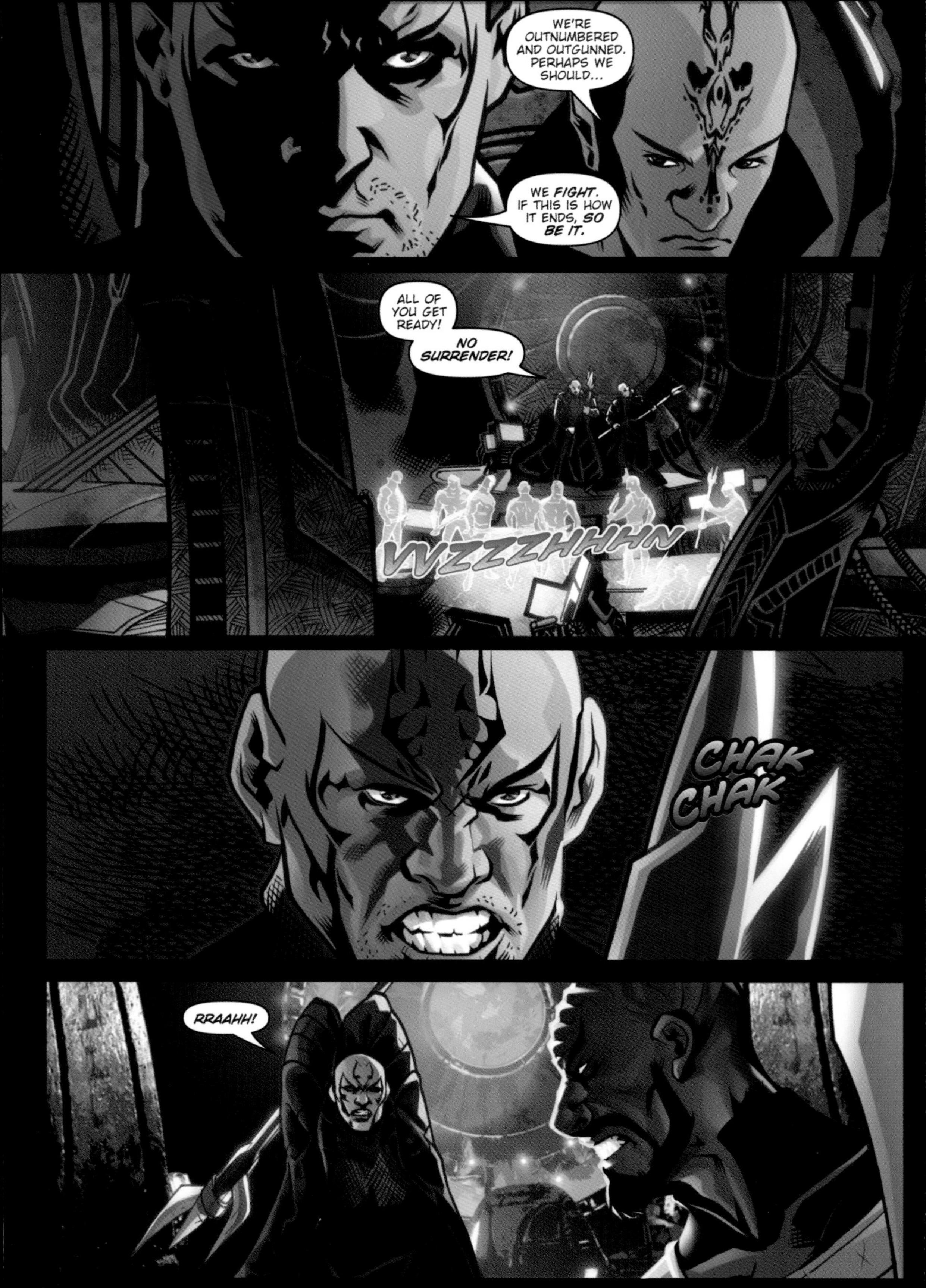
WE'RE OUTNUMBERED AND OUTGUNNED. PERHAPS WE SHOULD...
WE FIGHT. IF THIS IS HOW IT ENDS, SO BE IT.
ALL OF YOU GET READY!
NO SURRENDER!
VVZZZHHHN
CHAK CHAK
RRAAHH!

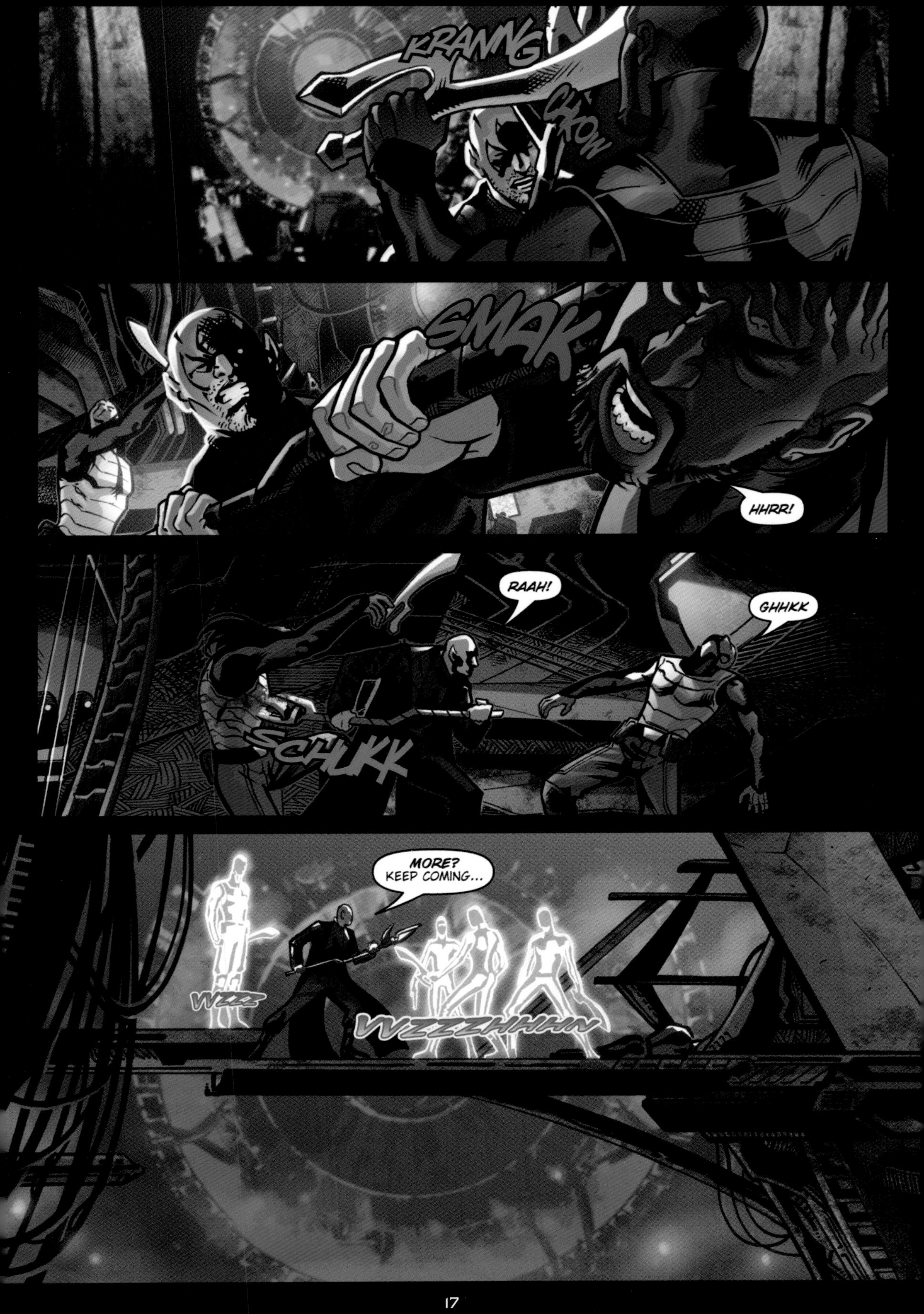
KRANNG
CHOW
SMAK
HHRR!
RAAH!
GHHKK
SCHUKK
MORE? KEEP COMING...
VVZZZ
VVZZZHHAAN

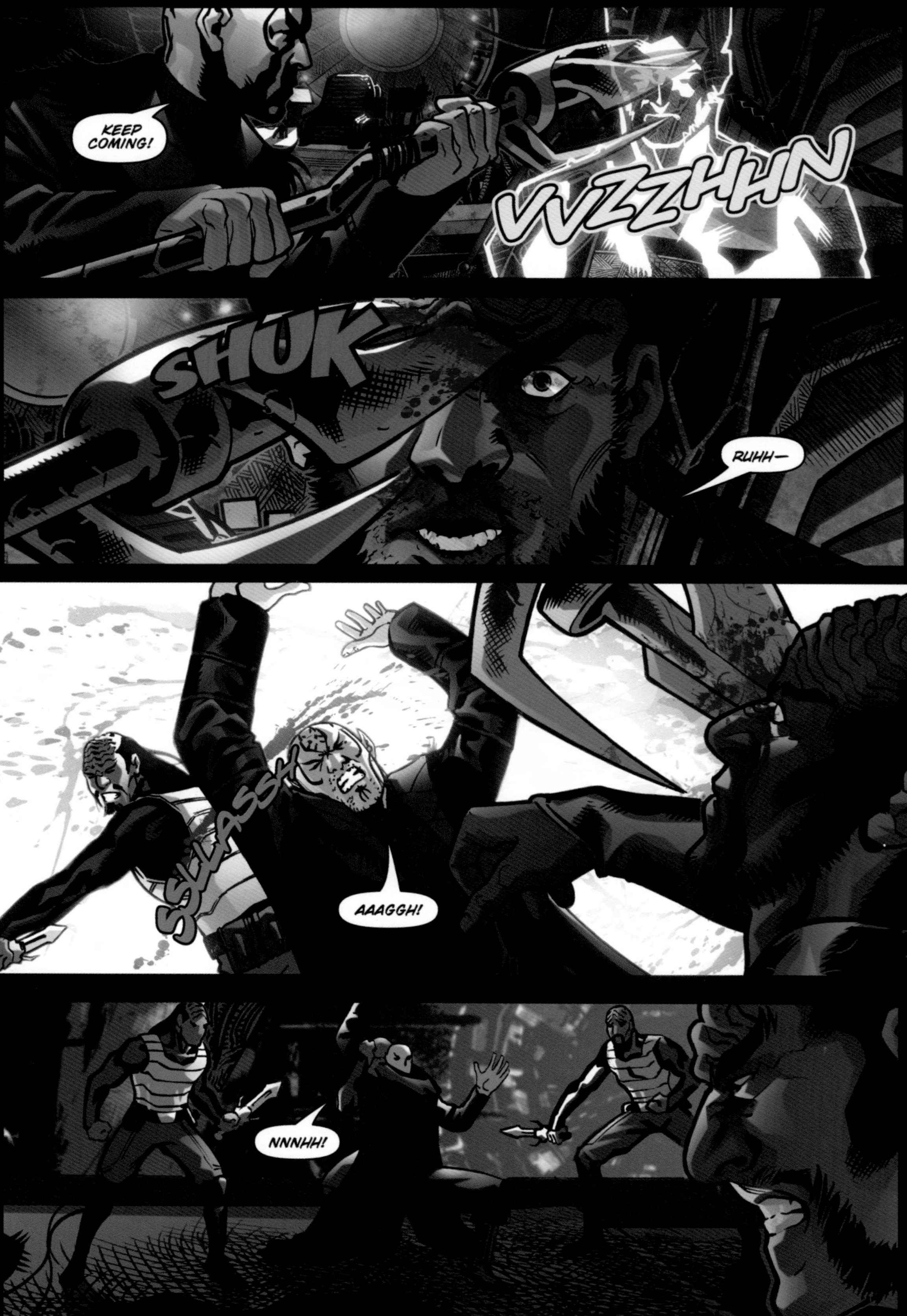
KEEP COMING!
VVZZHHN
SHUK
RUHH—
SSLLASSH
AAAGGH!
NNNHH!

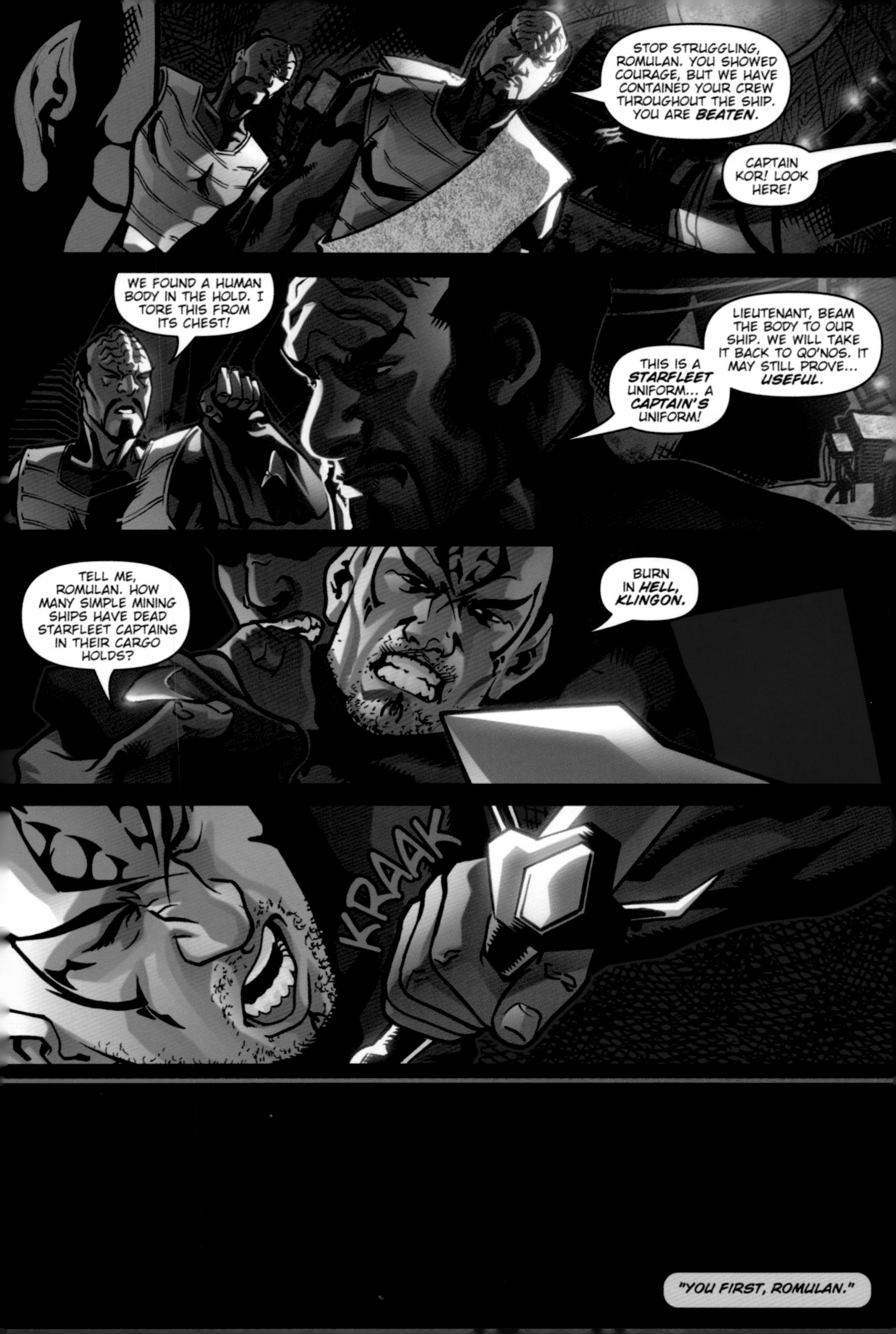
STOP STRUGGLING, ROMULAN. YOU SHOWED COURAGE, BUT WE HAVE CONTAINED YOUR CREW THROUGHOUT THE SHIP. YOU ARE BEATEN.
CAPTAIN KOR! LOOK HERE!
WE FOUND A HUMAN BODY IN THE HOLD. I TORE THIS FROM ITS CHEST!
THIS IS A STARFLEET UNIFORM... A CAPTAIN'S UNIFORM!
LIEUTENANT, BEAM THE BODY TO OUR SHIP. WE WILL TAKE IT BACK TO QO'NOS. IT MAY STILL PROVE... USEFUL.
TELL ME, ROMULAN. HOW MANY SIMPLE MINING SHIPS HAVE DEAD STARFLEET CAPTAINS IN THEIR CARGO HOLDS?
BURN IN HELL, KLINGON.
KRAAK
"YOU FIRST, ROMULAN."

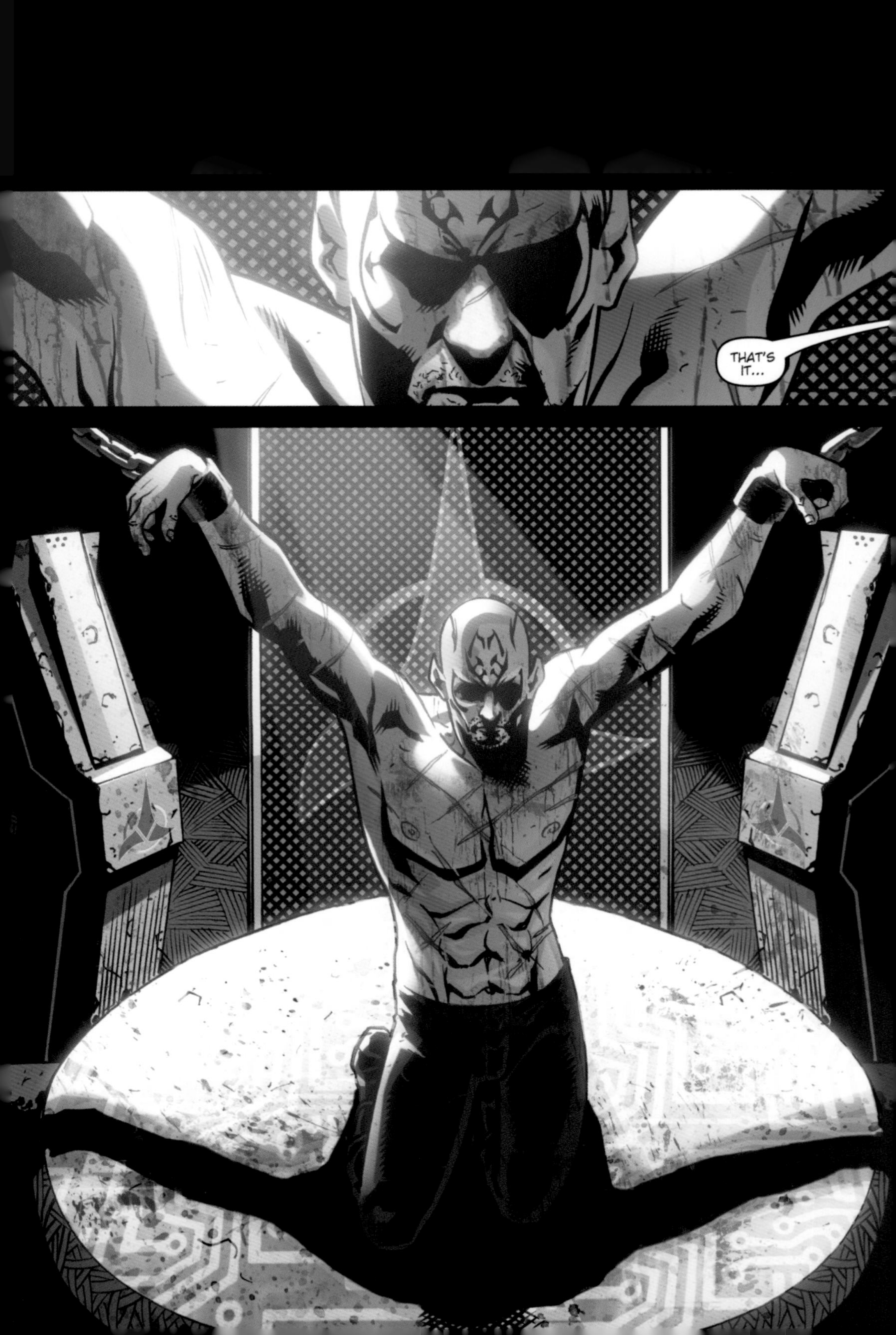
THAT'S IT...

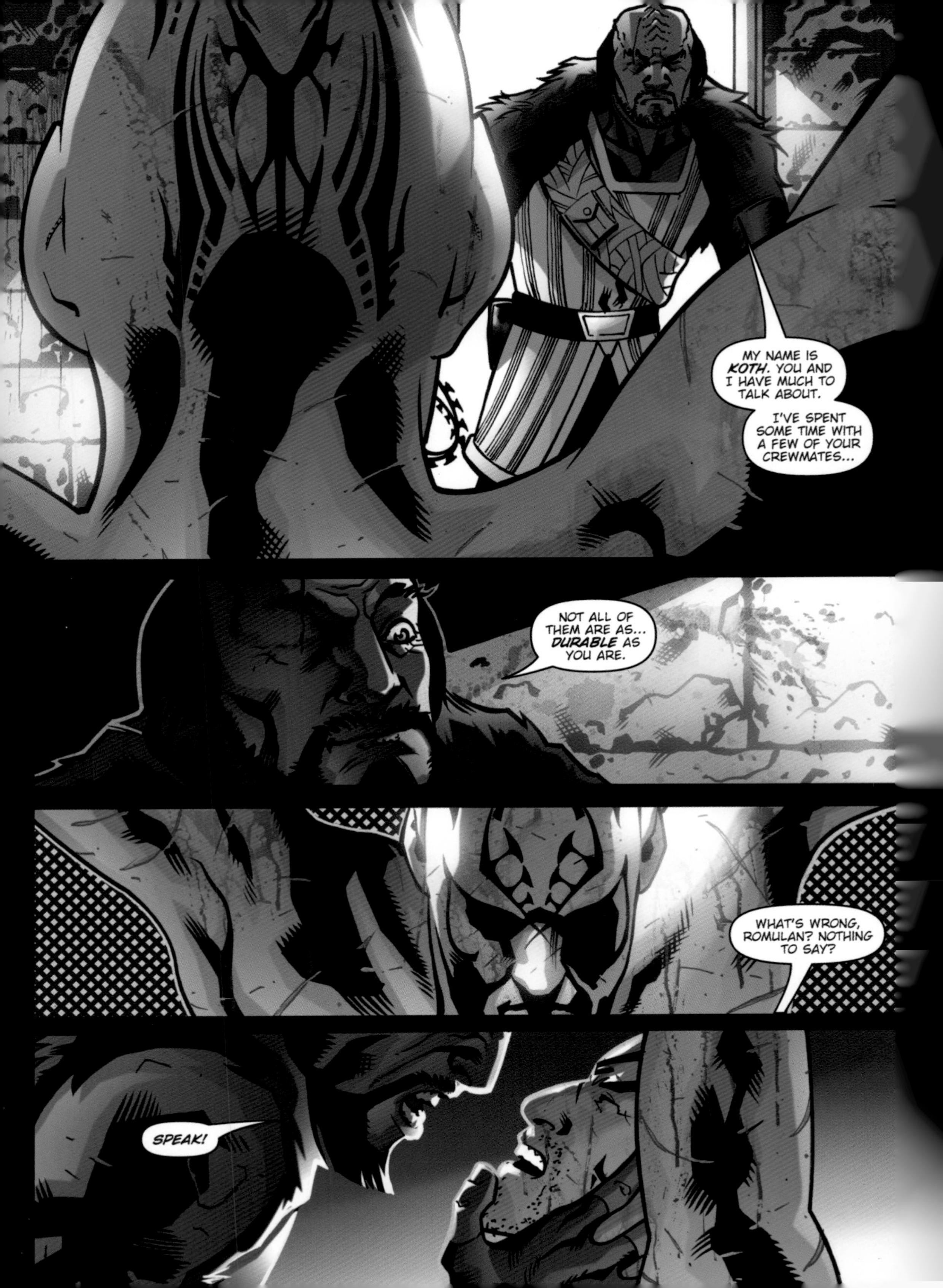
MY NAME IS KOTH. YOU AND I HAVE MUCH TO TALK ABOUT.
I'VE SPENT SOME TIME WITH A FEW OF YOUR CREWMATES...
NOT ALL OF THEM ARE AS... DURABLE AS YOU ARE.
WHAT'S WRONG, ROMULAN? NOTHING TO SAY?
SPEAK!

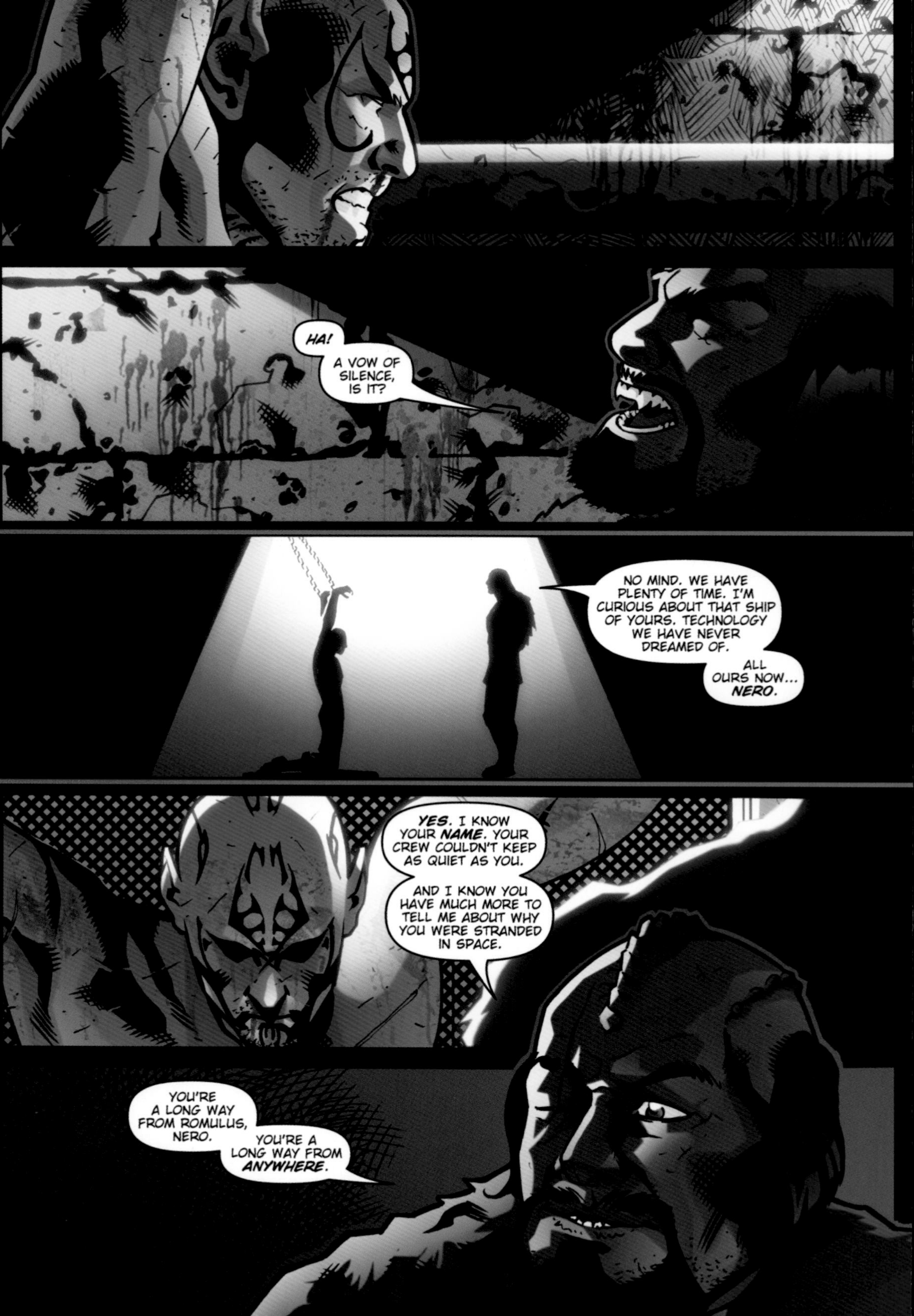
HA!
A VOW OF SILENCE, IS IT?
NO MIND. WE HAVE PLENTY OF TIME. I'M CURIOUS ABOUT THAT SHIP OF YOURS. TECHNOLOGY WE HAVE NEVER DREAMED OF.
ALL OURS NOW... NERO.
YES. I KNOW YOUR NAME. YOUR CREW COULDN'T KEEP AS QUIET AS YOU.
AND I KNOW YOU HAVE MUCH MORE TO TELL ME ABOUT WHY YOU WERE STRANDED IN SPACE.
YOU'RE A LONG WAY FROM ROMULUS, NERO.
YOU'RE A LONG WAY FROM ANYWHERE.

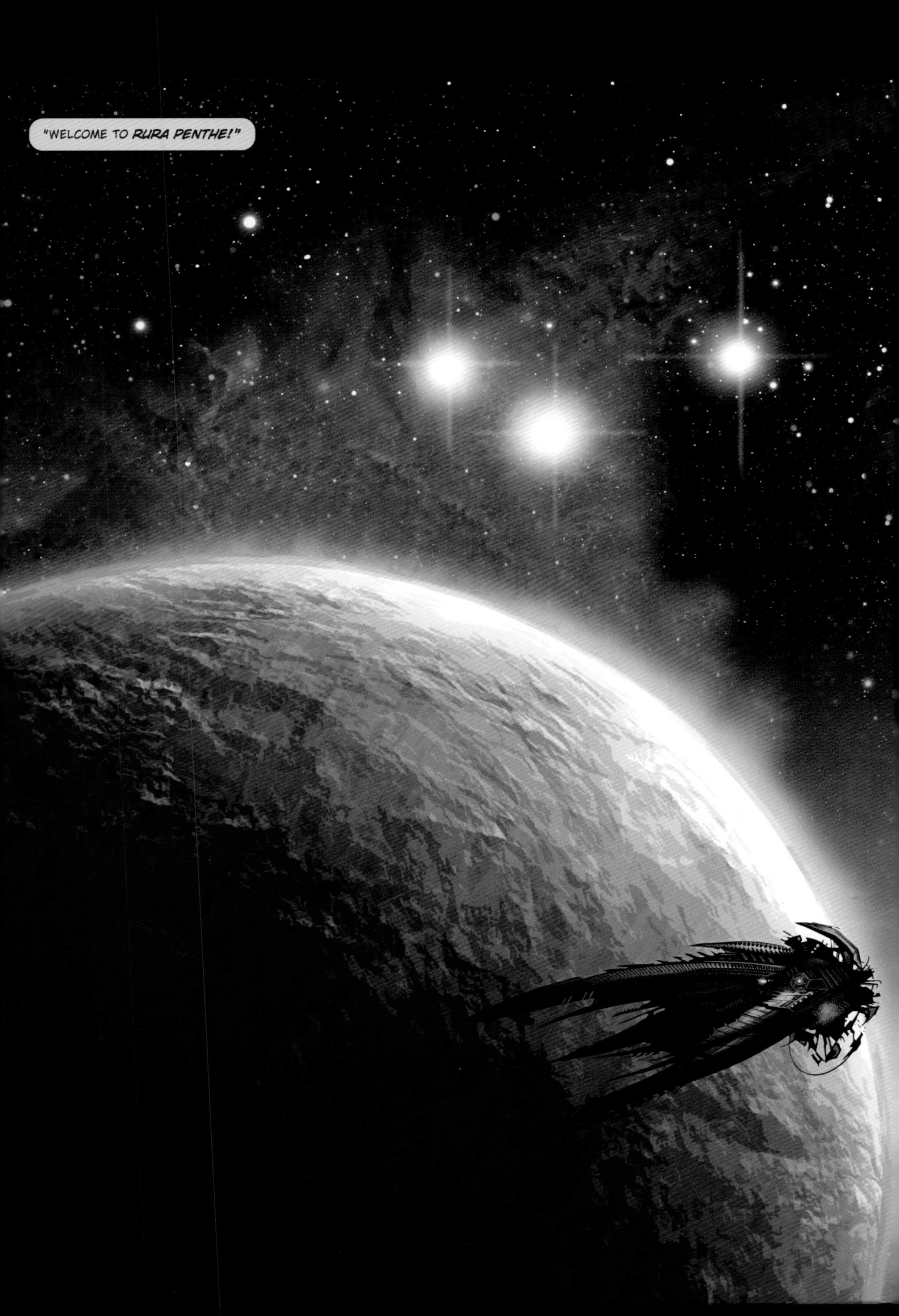
"WELCOME TO RURA PENTHE!"

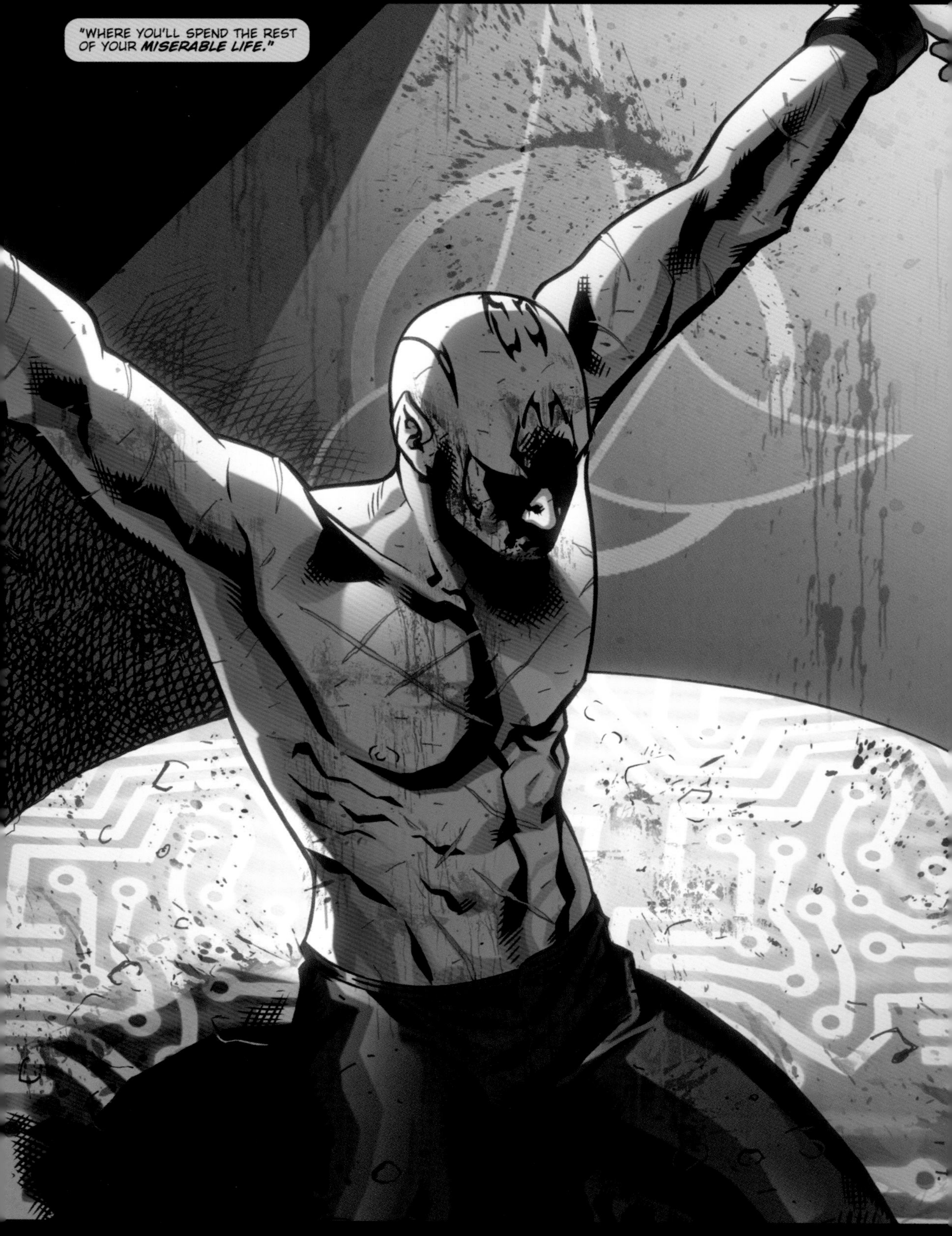
"WHERE YOU'LL SPEND THE REST OF YOUR MISERABLE LIFE."

THE KLINGON PRISON ASTEROID RURA PENTHE.

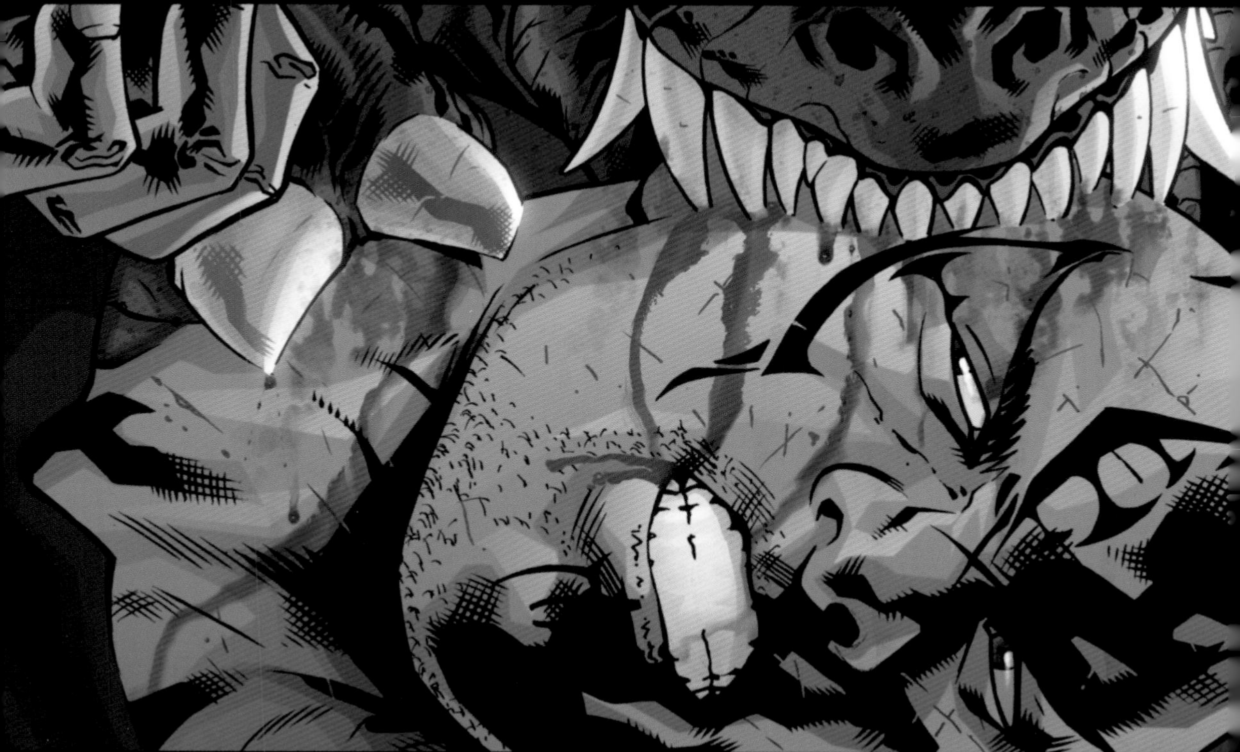

STAR TREK®

NERO

CHAPTER TWO

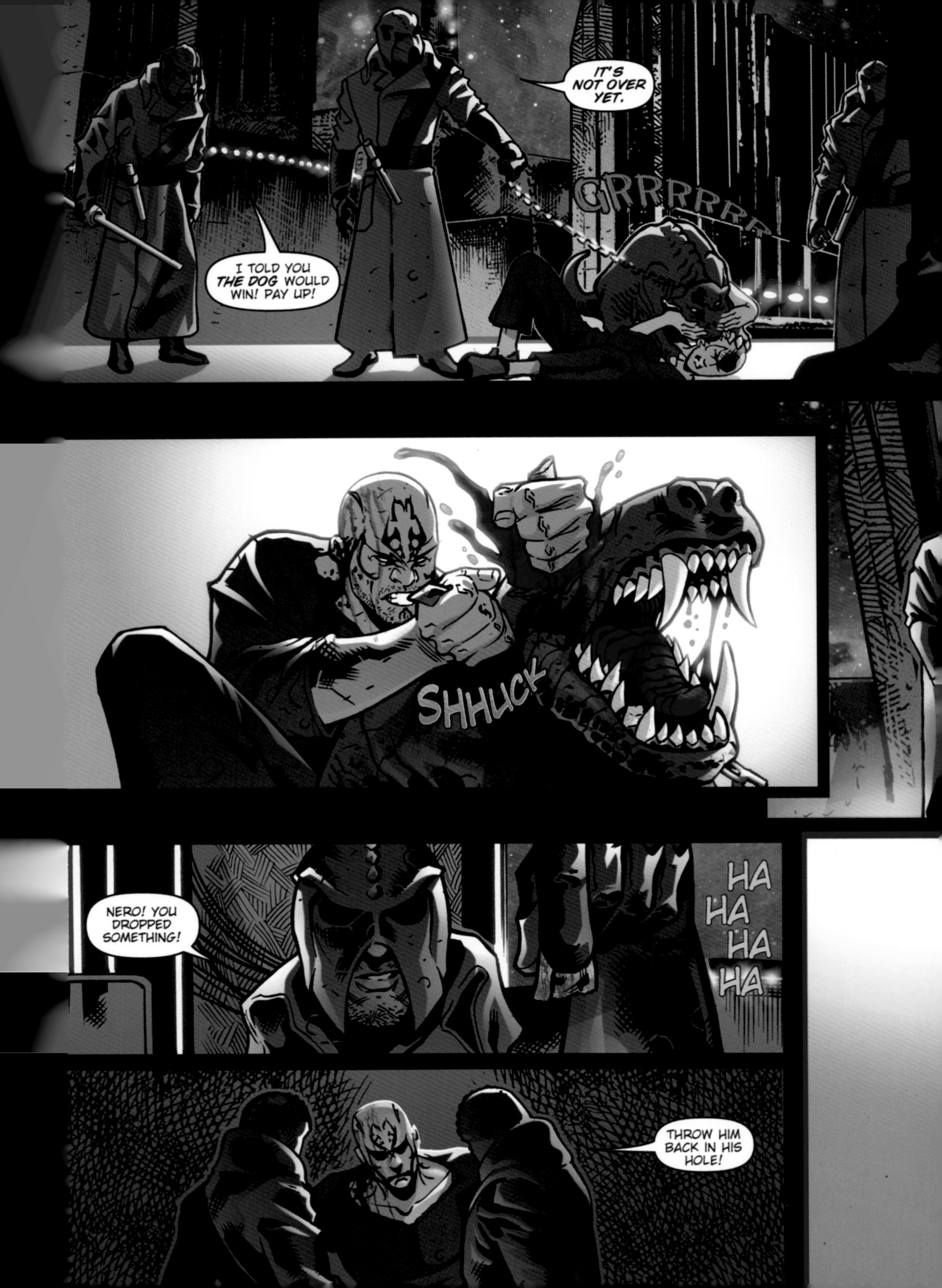
IT'S NOT OVER YET.
I TOLD YOU THE DOG WOULD WIN! PAY UP!
GRRRRRRR
SHHUCK
NERO! YOU DROPPED SOMETHING!
HA HA HA HA
THROW HIM BACK IN HIS HOLE!

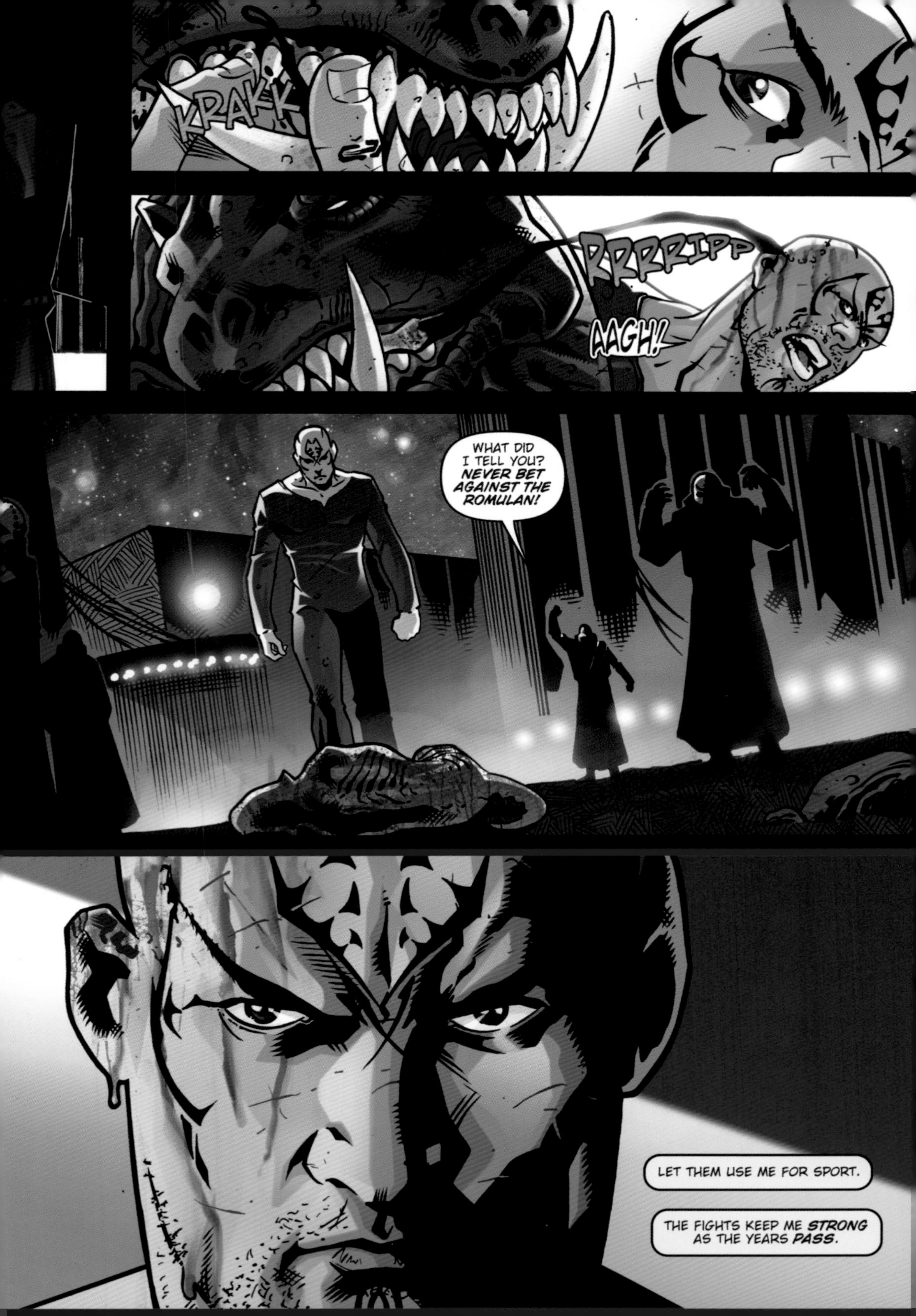
KRAKK!
RRRRIPP
AAGH!
WHAT DID I TELL YOU? NEVER BET AGAINST THE ROMULAN!
LET THEM USE ME FOR SPORT.
THE FIGHTS KEEP ME STRONG AS THE YEARS PASS.

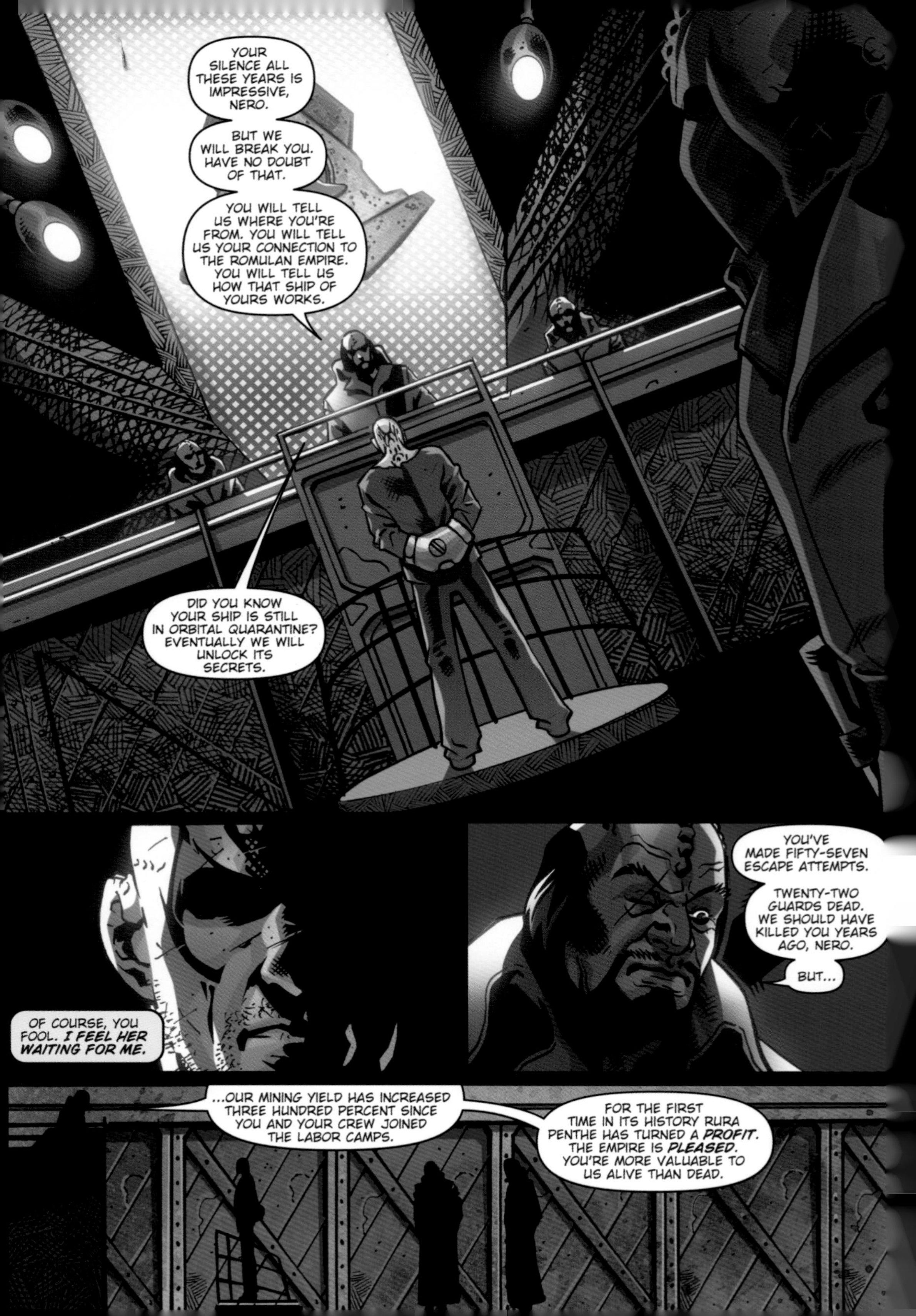
YOUR SILENCE ALL THESE YEARS IS IMPRESSIVE, NERO.
BUT WE WILL BREAK YOU. HAVE NO DOUBT OF THAT.
YOU WILL TELL US WHERE YOU'RE FROM. YOU WILL TELL US YOUR CONNECTION TO THE ROMULAN EMPIRE. YOU WILL TELL US HOW THAT SHIP OF YOURS WORKS.
DID YOU KNOW YOUR SHIP IS STILL IN ORBITAL QUARANTINE? EVENTUALLY WE WILL UNLOCK ITS SECRETS.
OF COURSE, YOU FOOL. *I FEEL HER WAITING FOR ME.*
YOU'VE MADE FIFTY-SEVEN ESCAPE ATTEMPTS.
TWENTY-TWO GUARDS DEAD. WE SHOULD HAVE KILLED YOU YEARS AGO, NERO.
BUT...
...OUR MINING YIELD HAS INCREASED THREE HUNDRED PERCENT SINCE YOU AND YOUR CREW JOINED THE LABOR CAMPS.
FOR THE FIRST TIME IN ITS HISTORY RURA PENTHE HAS TURNED A *PROFIT*. THE EMPIRE IS *PLEASED*. YOU'RE MORE VALUABLE TO US ALIVE THAN DEAD.

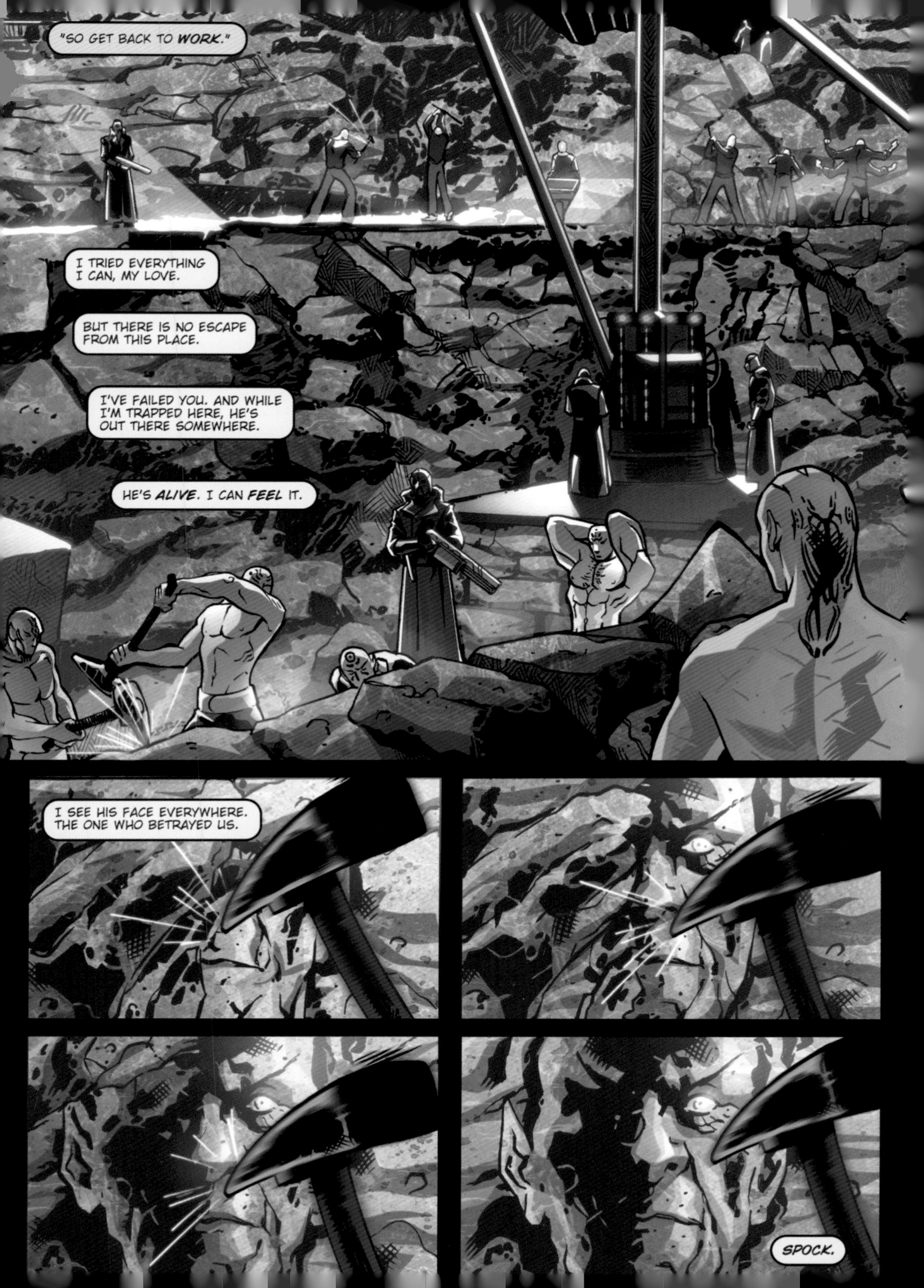
"SO GET BACK TO WORK."
I TRIED EVERYTHING I CAN, MY LOVE.
BUT THERE IS NO ESCAPE FROM THIS PLACE.
I'VE FAILED YOU. AND WHILE I'M TRAPPED HERE, HE'S OUT THERE SOMEWHERE.
HE'S ALIVE. I CAN FEEL IT.
I SEE HIS FACE EVERYWHERE. THE ONE WHO BETRAYED US.
SPOCK.

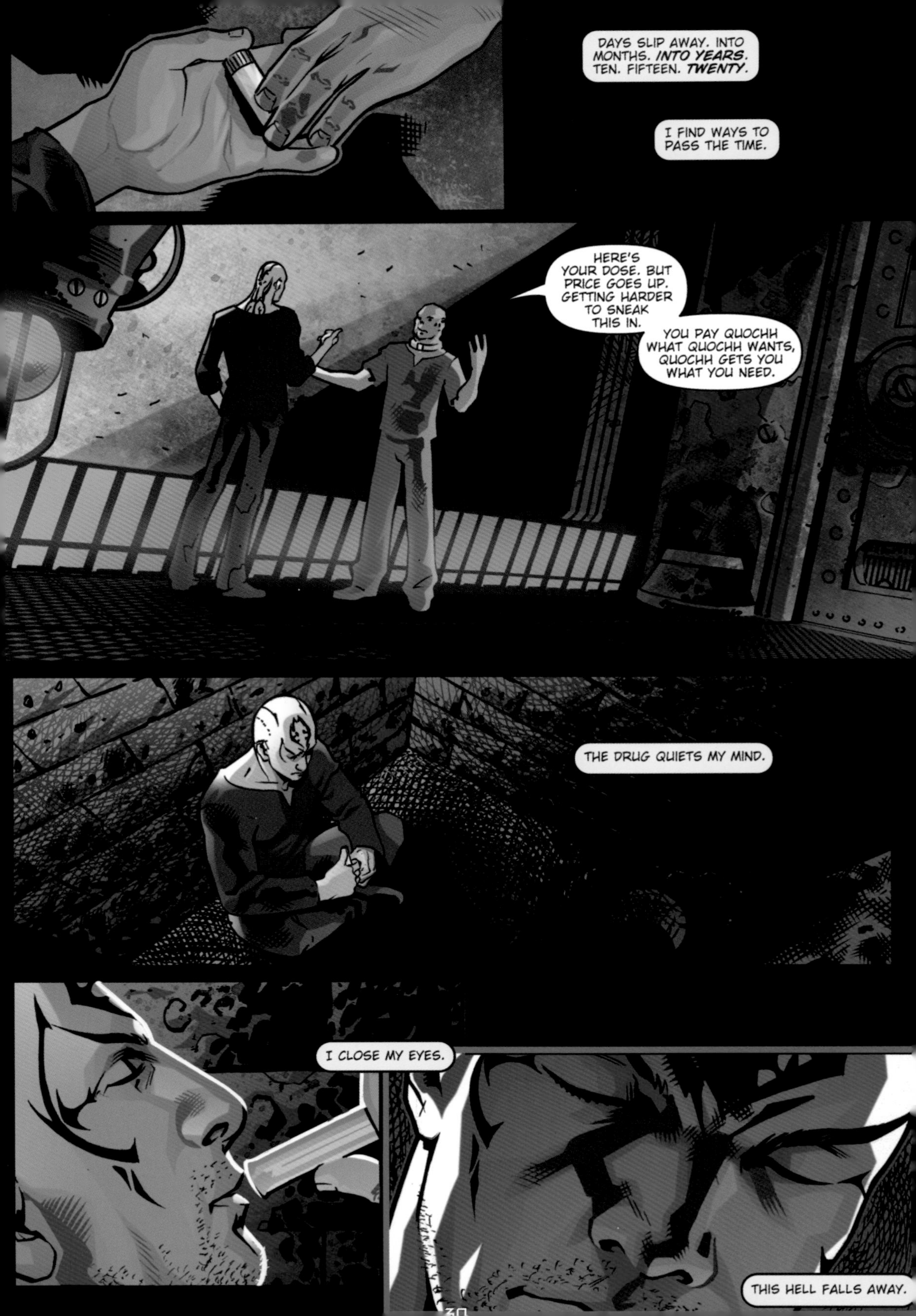
DAYS SLIP AWAY. INTO MONTHS. ***INTO YEARS.*** TEN. FIFTEEN. ***TWENTY.***
I FIND WAYS TO PASS THE TIME.
HERE'S YOUR DOSE. BUT PRICE GOES UP. GETTING HARDER TO SNEAK THIS IN.
YOU PAY QUOCHH WHAT QUOCHH WANTS, QUOCHH GETS YOU WHAT YOU NEED.
THE DRUG QUIETS MY MIND.
I CLOSE MY EYES.
THIS HELL FALLS AWAY.

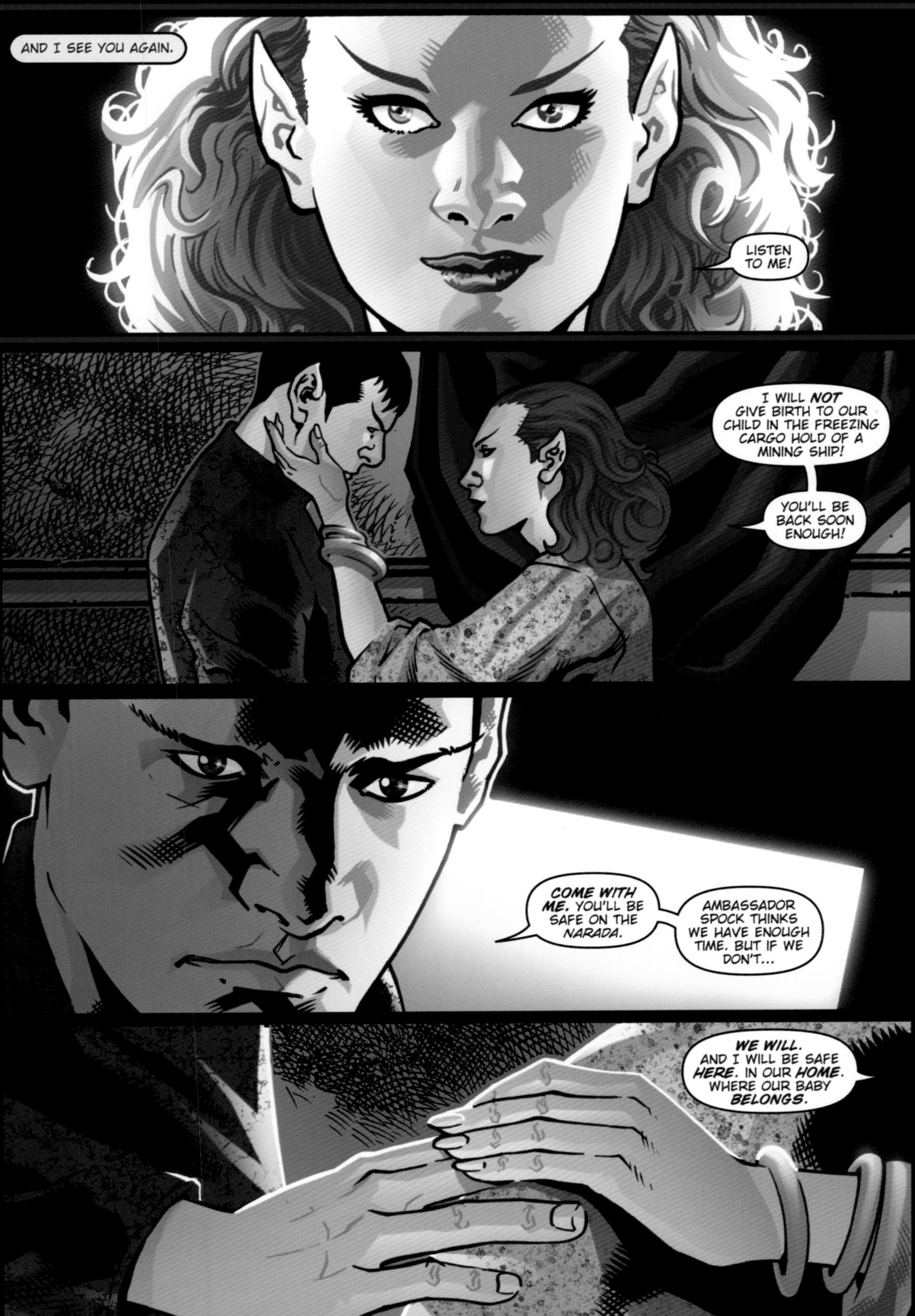
AND I SEE YOU AGAIN.
LISTEN TO ME!
I WILL NOT GIVE BIRTH TO OUR CHILD IN THE FREEZING CARGO HOLD OF A MINING SHIP!
YOU'LL BE BACK SOON ENOUGH!
COME WITH ME. YOU'LL BE SAFE ON THE NARADA.
AMBASSADOR SPOCK THINKS WE HAVE ENOUGH TIME. BUT IF WE DON'T...
WE WILL. AND I WILL BE SAFE HERE. IN OUR HOME. WHERE OUR BABY BELONGS.

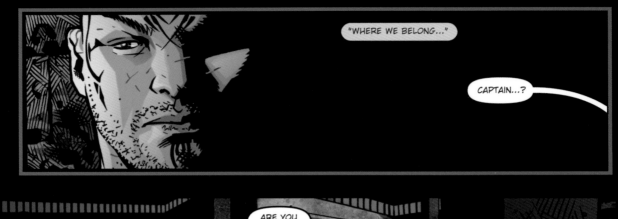

"WHERE WE BELONG..."

CAPTAIN...?

ARE YOU ALL RIGHT?

I'VE FOUND SOMEONE, CAPTAIN. SOMEONE I THINK CAN HELP US. HE CALLS HIMSELF—

CALL ME CLAVELL.

SO. NERO. "THE ONE WHO DOES NOT SPEAK."

YOU'RE SOMETHING OF A LEGEND AROUND HERE. THE GUARDS THINK YOU'RE A DEMON STRAIGHT FROM GRE'THOR.

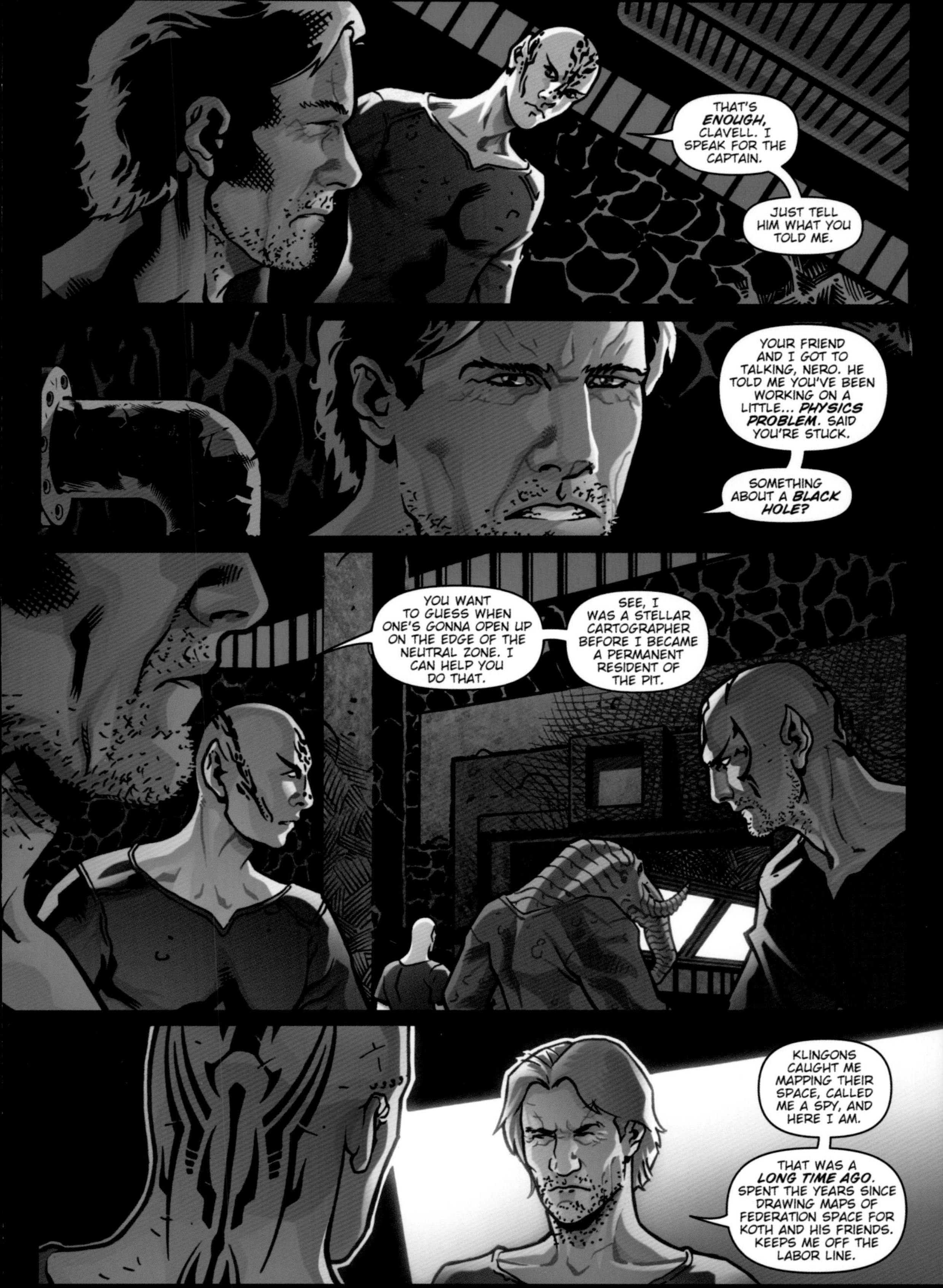
THAT'S ENOUGH, CLAVELL. I SPEAK FOR THE CAPTAIN.
JUST TELL HIM WHAT YOU TOLD ME.
YOUR FRIEND AND I GOT TO TALKING, NERO. HE TOLD ME YOU'VE BEEN WORKING ON A LITTLE... PHYSICS PROBLEM. SAID YOU'RE STUCK.
SOMETHING ABOUT A BLACK HOLE?
YOU WANT TO GUESS WHEN ONE'S GONNA OPEN UP ON THE EDGE OF THE NEUTRAL ZONE. I CAN HELP YOU DO THAT.
SEE, I WAS A STELLAR CARTOGRAPHER BEFORE I BECAME A PERMANENT RESIDENT OF THE PIT.
KLINGONS CAUGHT ME MAPPING THEIR SPACE, CALLED ME A SPY, AND HERE I AM.
THAT WAS A LONG TIME AGO. SPENT THE YEARS SINCE DRAWING MAPS OF FEDERATION SPACE FOR KOTH AND HIS FRIENDS. KEEPS ME OFF THE LABOR LINE.

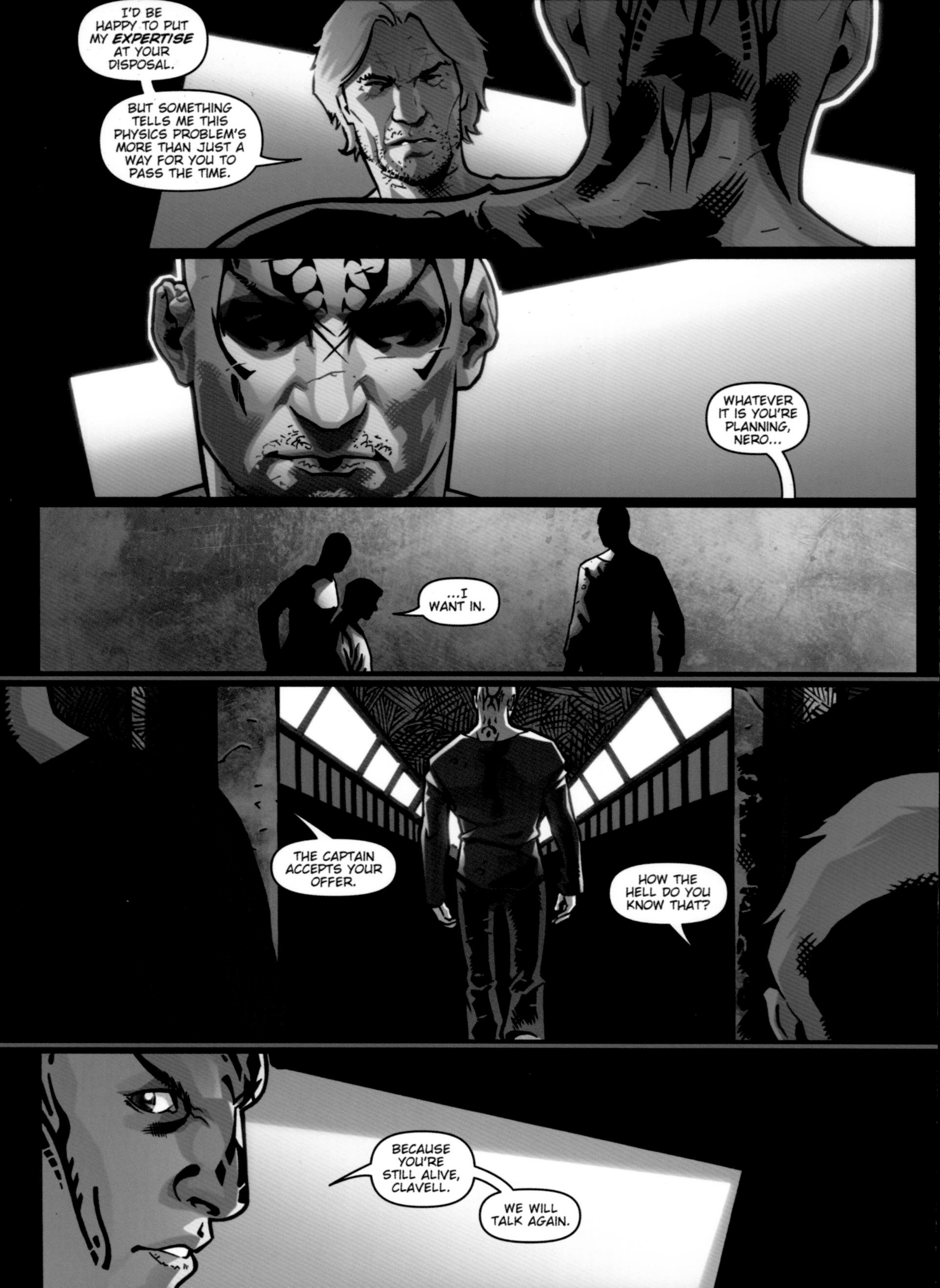
I'D BE HAPPY TO PUT MY ***EXPERTISE*** AT YOUR DISPOSAL.
BUT SOMETHING TELLS ME THIS PHYSICS PROBLEM'S MORE THAN JUST A WAY FOR YOU TO PASS THE TIME.
WHATEVER IT IS YOU'RE PLANNING, NERO...
...I WANT IN.
THE CAPTAIN ACCEPTS YOUR OFFER.
HOW THE HELL DO YOU KNOW THAT?
BECAUSE YOU'RE STILL ALIVE, CLAVELL.
WE WILL TALK AGAIN.

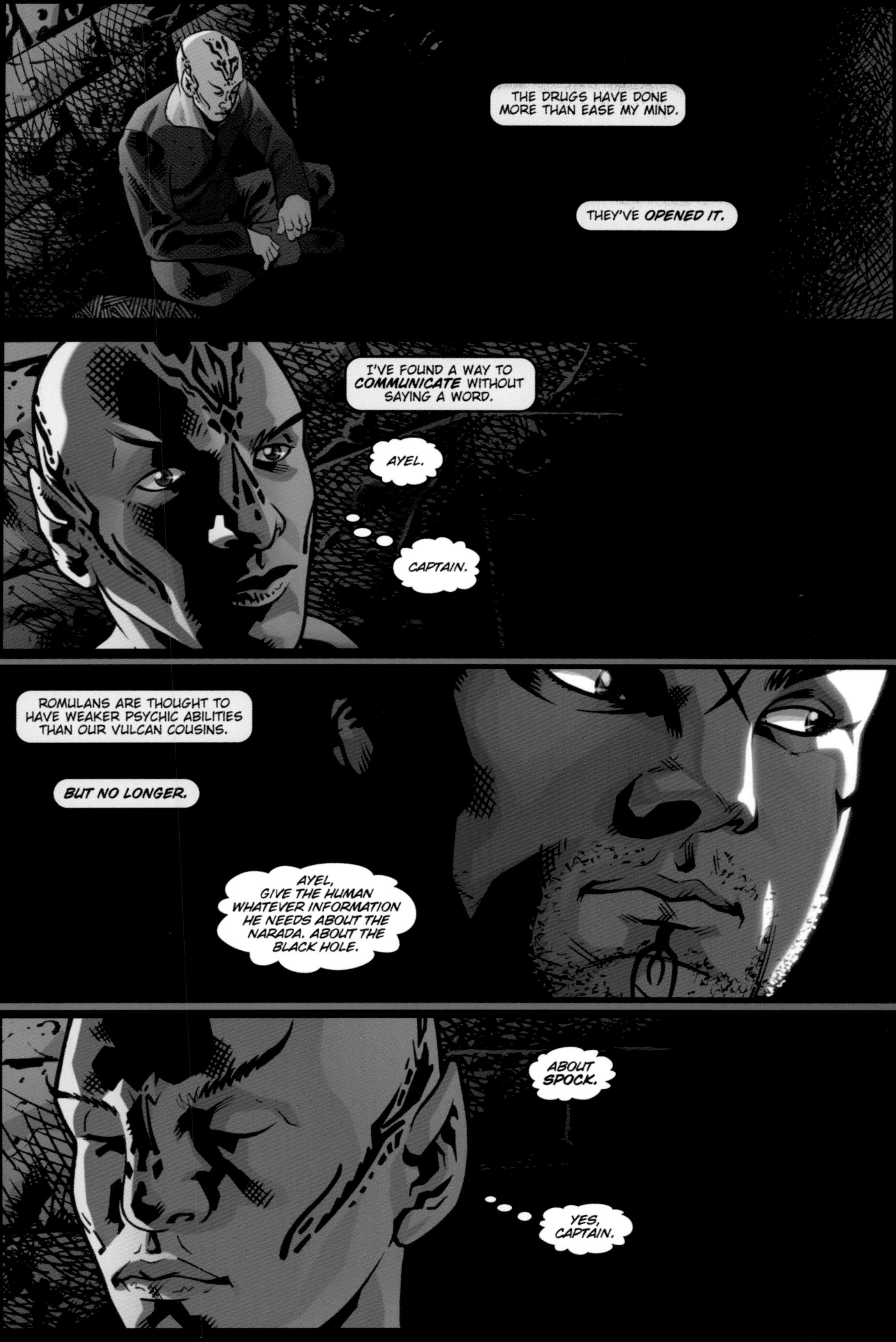
THE DRUGS HAVE DONE MORE THAN EASE MY MIND.
THEY'VE *OPENED IT.*
I'VE FOUND A WAY TO **COMMUNICATE** WITHOUT SAYING A WORD.
AYEL.
CAPTAIN.
ROMULANS ARE THOUGHT TO HAVE WEAKER PSYCHIC ABILITIES THAN OUR VULCAN COUSINS.
BUT NO LONGER.
AYEL, GIVE THE HUMAN WHATEVER INFORMATION HE NEEDS ABOUT THE NARADA. ABOUT THE BLACK HOLE.
*ABOUT **SPOCK.***
YES, CAPTAIN.

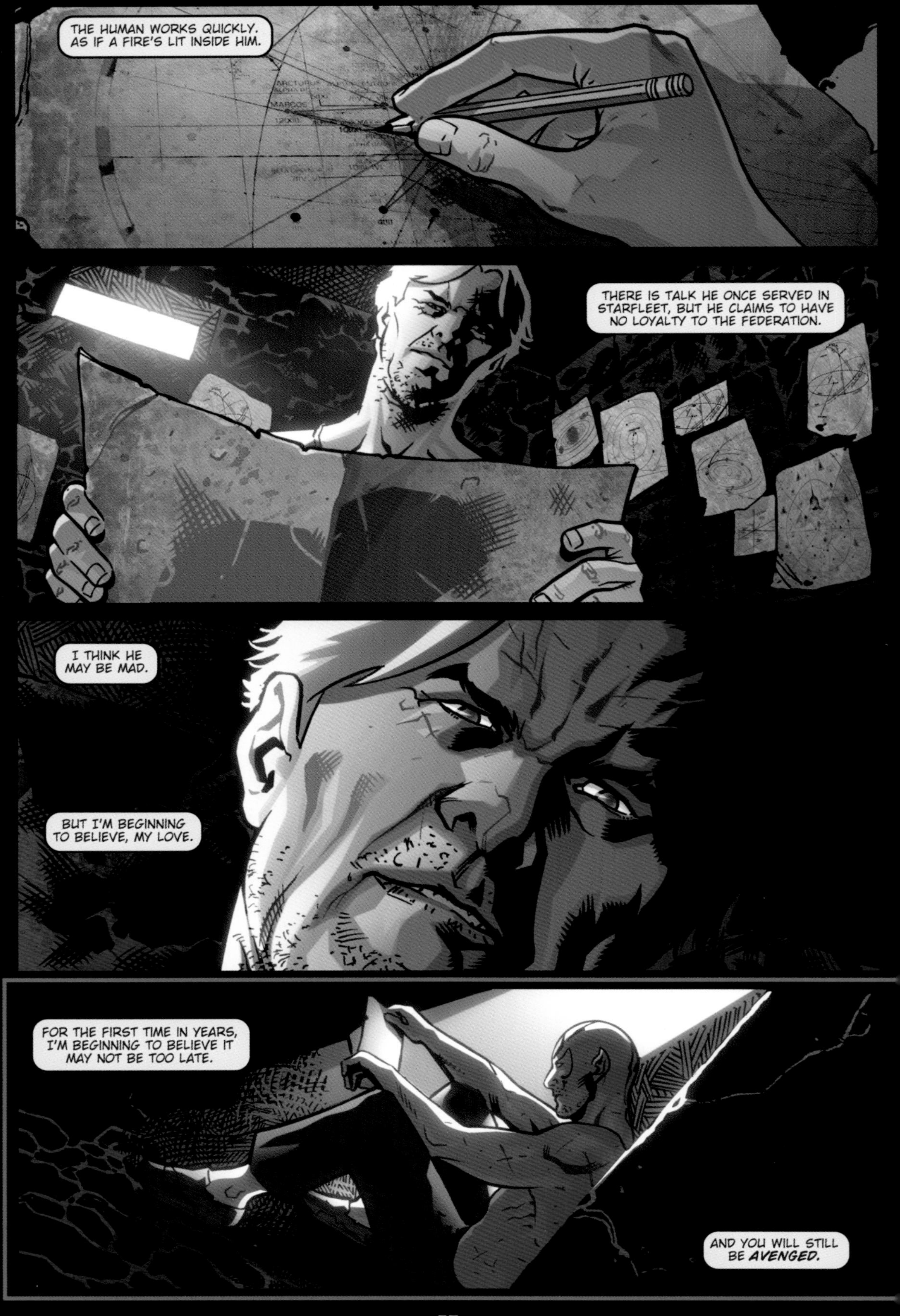
THE HUMAN WORKS QUICKLY. AS IF A FIRE'S LIT INSIDE HIM.
THERE IS TALK HE ONCE SERVED IN STARFLEET, BUT HE CLAIMS TO HAVE NO LOYALTY TO THE FEDERATION.
I THINK HE MAY BE MAD.
BUT I'M BEGINNING TO BELIEVE, MY LOVE.
FOR THE FIRST TIME IN YEARS, I'M BEGINNING TO BELIEVE IT MAY NOT BE TOO LATE.
AND YOU WILL STILL BE *AVENGED.*

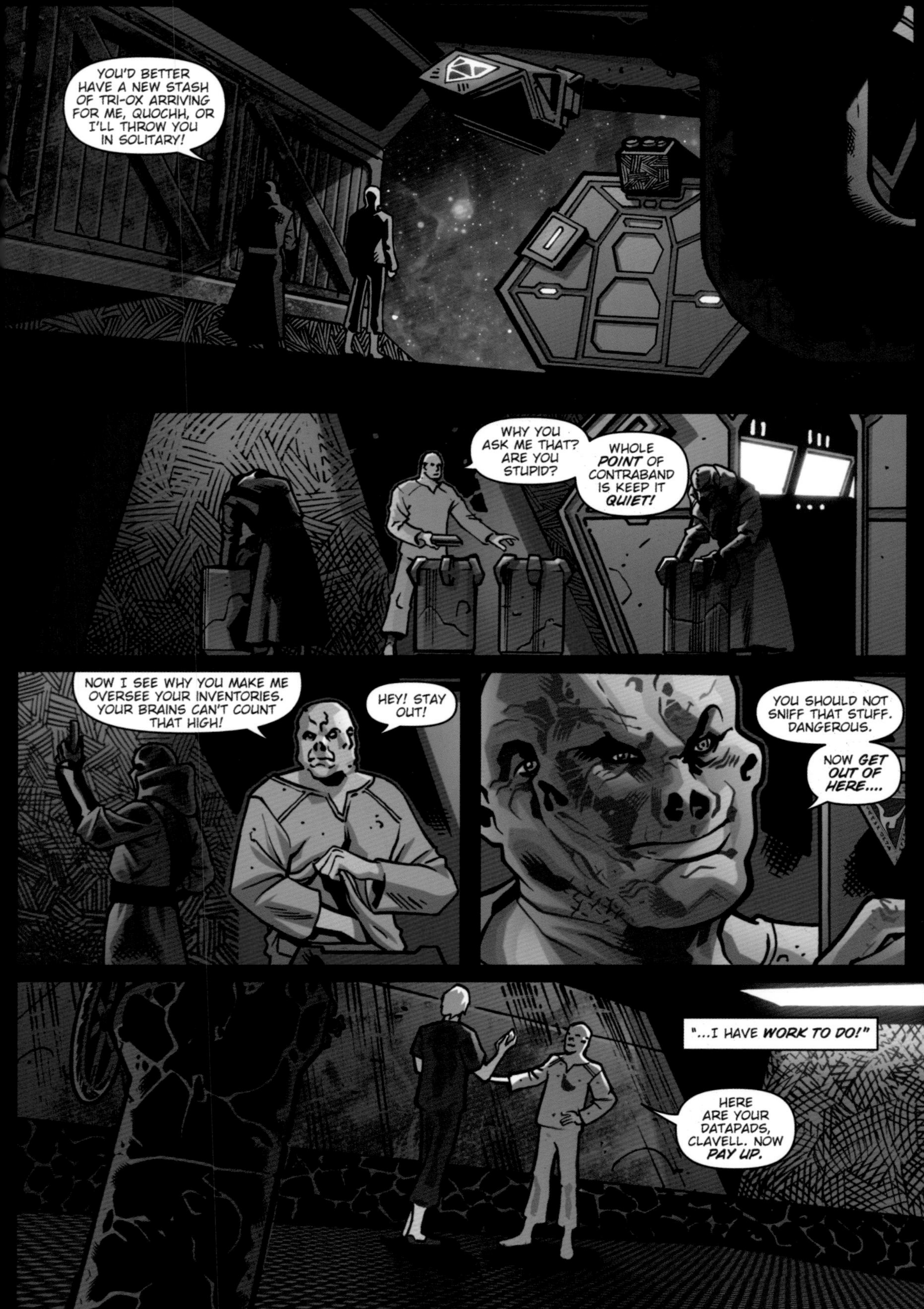
YOU'D BETTER HAVE A NEW STASH OF TRI-OX ARRIVING FOR ME, QUOCHH, OR I'LL THROW YOU IN SOLITARY!
WHY YOU ASK ME THAT? ARE YOU STUPID?
WHOLE POINT OF CONTRABAND IS KEEP IT QUIET!
NOW I SEE WHY YOU MAKE ME OVERSEE YOUR INVENTORIES. YOUR BRAINS CAN'T COUNT THAT HIGH!
HEY! STAY OUT!
YOU SHOULD NOT SNIFF THAT STUFF. DANGEROUS.
NOW GET OUT OF HERE....
"...I HAVE WORK TO DO!"
HERE ARE YOUR DATAPADS, CLAVELL. NOW PAY UP.

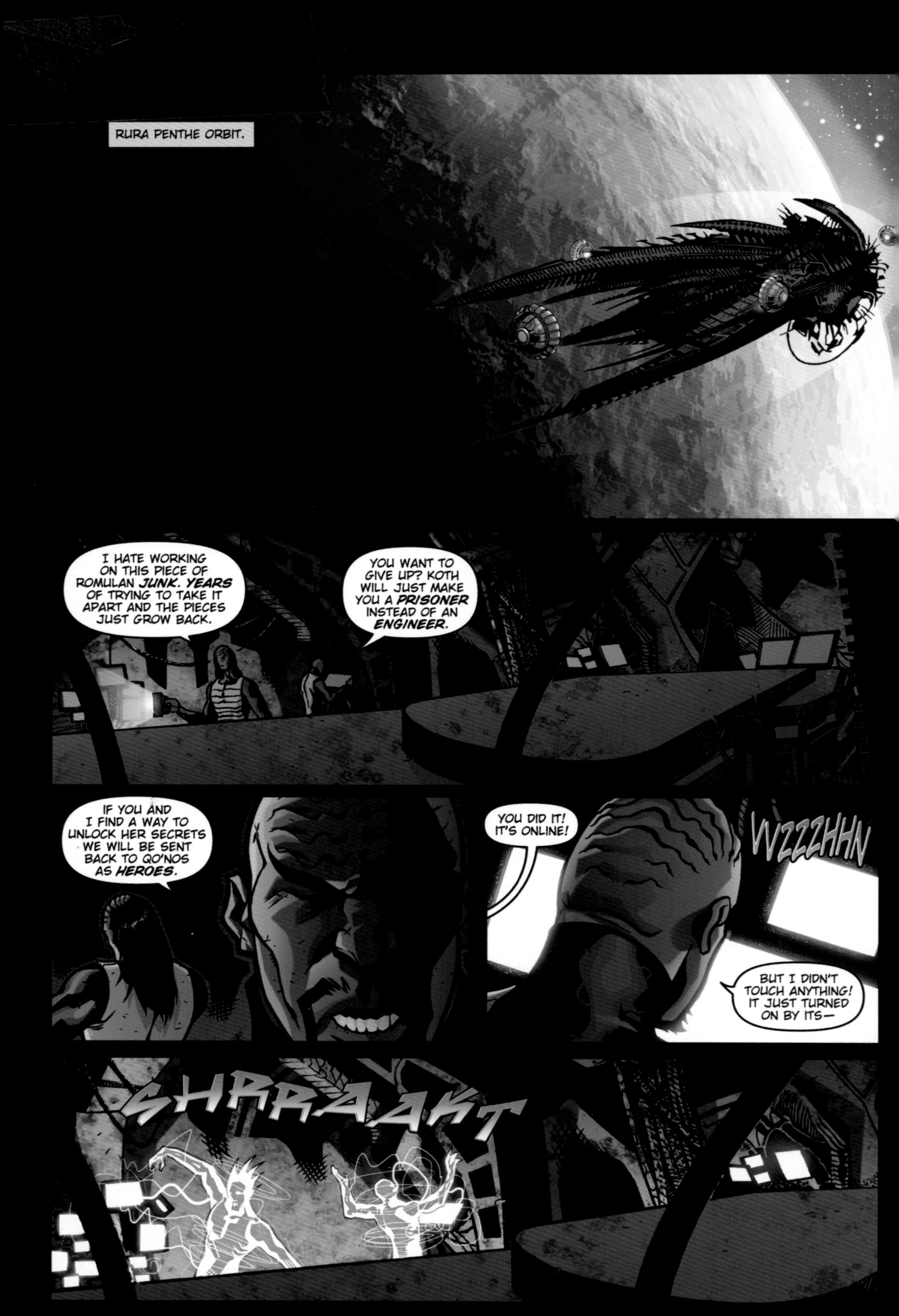
RURA PENTHE ORBIT.
I HATE WORKING ON THIS PIECE OF ROMULAN JUNK. YEARS OF TRYING TO TAKE IT APART AND THE PIECES JUST GROW BACK.
YOU WANT TO GIVE UP? KOTH WILL JUST MAKE YOU A PRISONER INSTEAD OF AN ENGINEER.
IF YOU AND I FIND A WAY TO UNLOCK HER SECRETS WE WILL BE SENT BACK TO QO'NOS AS HEROES.
YOU DID IT! IT'S ONLINE!
VVZZZHHN
BUT I DIDN'T TOUCH ANYTHING! IT JUST TURNED ON BY ITS—
SHRRAAKT

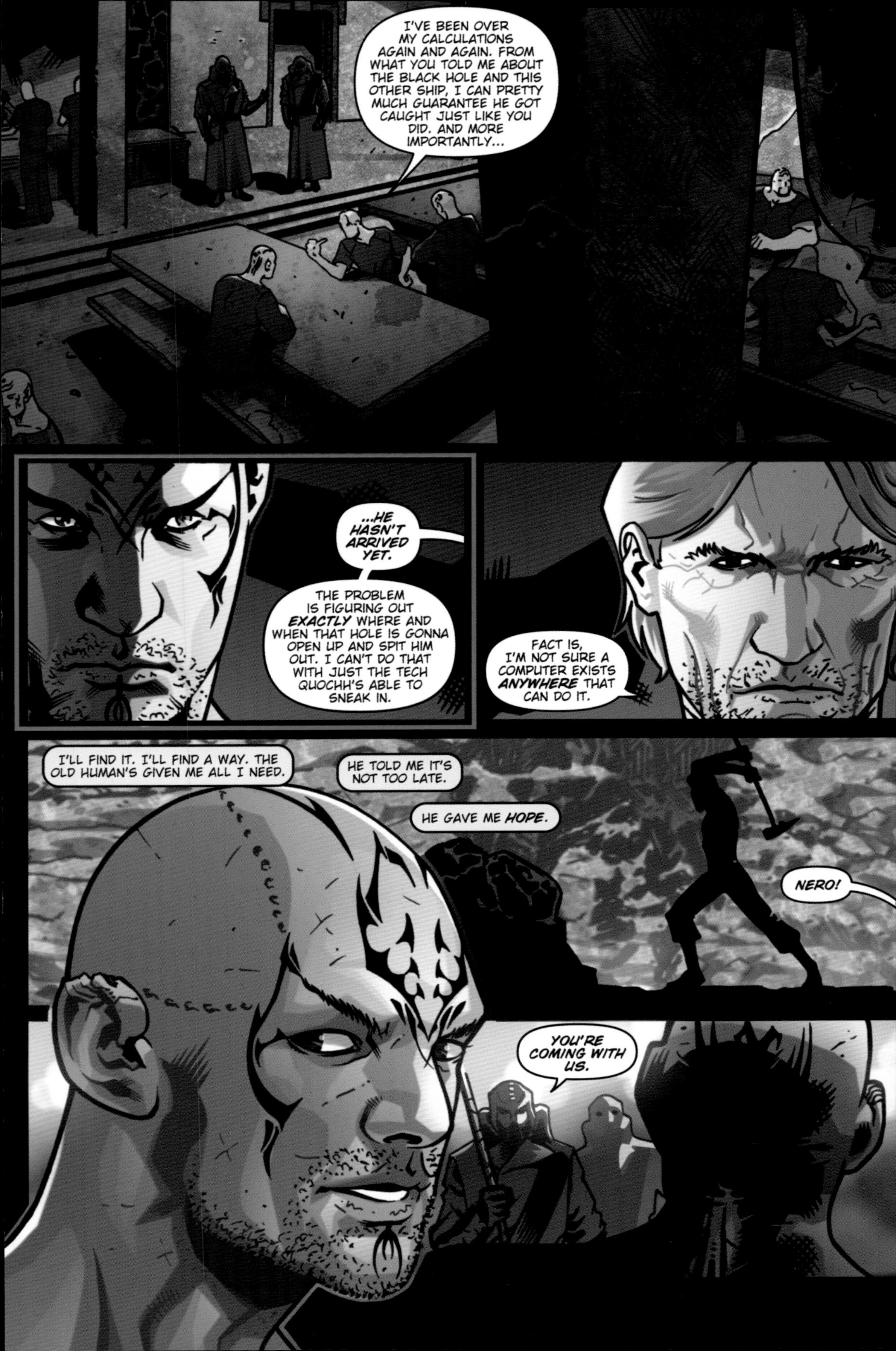
I'VE BEEN OVER MY CALCULATIONS AGAIN AND AGAIN. FROM WHAT YOU TOLD ME ABOUT THE BLACK HOLE AND THIS OTHER SHIP, I CAN PRETTY MUCH GUARANTEE HE GOT CAUGHT JUST LIKE YOU DID. AND MORE IMPORTANTLY...
...HE HASN'T ARRIVED YET.
THE PROBLEM IS FIGURING OUT EXACTLY WHERE AND WHEN THAT HOLE IS GONNA OPEN UP AND SPIT HIM OUT. I CAN'T DO THAT WITH JUST THE TECH QUOCHH'S ABLE TO SNEAK IN.
FACT IS, I'M NOT SURE A COMPUTER EXISTS ANYWHERE THAT CAN DO IT.
I'LL FIND IT. I'LL FIND A WAY. THE OLD HUMAN'S GIVEN ME ALL I NEED.
HE TOLD ME IT'S NOT TOO LATE.
HE GAVE ME HOPE.
NERO!
YOU'RE COMING WITH US.

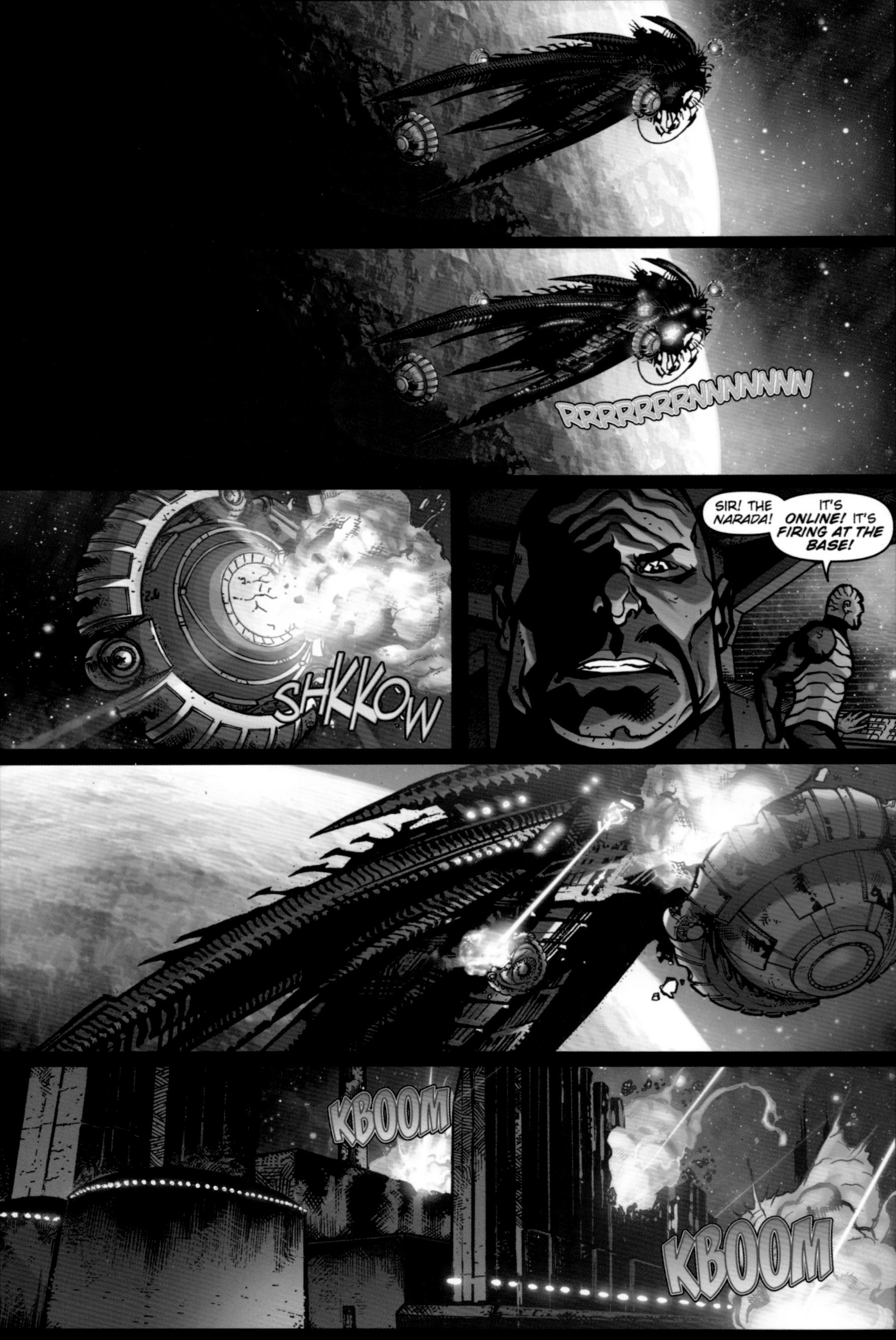
RRRRRRRNNNNNNNN
SHKKOW
SIR! THE NARADA!
IT'S ONLINE! IT'S FIRING AT THE BASE!
KBOOM
KBOOM

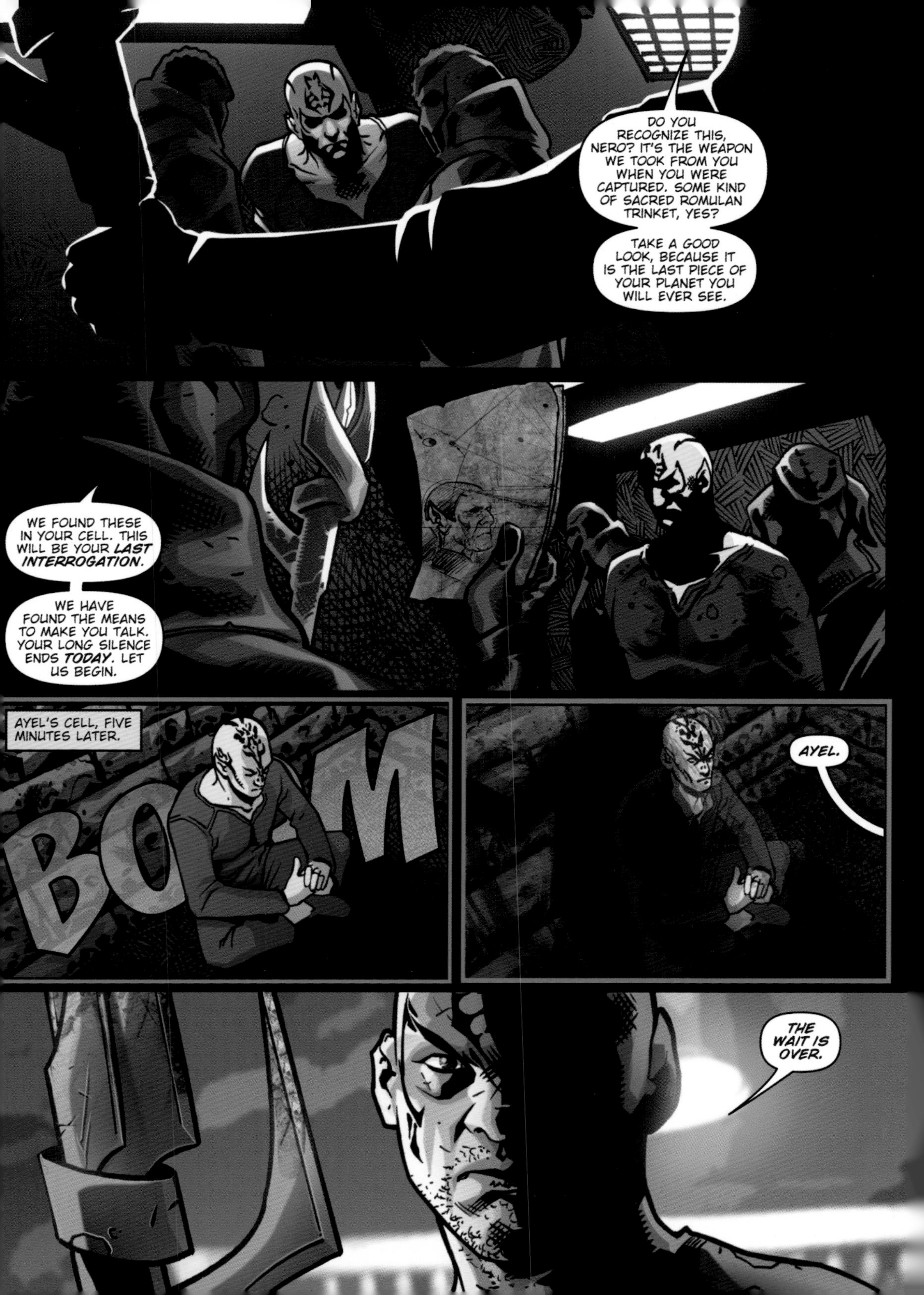
DO YOU RECOGNIZE THIS, NERO? IT'S THE WEAPON WE TOOK FROM YOU WHEN YOU WERE CAPTURED. SOME KIND OF SACRED ROMULAN TRINKET, YES?
TAKE A GOOD LOOK, BECAUSE IT IS THE LAST PIECE OF YOUR PLANET YOU WILL EVER SEE.
WE FOUND THESE IN YOUR CELL. THIS WILL BE YOUR *LAST INTERROGATION*.
WE HAVE FOUND THE MEANS TO MAKE YOU TALK. YOUR LONG SILENCE ENDS *TODAY*. LET US BEGIN.
AYEL'S CELL, FIVE MINUTES LATER.
BOOM
AYEL.
THE WAIT IS OVER.

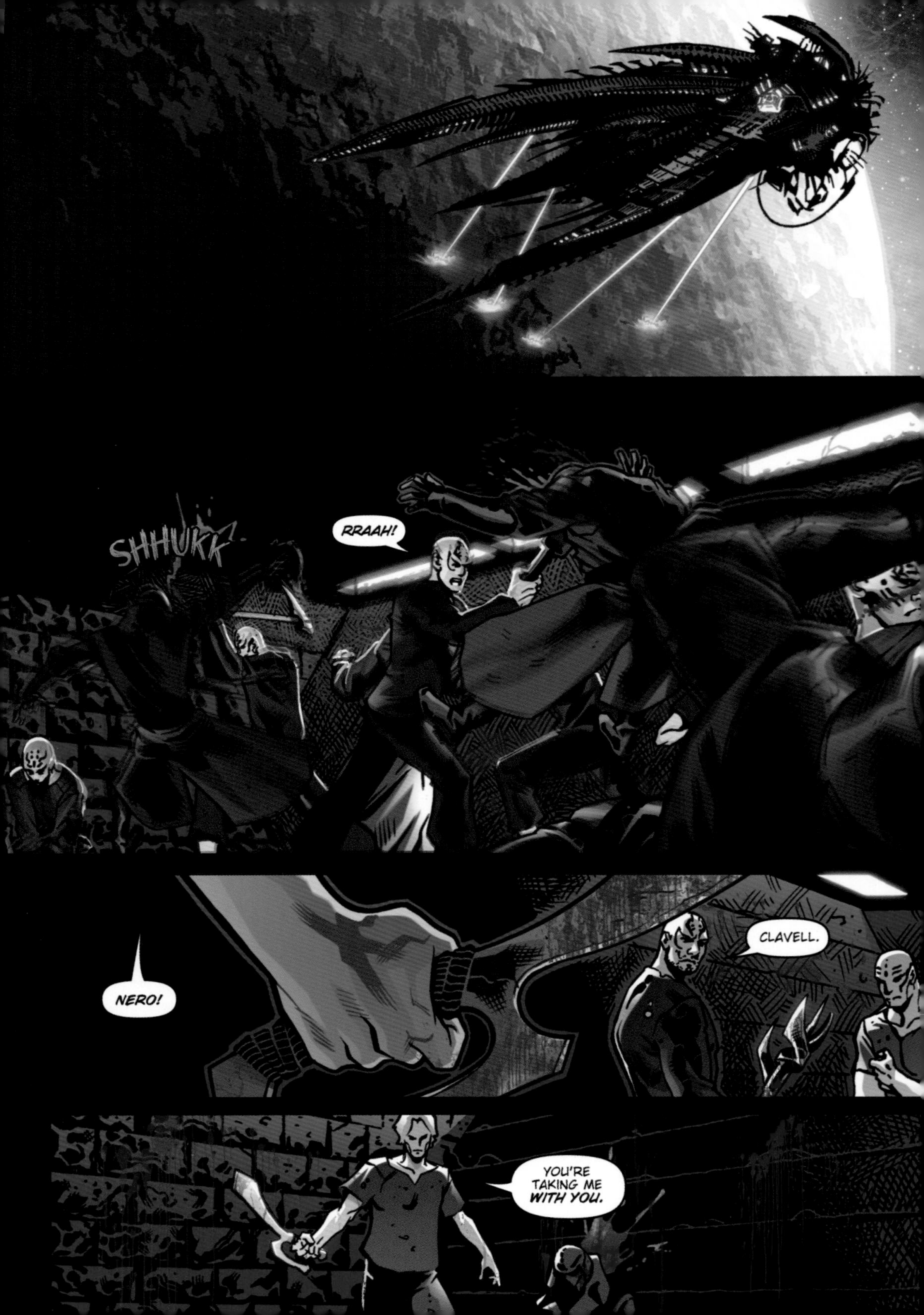
SHHUKK
RRAAH!
NERO!
CLAVELL.
YOU'RE TAKING ME WITH YOU.

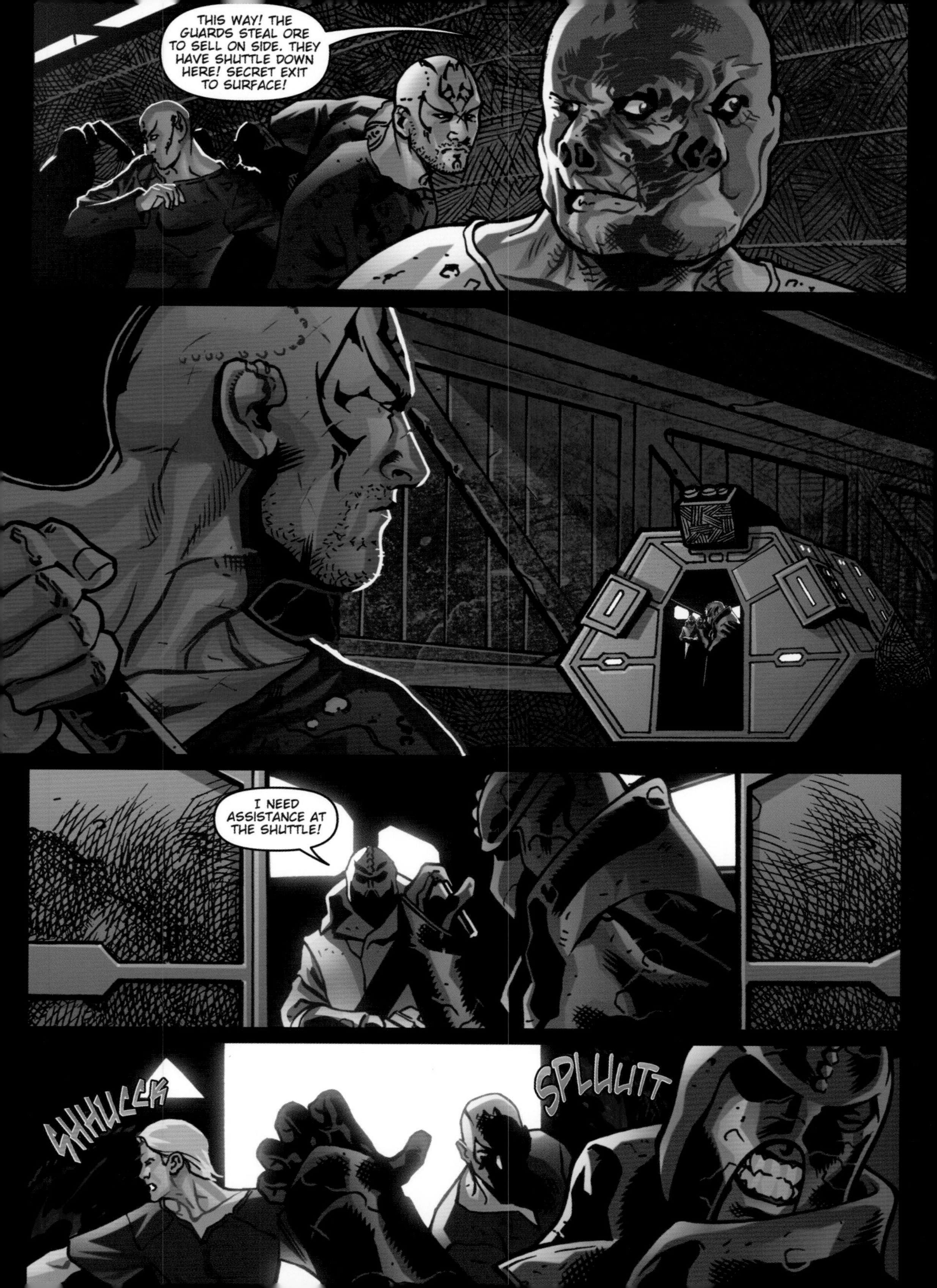
THIS WAY! THE GUARDS STEAL ORE TO SELL ON SIDE. THEY HAVE SHUTTLE DOWN HERE! SECRET EXIT TO SURFACE!
I NEED ASSISTANCE AT THE SHUTTLE!
SHHUCCK
SPLUUTT

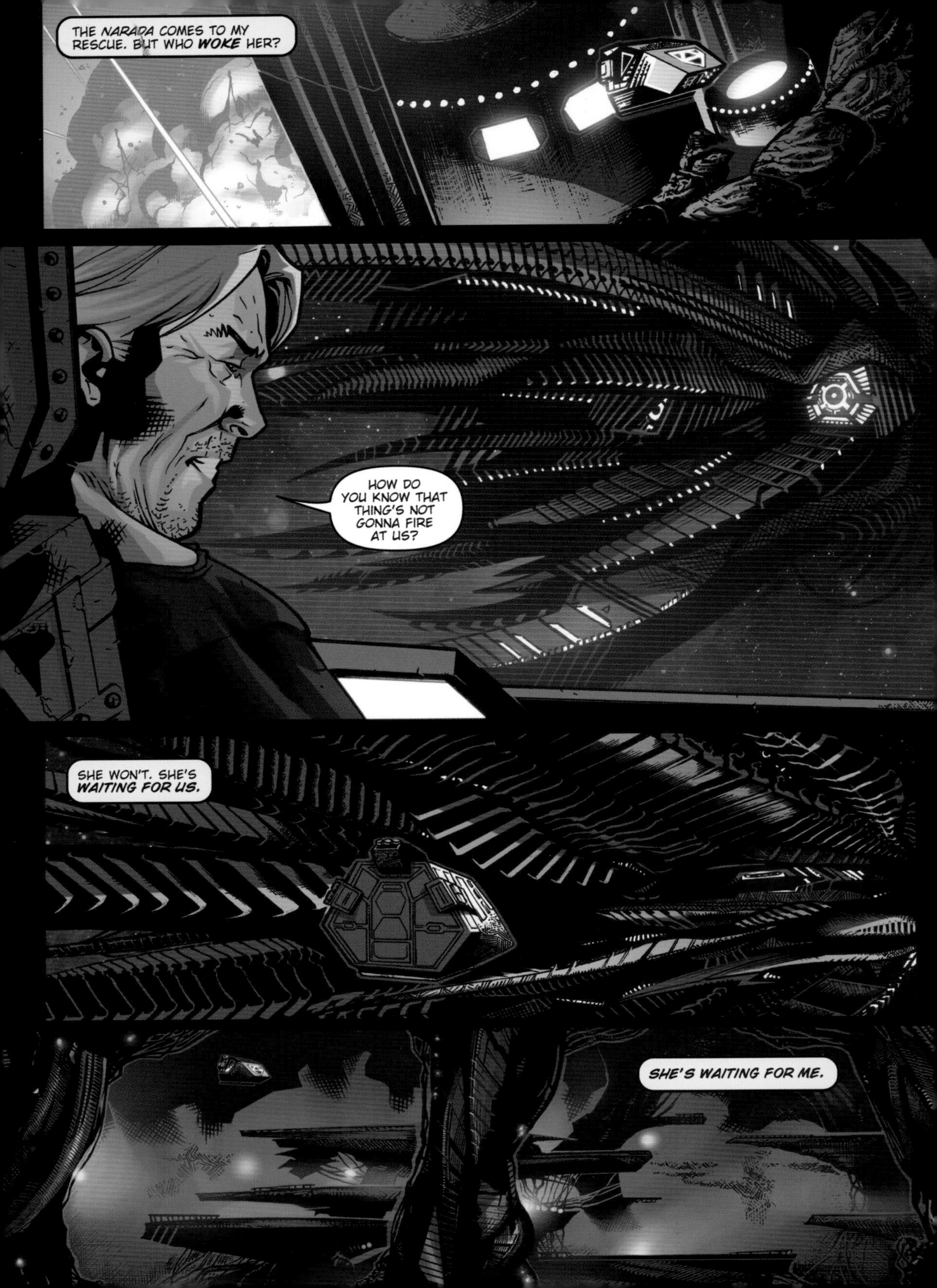
THE *NARADA* COMES TO MY RESCUE. BUT WHO **WOKE** HER?
HOW DO YOU KNOW THAT THING'S NOT GONNA FIRE AT US?
SHE WON'T. SHE'S ***WAITING FOR US.***
SHE'S WAITING FOR ME.

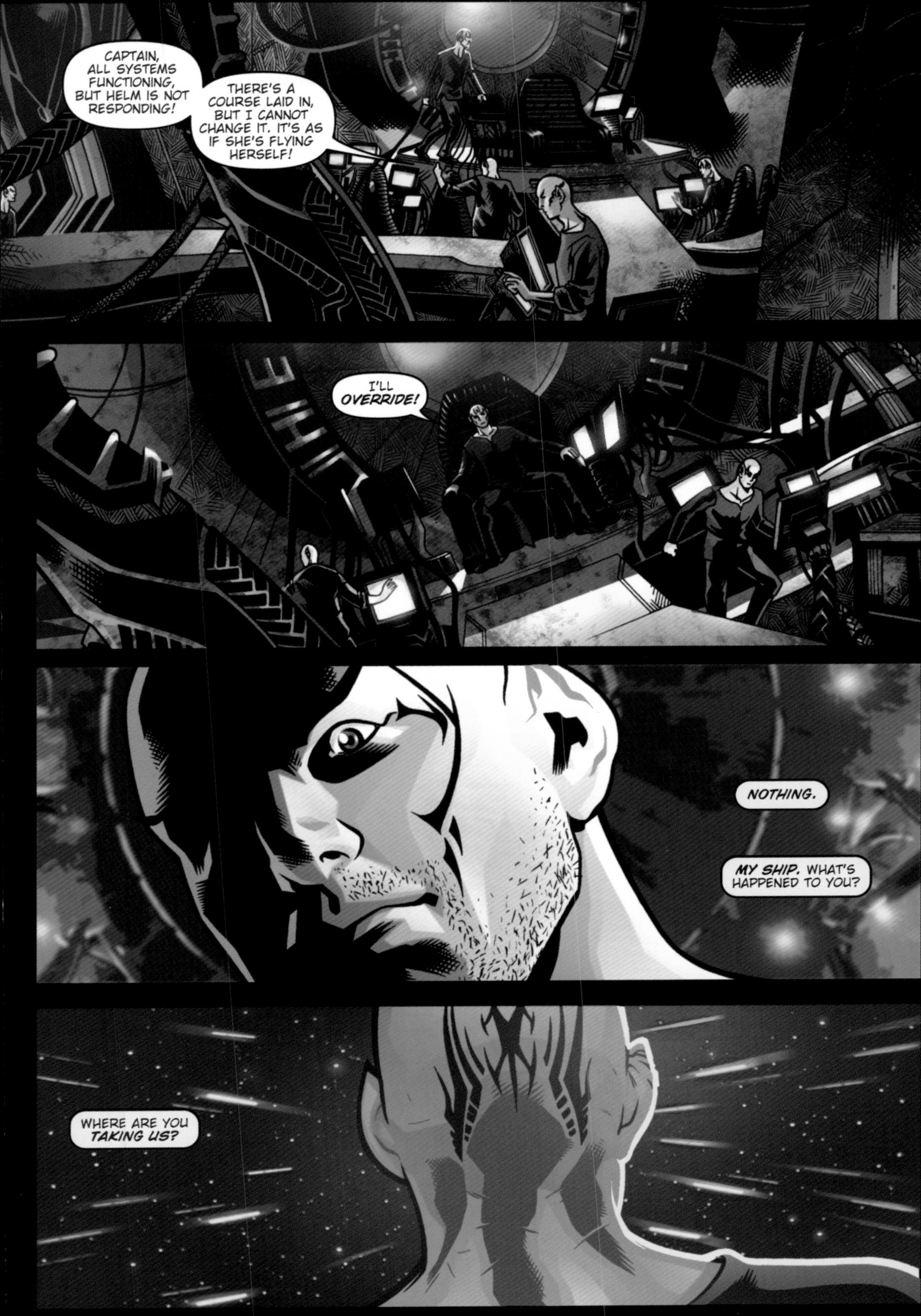
CAPTAIN, ALL SYSTEMS FUNCTIONING, BUT HELM IS NOT RESPONDING!
THERE'S A COURSE LAID IN, BUT I CANNOT CHANGE IT. IT'S AS IF SHE'S FLYING HERSELF!
I'LL OVERRIDE!
NOTHING.
MY SHIP. WHAT'S HAPPENED TO YOU?
WHERE ARE YOU TAKING US?

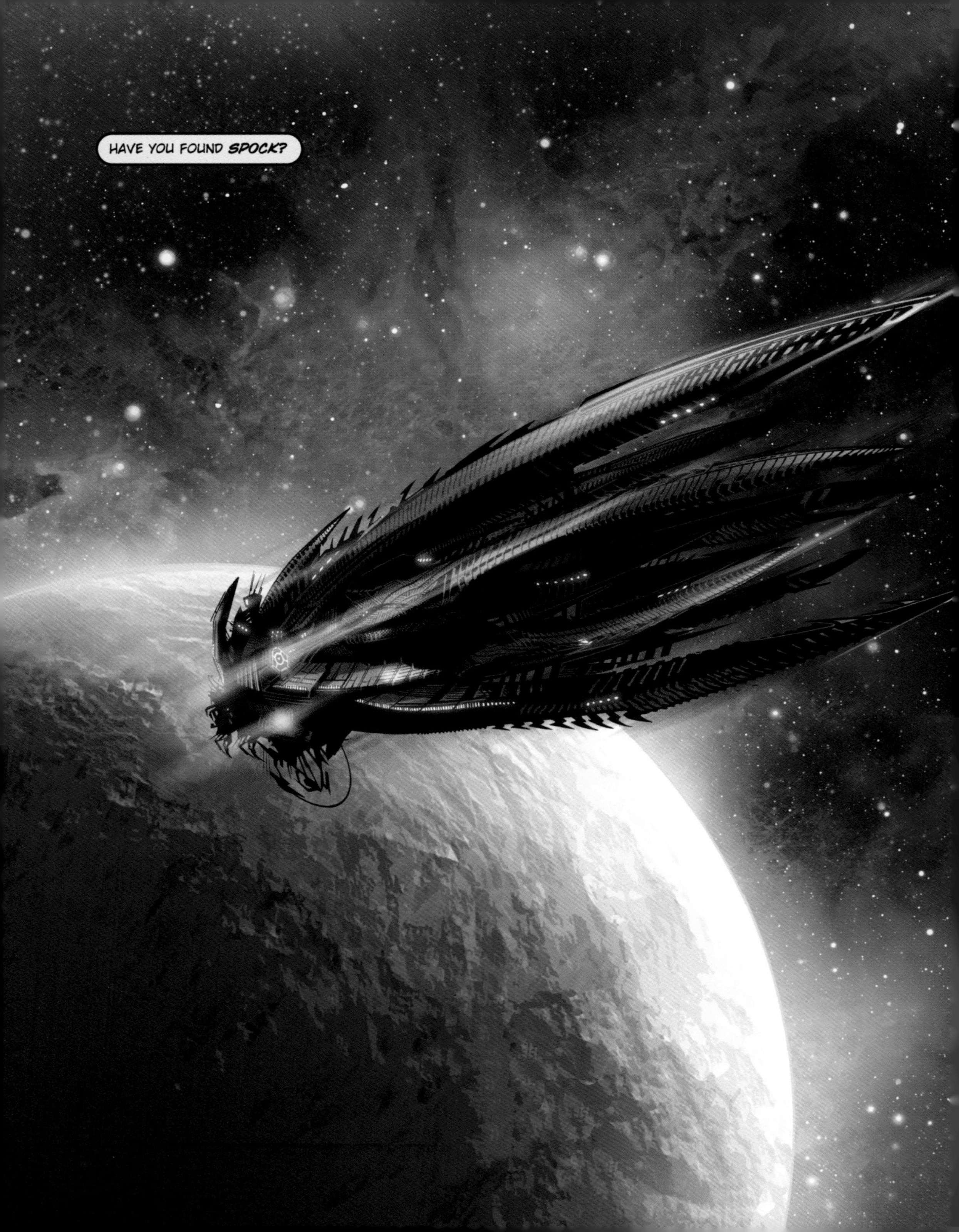
HAVE YOU FOUND SPOCK?

THE EDGE OF THE DELTA QUADRANT.

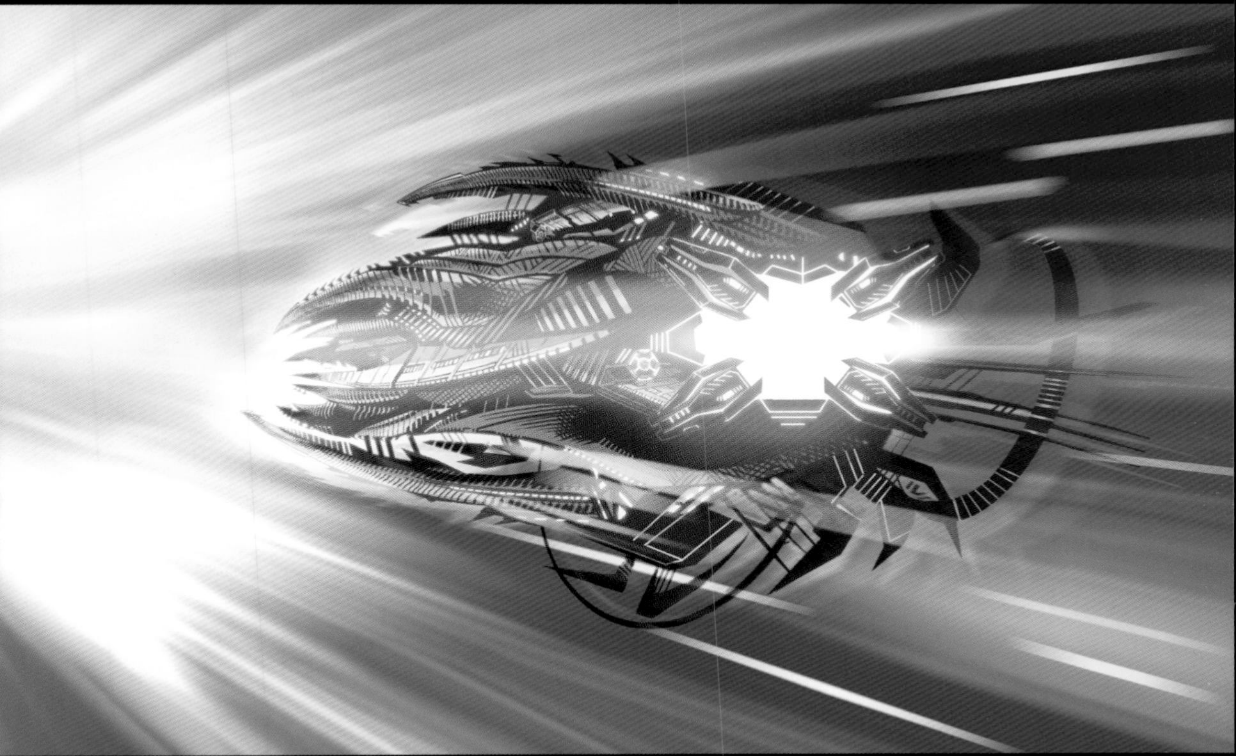

STAR TREK®
NERO
CHAPTER THREE

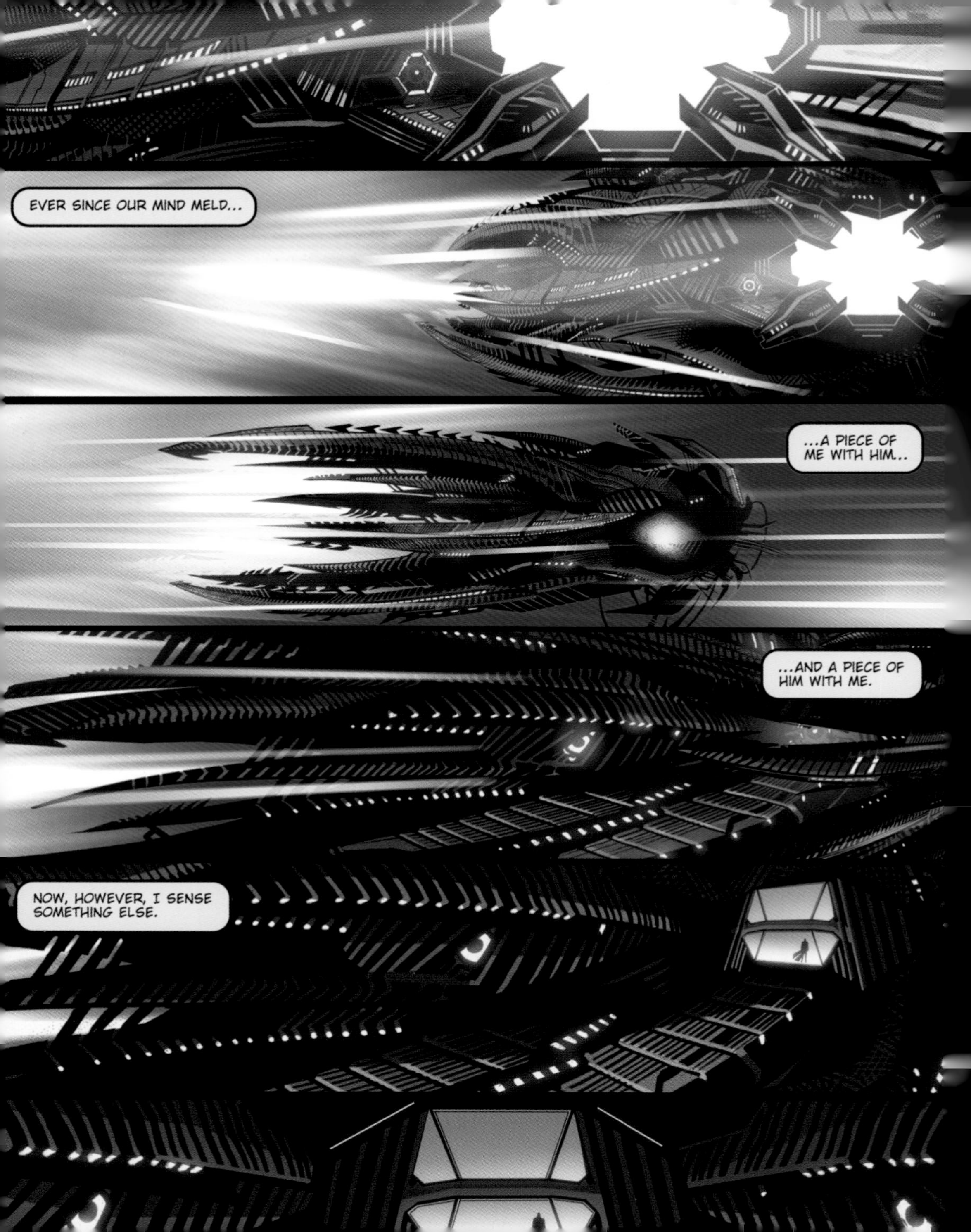
EVER SINCE OUR MIND MELD...
...A PIECE OF ME WITH HIM...
...AND A PIECE OF HIM WITH ME.
NOW, HOWEVER, I SENSE SOMETHING ELSE.

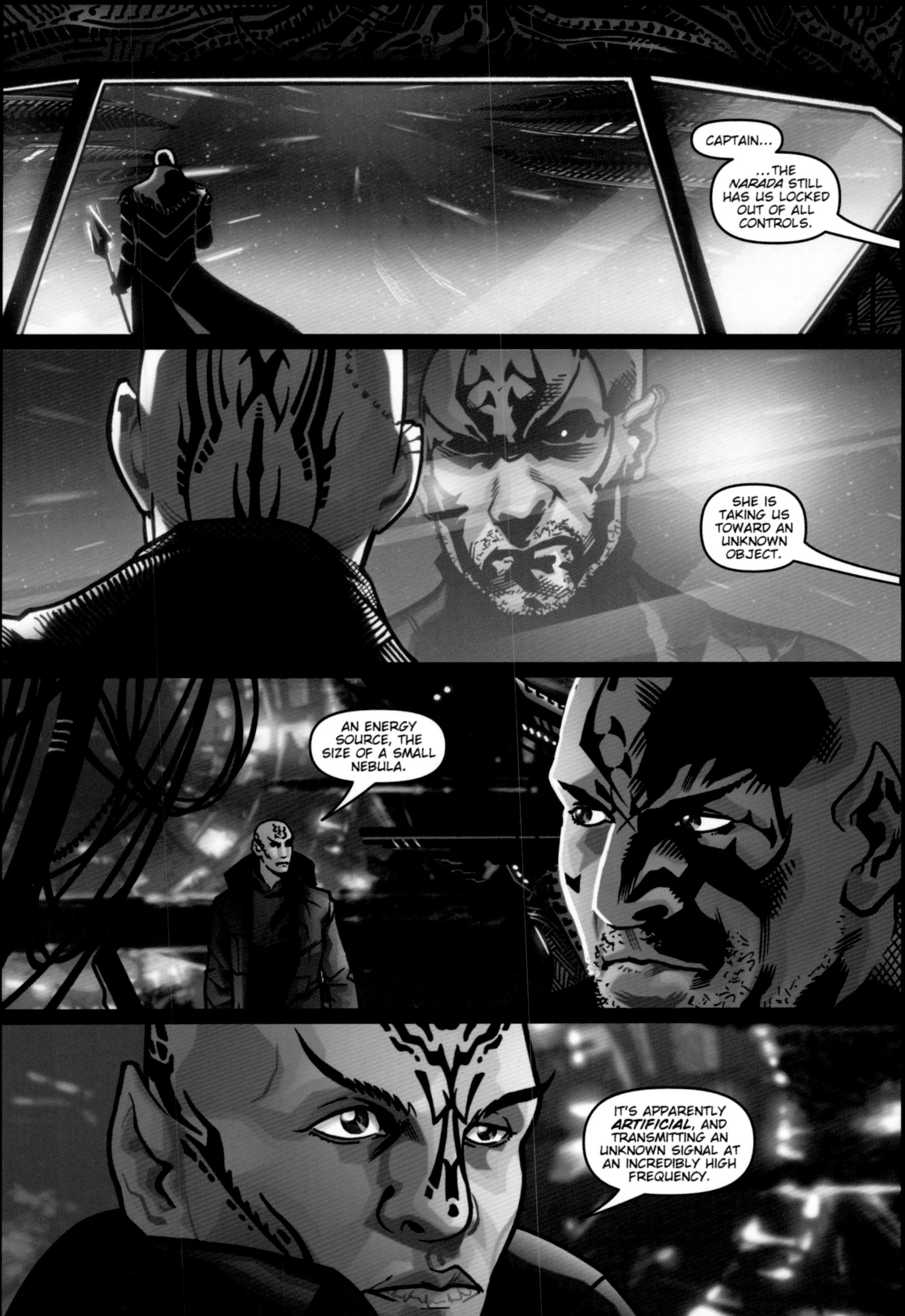
CAPTAIN...
...THE *NARADA* STILL HAS US LOCKED OUT OF ALL CONTROLS.
SHE IS TAKING US TOWARD AN UNKNOWN OBJECT.
AN ENERGY SOURCE, THE SIZE OF A SMALL NEBULA.
IT'S APPARENTLY ***ARTIFICIAL***, AND TRANSMITTING AN UNKNOWN SIGNAL AT AN INCREDIBLY HIGH FREQUENCY.

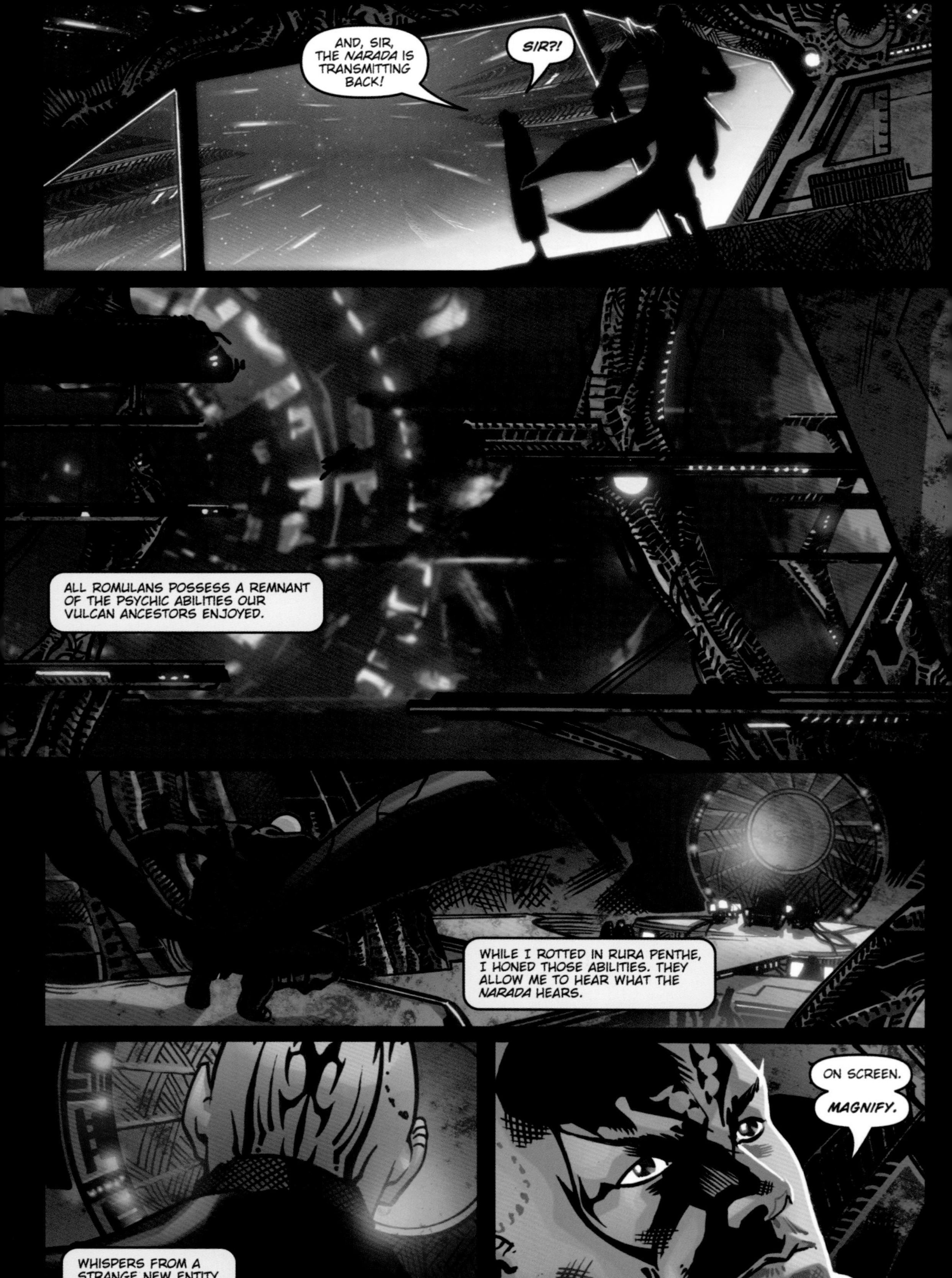
AND, SIR, THE NARADA IS TRANSMITTING BACK!
SIR?!
ALL ROMULANS POSSESS A REMNANT OF THE PSYCHIC ABILITIES OUR VULCAN ANCESTORS ENJOYED.
WHILE I ROTTED IN RURA PENTHE, I HONED THOSE ABILITIES. THEY ALLOW ME TO HEAR WHAT THE NARADA HEARS.
WHISPERS FROM A STRANGE NEW ENTITY.
ON SCREEN.
MAGNIFY.

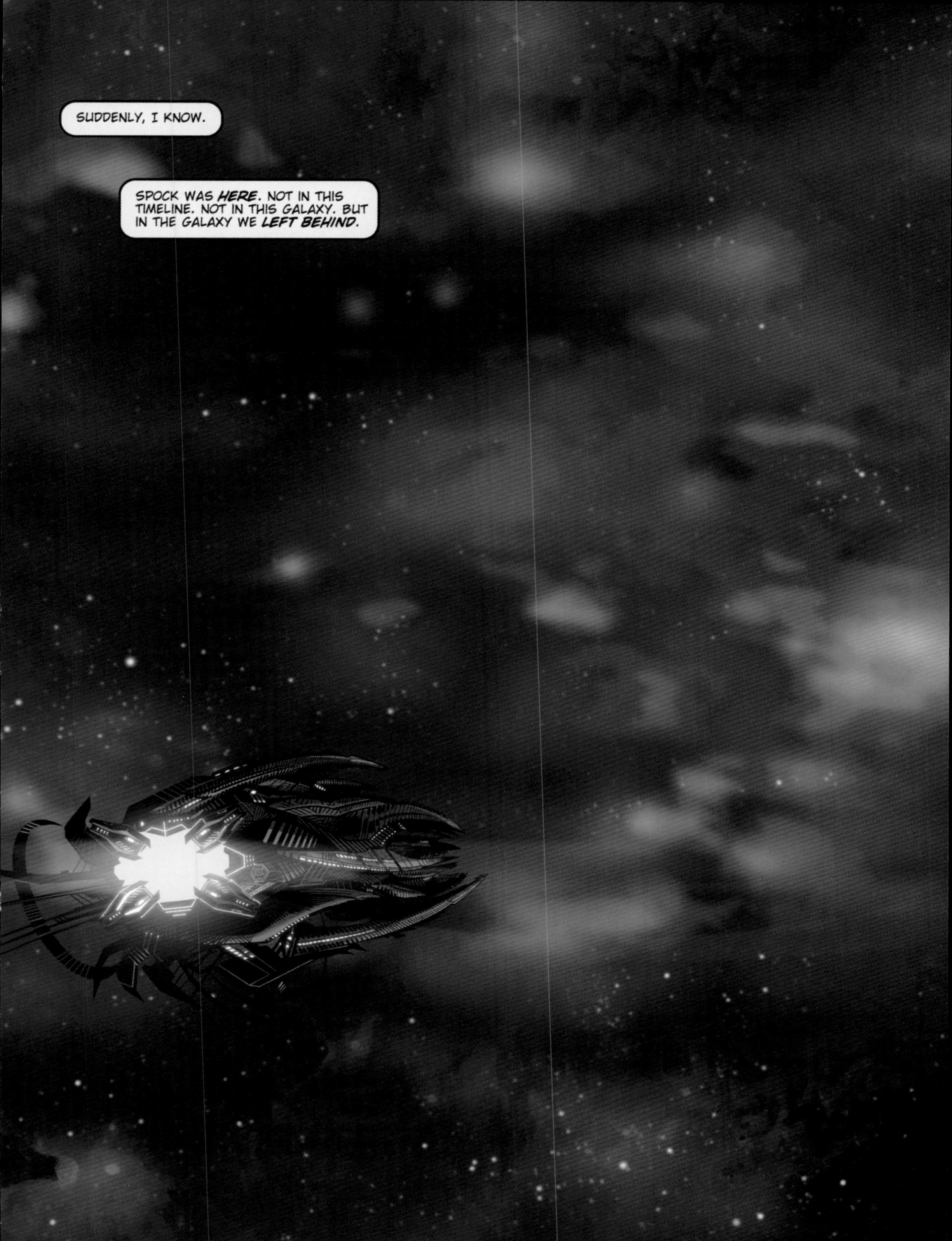
SUDDENLY, I KNOW.
SPOCK WAS HERE. NOT IN THIS TIMELINE. NOT IN THIS GALAXY. BUT IN THE GALAXY WE LEFT BEHIND.

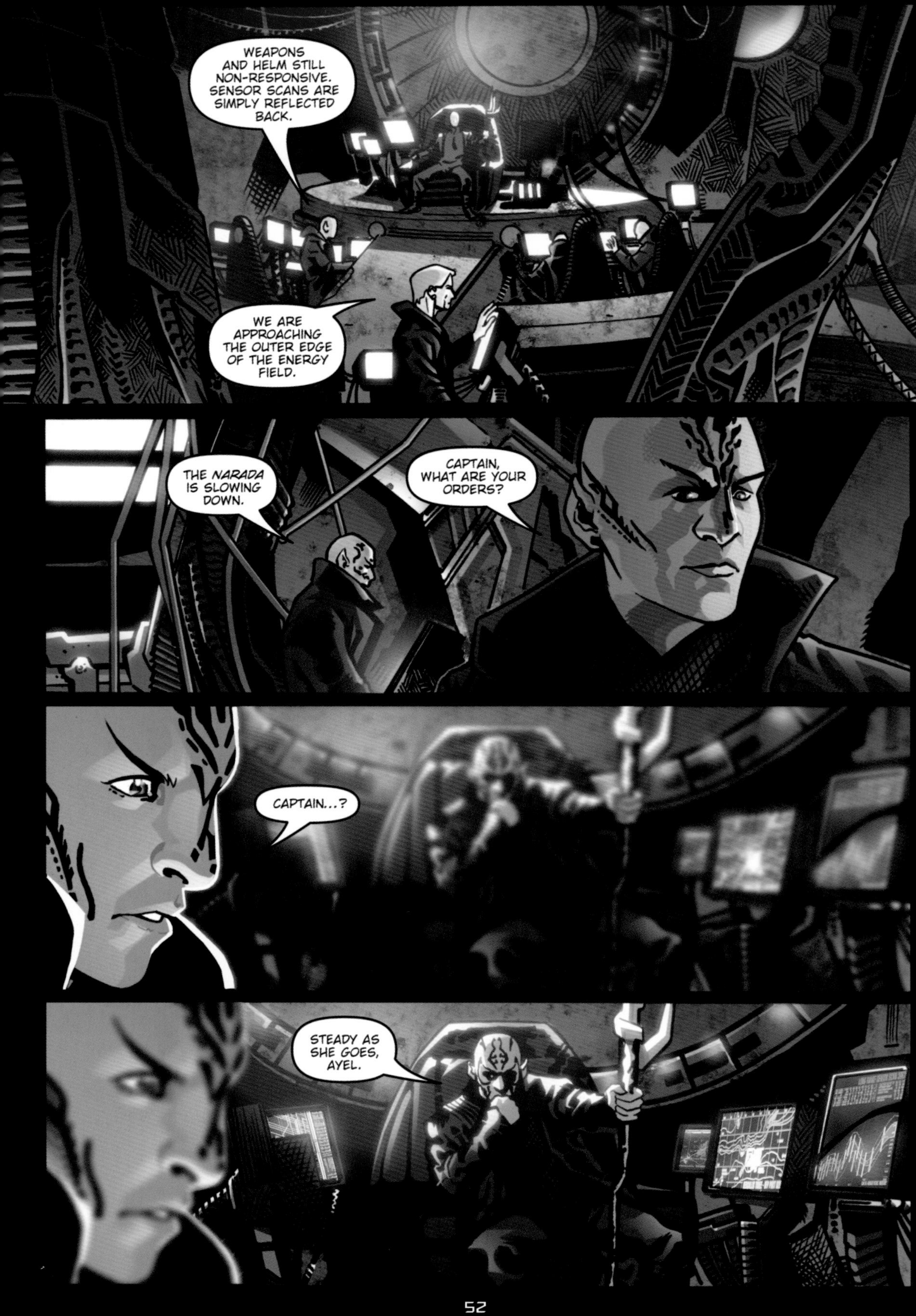
WEAPONS AND HELM STILL NON-RESPONSIVE. SENSOR SCANS ARE SIMPLY REFLECTED BACK.
WE ARE APPROACHING THE OUTER EDGE OF THE ENERGY FIELD.
THE *NARADA* IS SLOWING DOWN.
CAPTAIN, WHAT ARE YOUR ORDERS?
CAPTAIN...?
STEADY AS SHE GOES, AYEL.

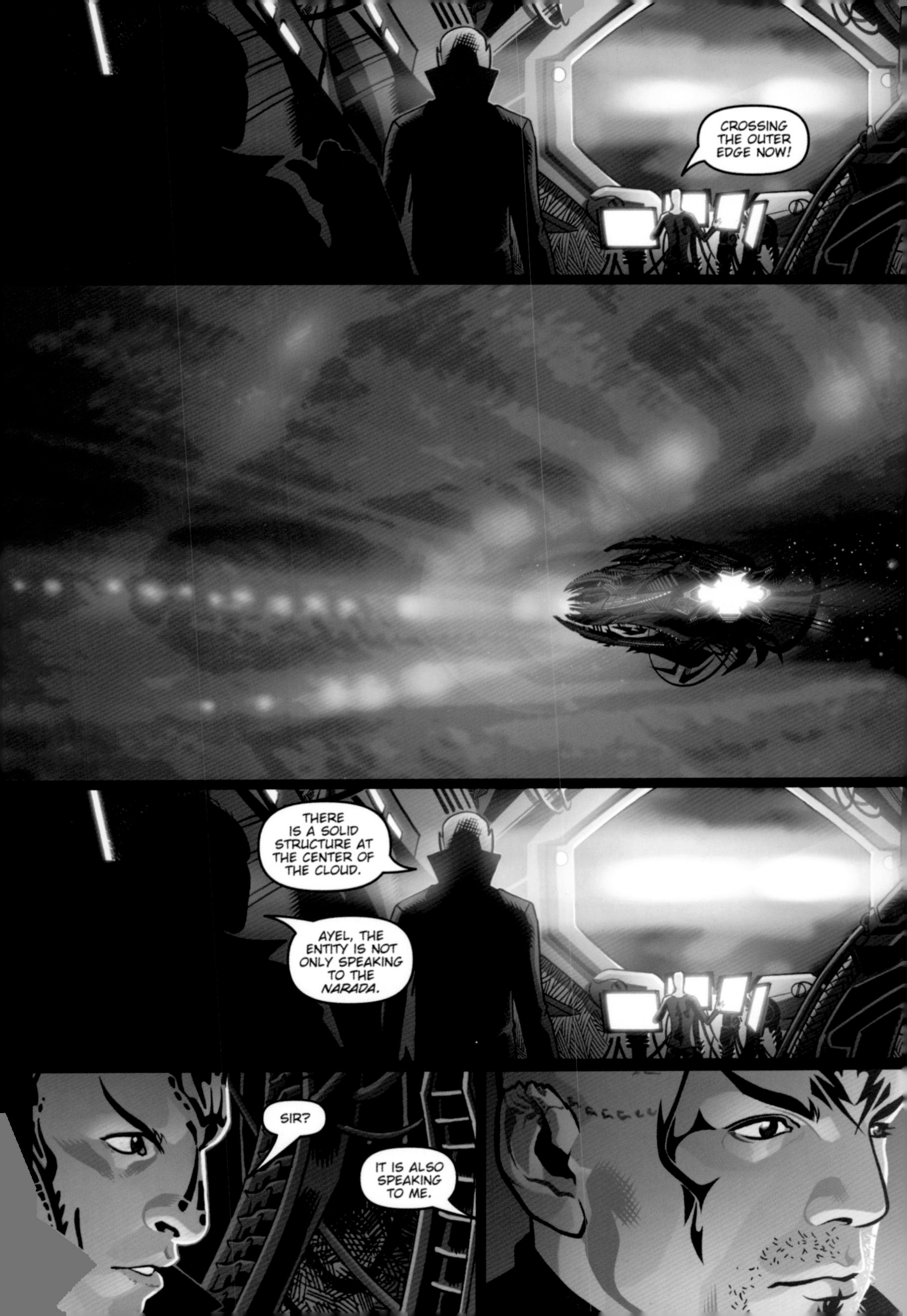
CROSSING THE OUTER EDGE NOW!
THERE IS A SOLID STRUCTURE AT THE CENTER OF THE CLOUD.
AYEL, THE ENTITY IS NOT ONLY SPEAKING TO THE *NARADA*.
SIR?
IT IS ALSO SPEAKING TO ME.

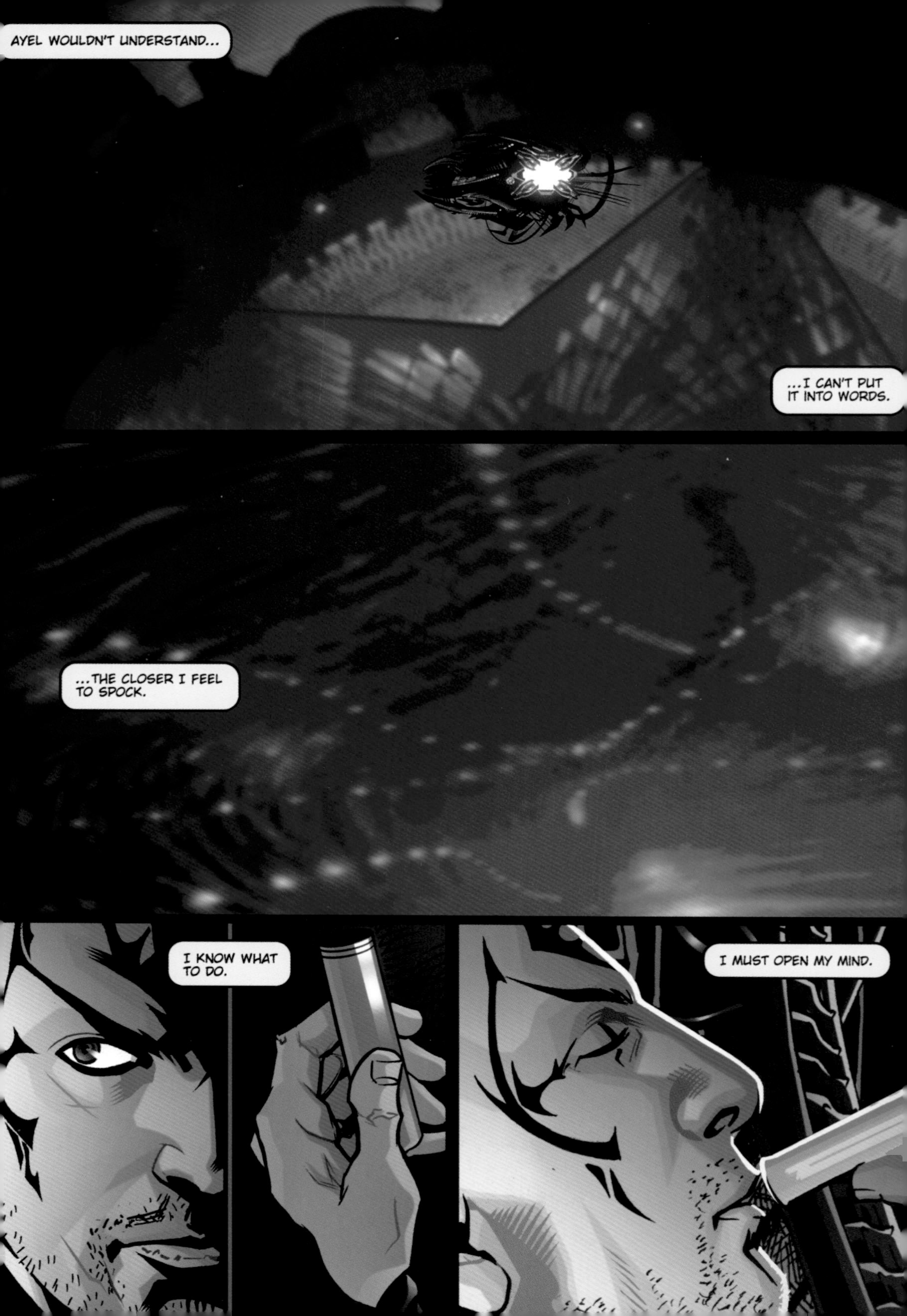
AYEL WOULDN'T UNDERSTAND...
...I CAN'T PUT IT INTO WORDS.
...THE CLOSER I FEEL TO SPOCK.
I KNOW WHAT TO DO.
I MUST OPEN MY MIND.

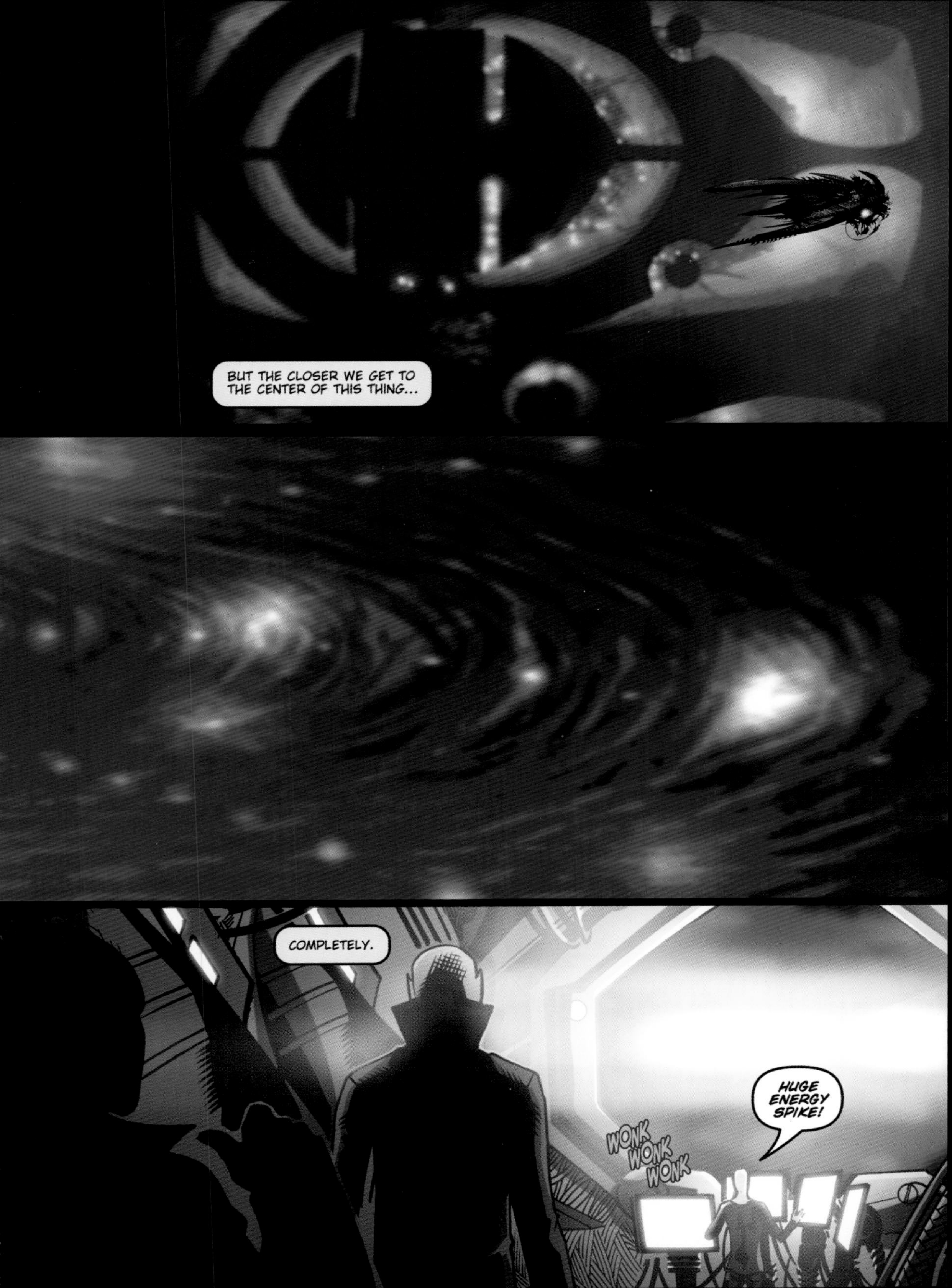
BUT THE CLOSER WE GET TO THE CENTER OF THIS THING...
COMPLETELY.
WONK WONK WONK
HUGE ENERGY SPIKE!

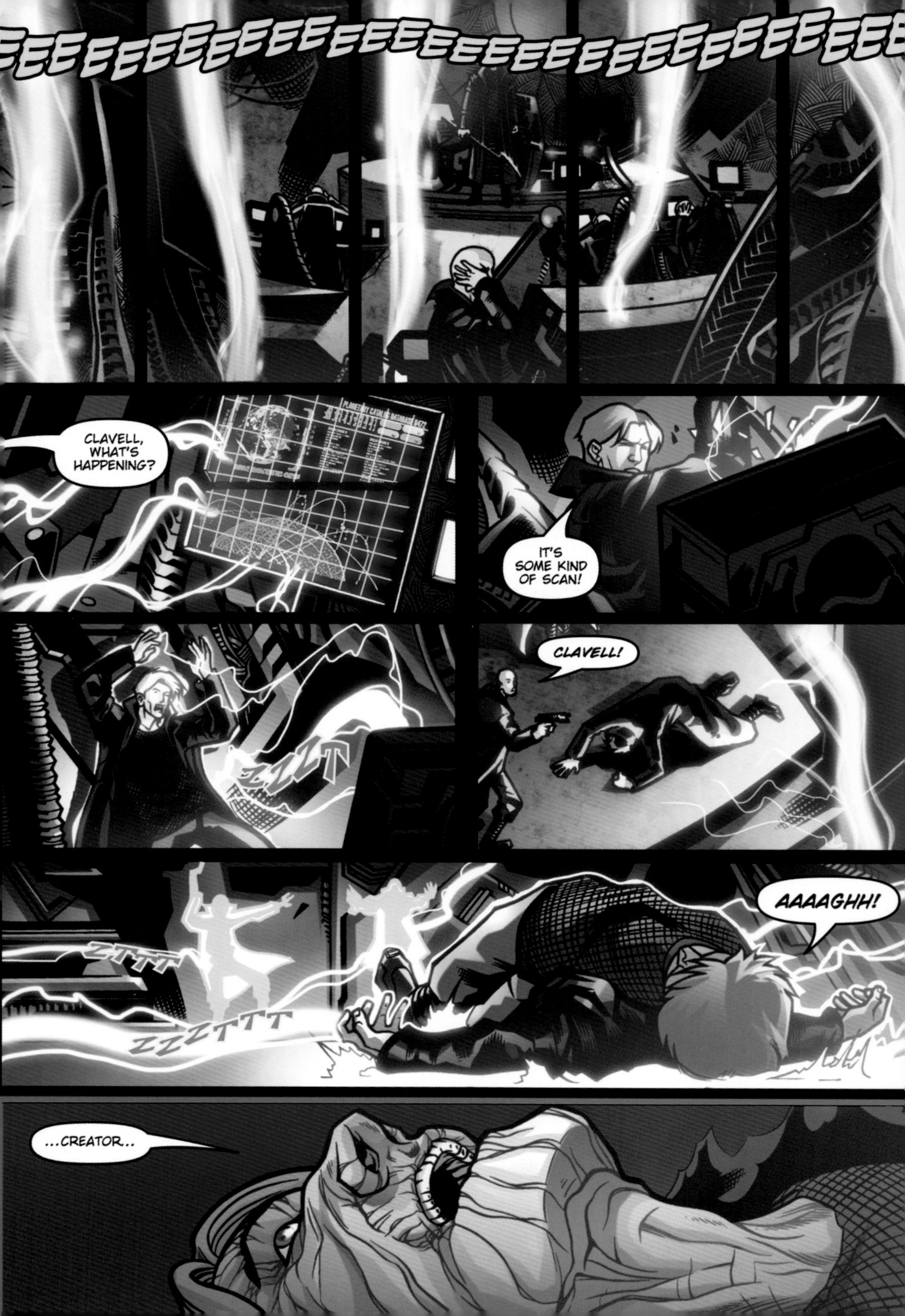
EEEEEEEEEEEEEEEEEEEEEEEEEEEEE
CLAVELL, WHAT'S HAPPENING?
IT'S SOME KIND OF SCAN!
ZZZT
CLAVELL!
ZTTT
ZZZTTTT
AAAAGHH!
...CREATOR...

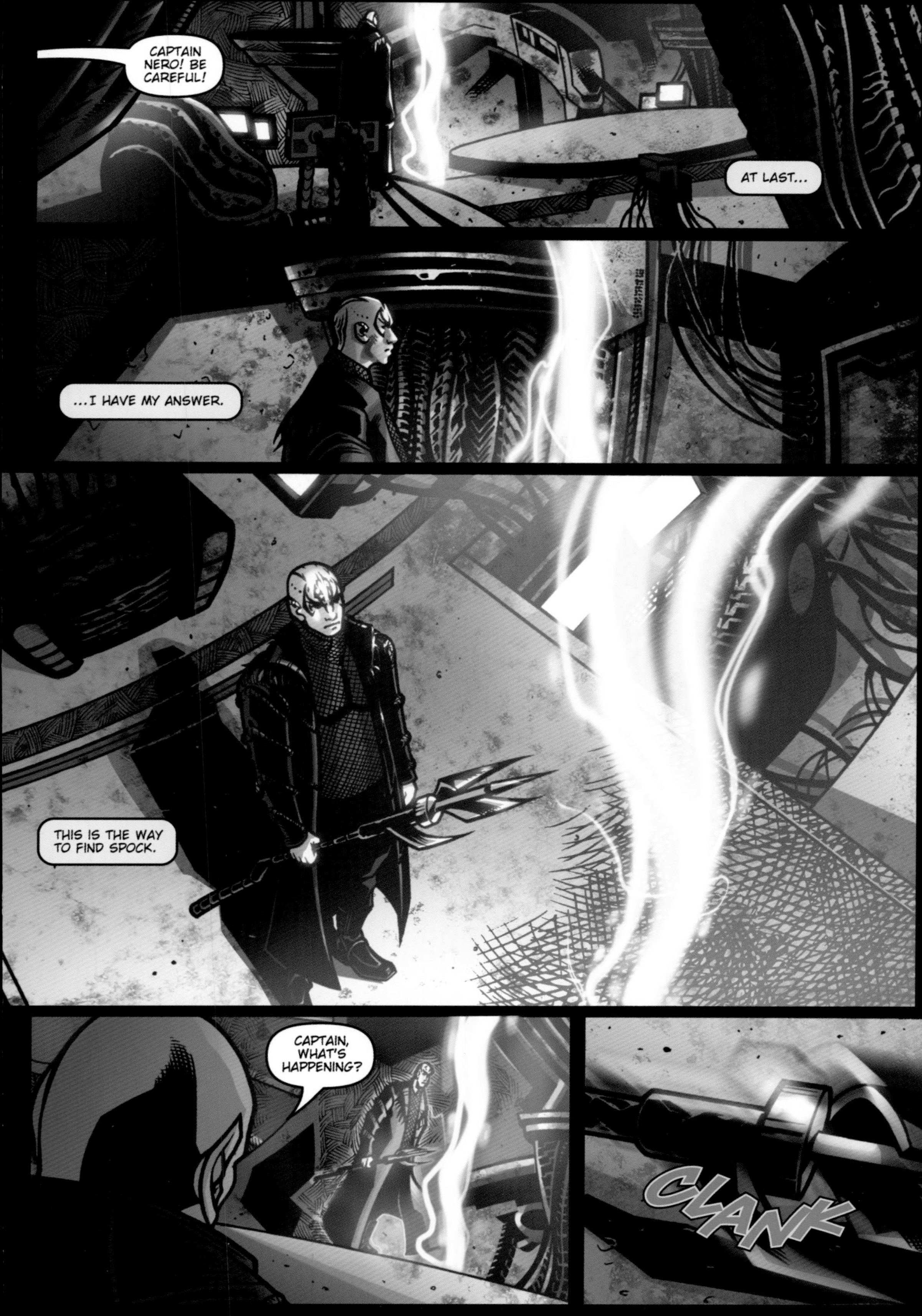
CAPTAIN NERO! BE CAREFUL!
AT LAST...
...I HAVE MY ANSWER.
THIS IS THE WAY TO FIND SPOCK.
CAPTAIN, WHAT'S HAPPENING?
CLANK

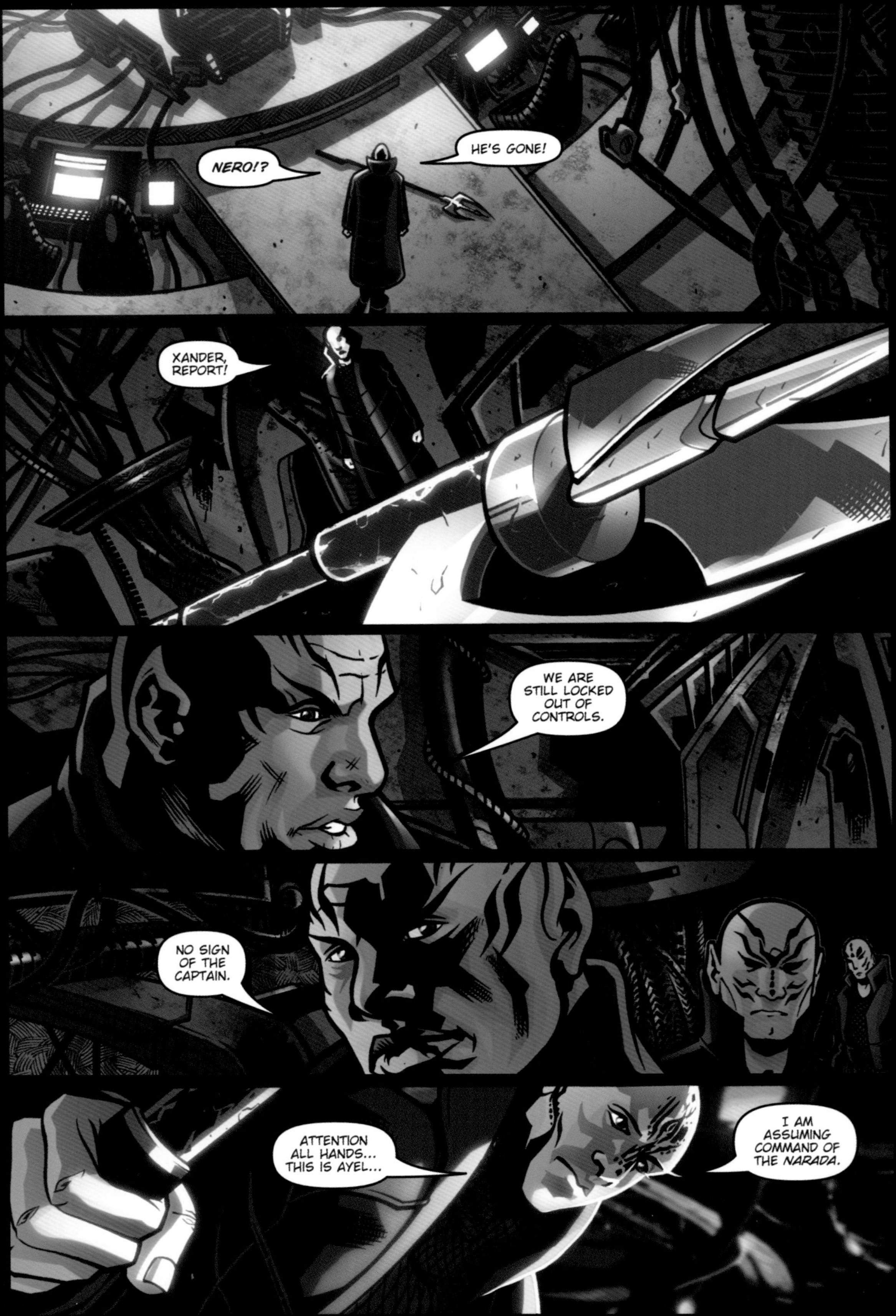
NERO!?
HE'S GONE!
XANDER, REPORT!
WE ARE STILL LOCKED OUT OF CONTROLS.
NO SIGN OF THE CAPTAIN.
ATTENTION ALL HANDS... THIS IS AYEL...
I AM ASSUMING COMMAND OF THE *NARADA*.

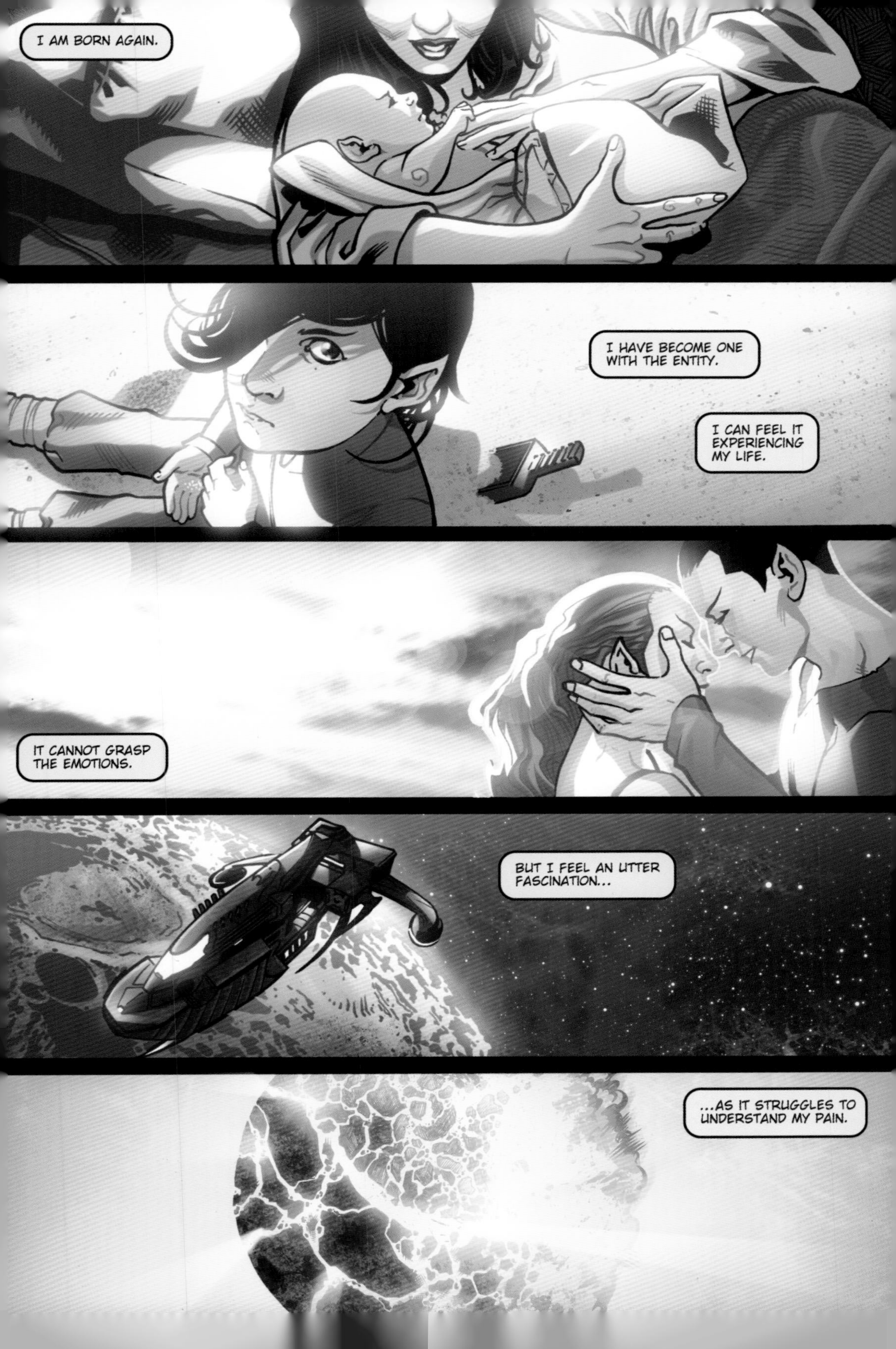
I AM BORN AGAIN.
I HAVE BECOME ONE WITH THE ENTITY.
I CAN FEEL IT EXPERIENCING MY LIFE.
IT CANNOT GRASP THE EMOTIONS.
BUT I FEEL AN UTTER FASCINATION...
...AS IT STRUGGLES TO UNDERSTAND MY PAIN.

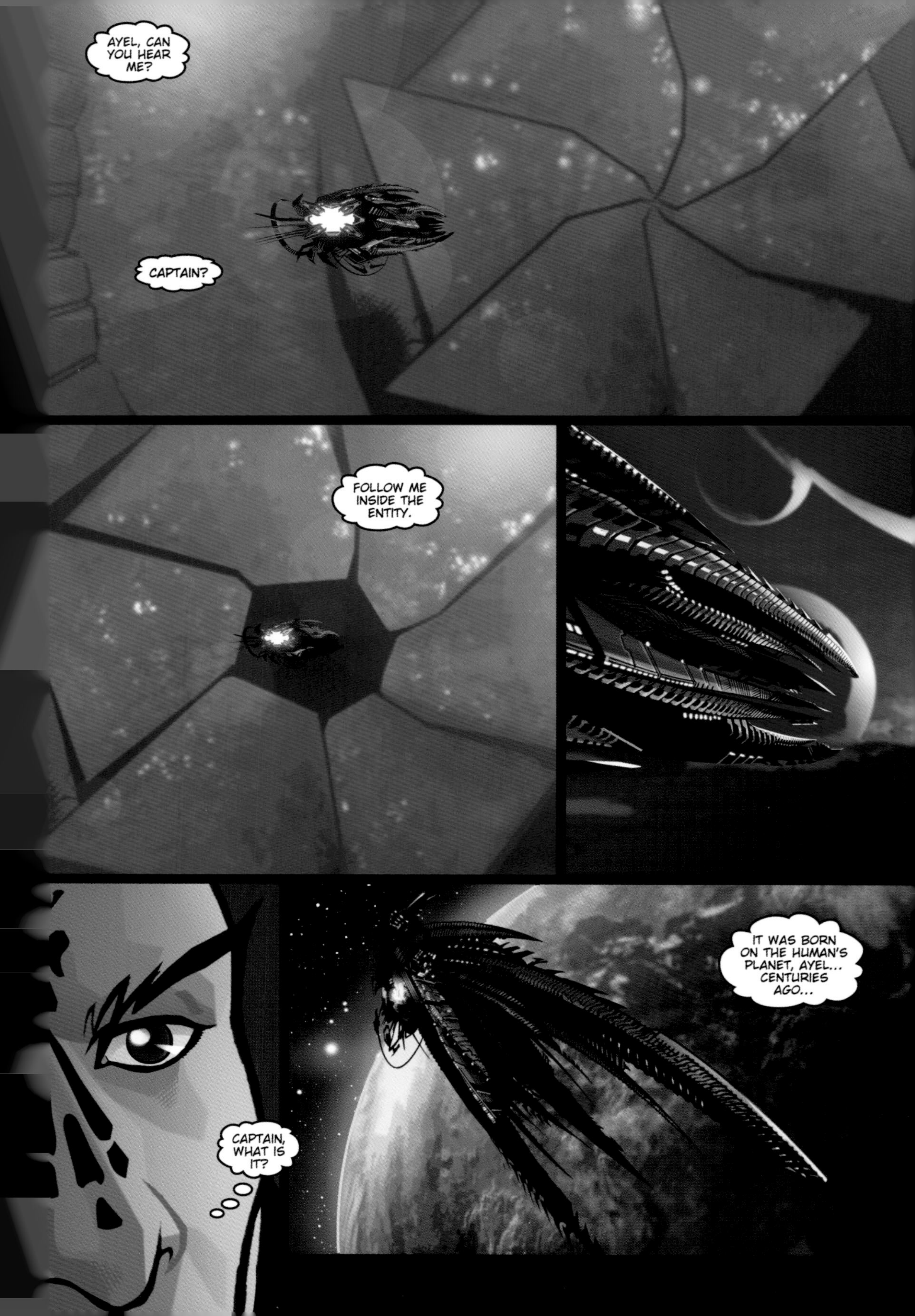
AYEL, CAN YOU HEAR ME?
CAPTAIN?
FOLLOW ME INSIDE THE ENTITY.
IT WAS BORN ON THE HUMAN'S PLANET, AYEL... CENTURIES AGO...
CAPTAIN, WHAT IS IT?

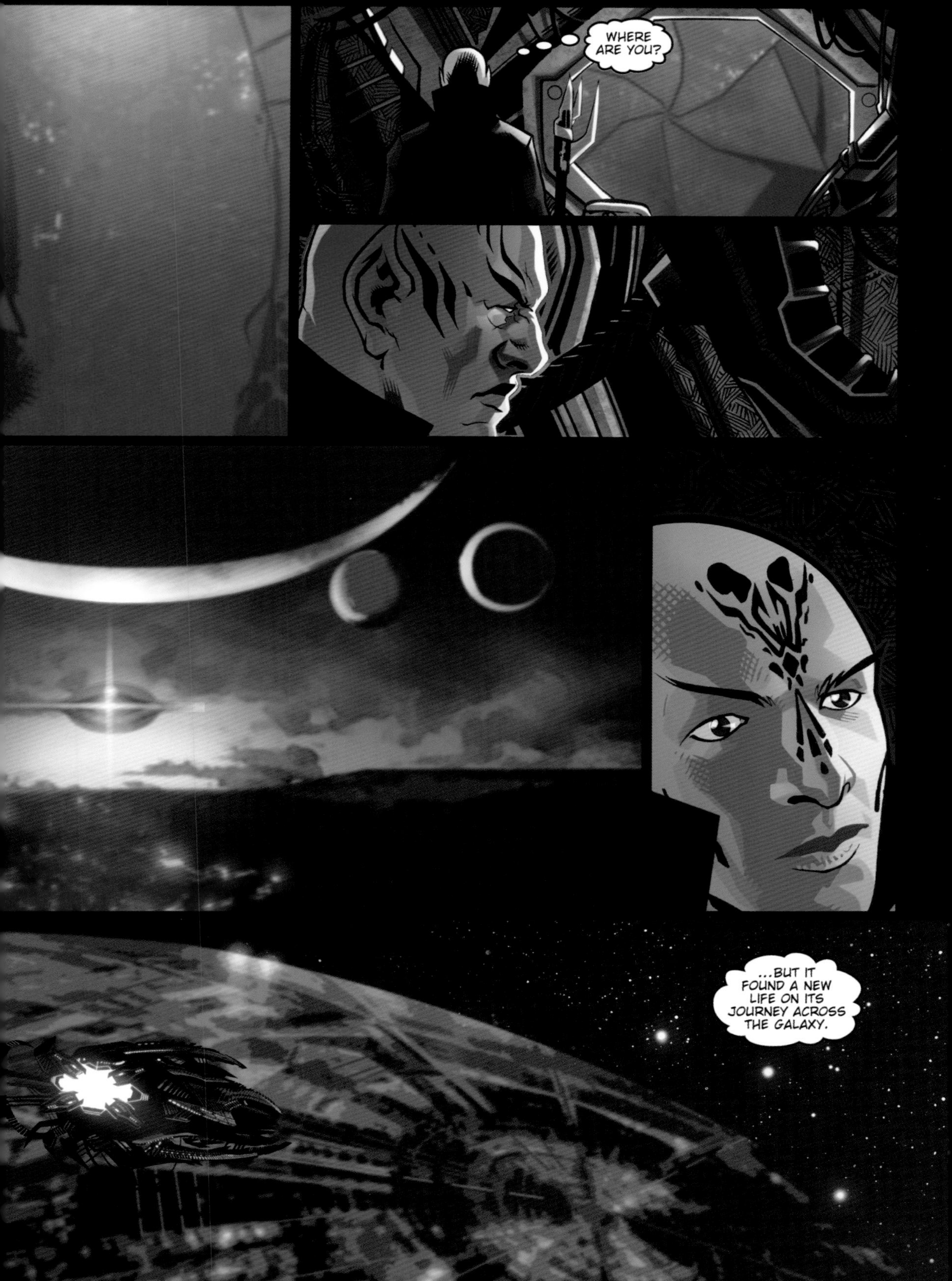
WHERE ARE YOU?
...BUT IT FOUND A NEW LIFE ON ITS JOURNEY ACROSS THE GALAXY.

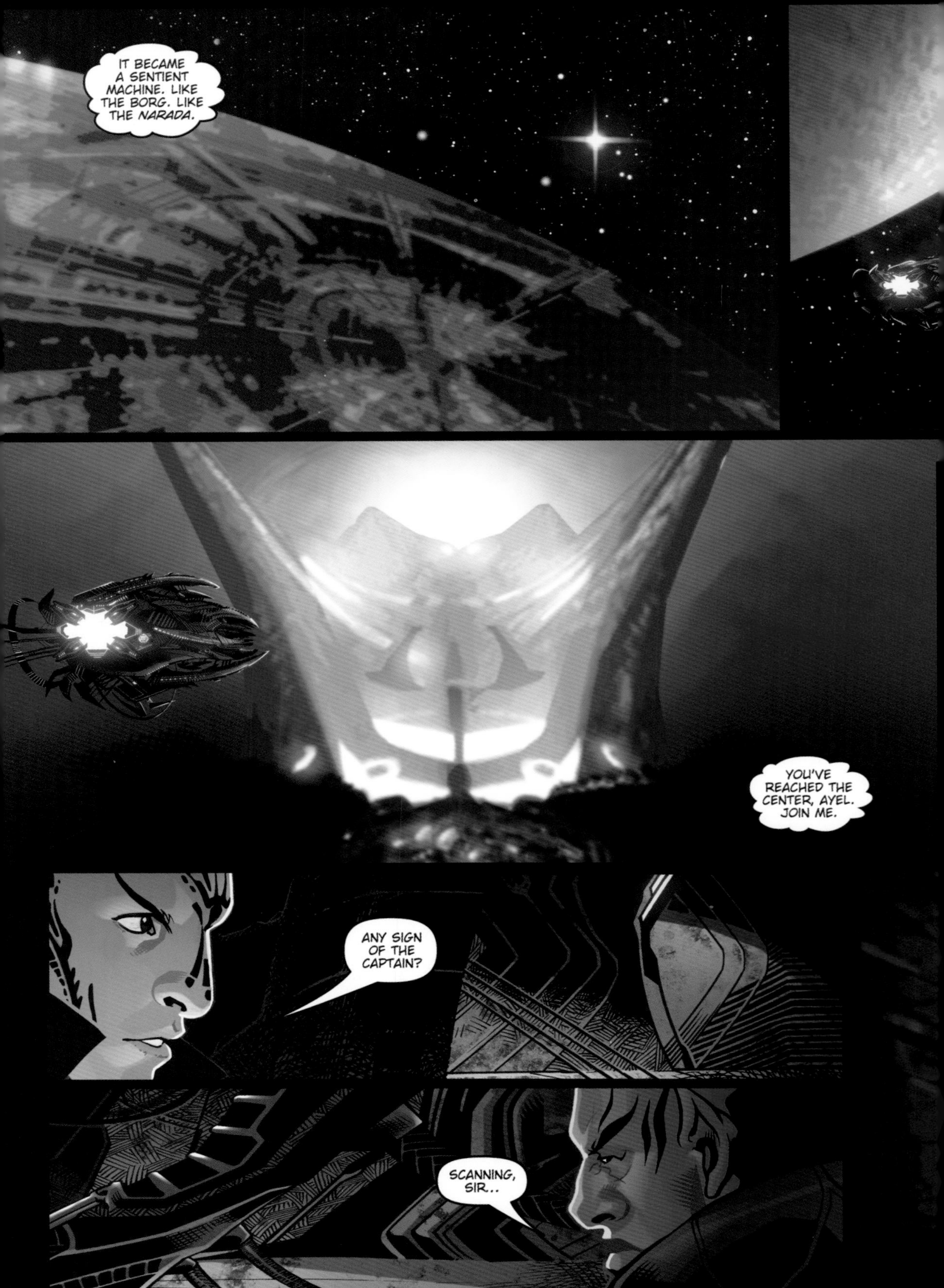
IT BECAME A SENTIENT MACHINE. LIKE THE BORG. LIKE THE *NARADA*.
YOU'VE REACHED THE CENTER, AYEL. JOIN ME.
ANY SIGN OF THE CAPTAIN?
SCANNING, SIR...

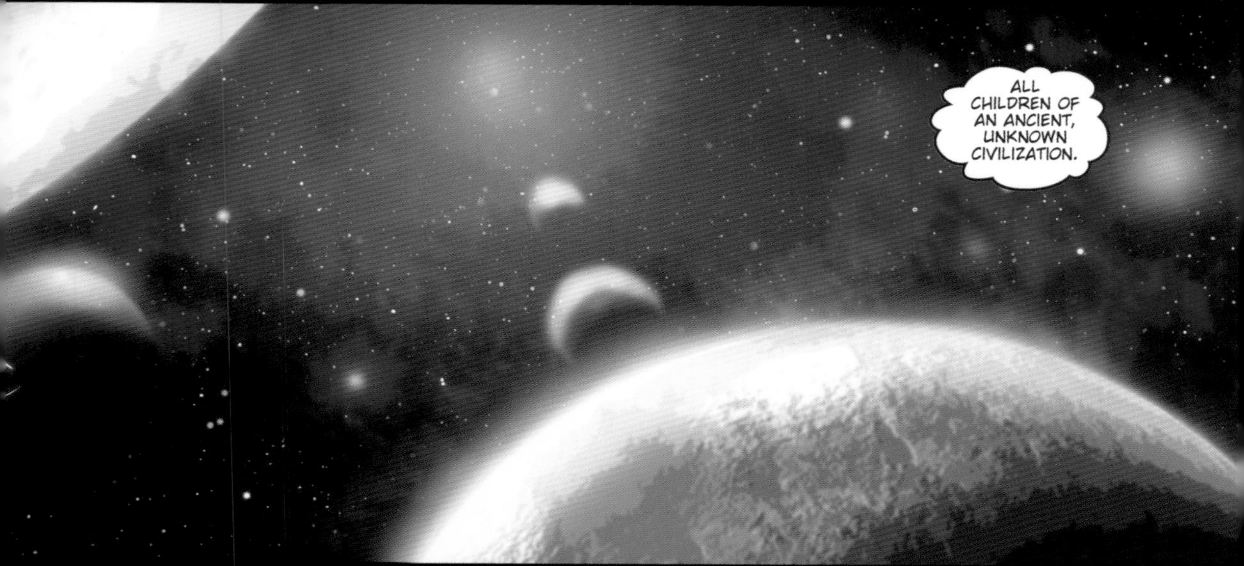
ALL CHILDREN OF AN ANCIENT, UNKNOWN CIVILIZATION.

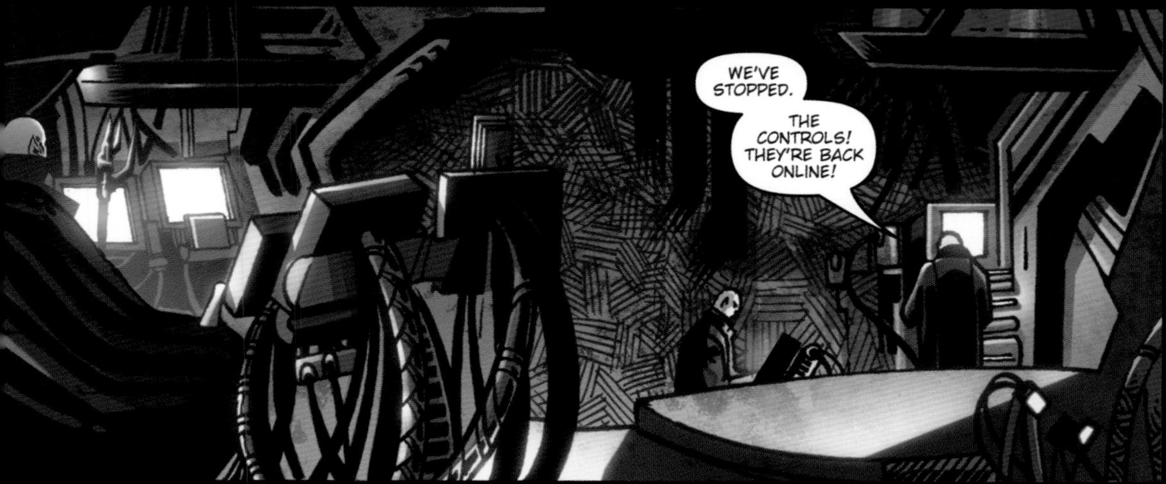
WE'VE STOPPED.
THE CONTROLS! THEY'RE BACK ONLINE!

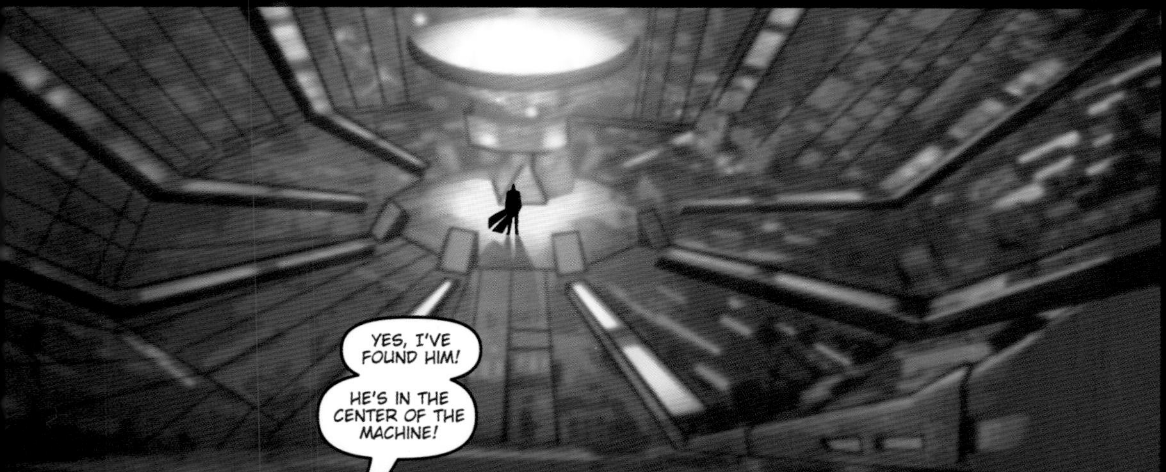
YES, I'VE FOUND HIM!
HE'S IN THE CENTER OF THE MACHINE!

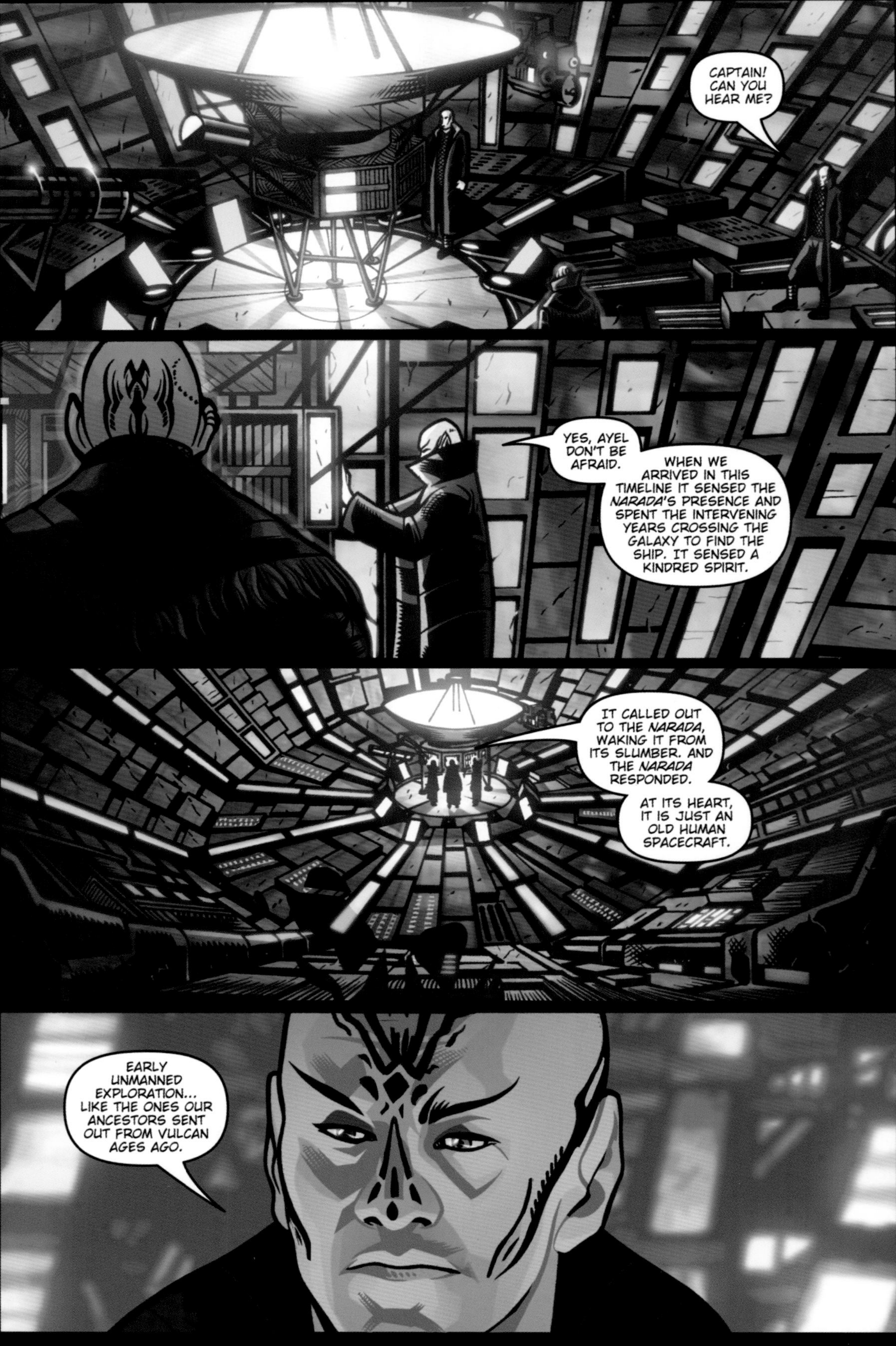
CAPTAIN! CAN YOU HEAR ME?
YES, AYEL DON'T BE AFRAID.
WHEN WE ARRIVED IN THIS TIMELINE IT SENSED THE *NARADA*'S PRESENCE AND SPENT THE INTERVENING YEARS CROSSING THE GALAXY TO FIND THE SHIP. IT SENSED A KINDRED SPIRIT.
IT CALLED OUT TO THE *NARADA*, WAKING IT FROM ITS SLUMBER. AND THE *NARADA* RESPONDED.
AT ITS HEART, IT IS JUST AN OLD HUMAN SPACECRAFT.
EARLY UNMANNED EXPLORATION... LIKE THE ONES OUR ANCESTORS SENT OUT FROM VULCAN AGES AGO.

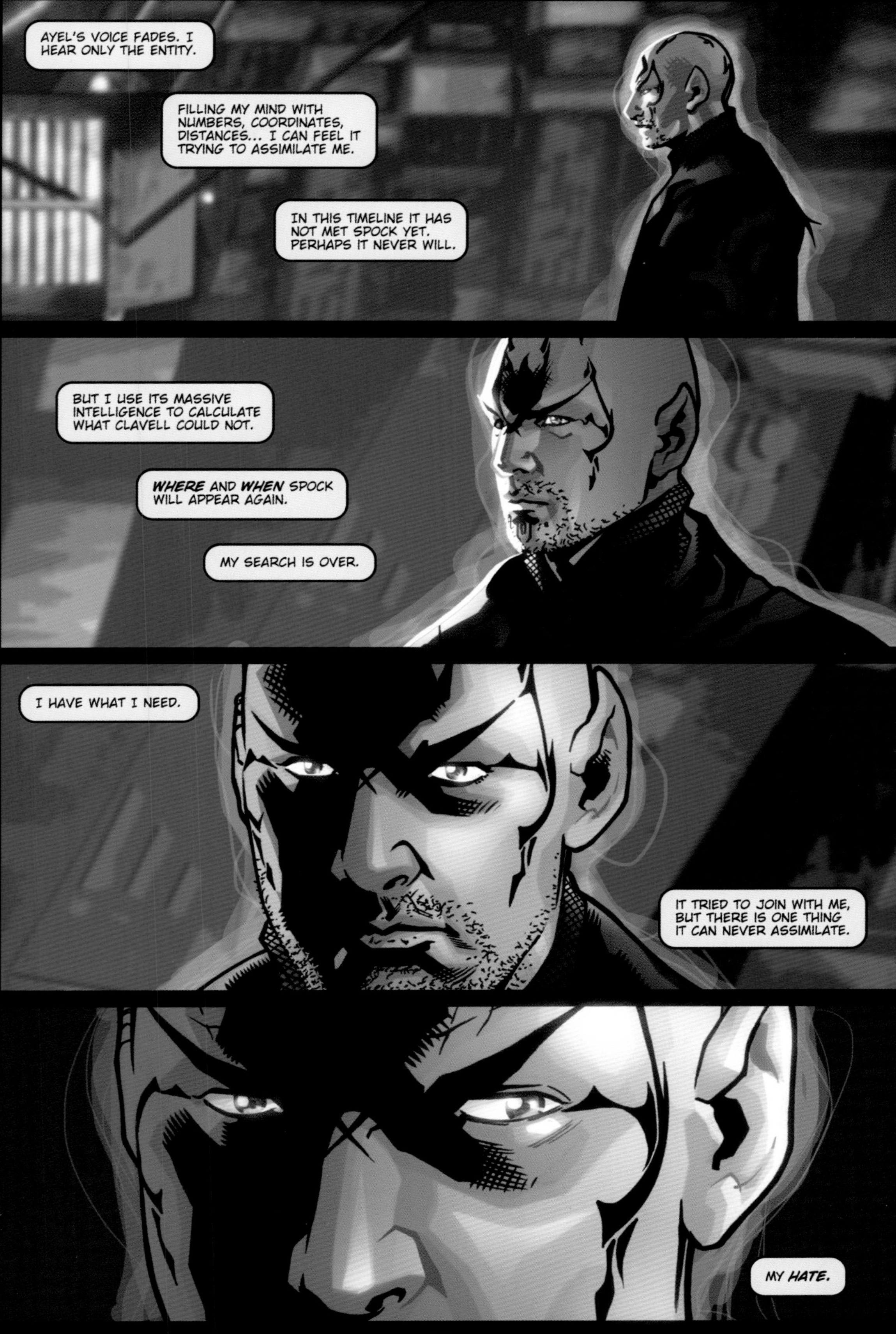
AYEL'S VOICE FADES. I HEAR ONLY THE ENTITY.
FILLING MY MIND WITH NUMBERS, COORDINATES, DISTANCES... I CAN FEEL IT TRYING TO ASSIMILATE ME.
IN THIS TIMELINE IT HAS NOT MET SPOCK YET. PERHAPS IT NEVER WILL.
BUT I USE ITS MASSIVE INTELLIGENCE TO CALCULATE WHAT CLAVELL COULD NOT.
WHERE AND *WHEN* SPOCK WILL APPEAR AGAIN.
MY SEARCH IS OVER.
I HAVE WHAT I NEED.
IT TRIED TO JOIN WITH ME, BUT THERE IS ONE THING IT CAN NEVER ASSIMILATE.
MY *HATE.*

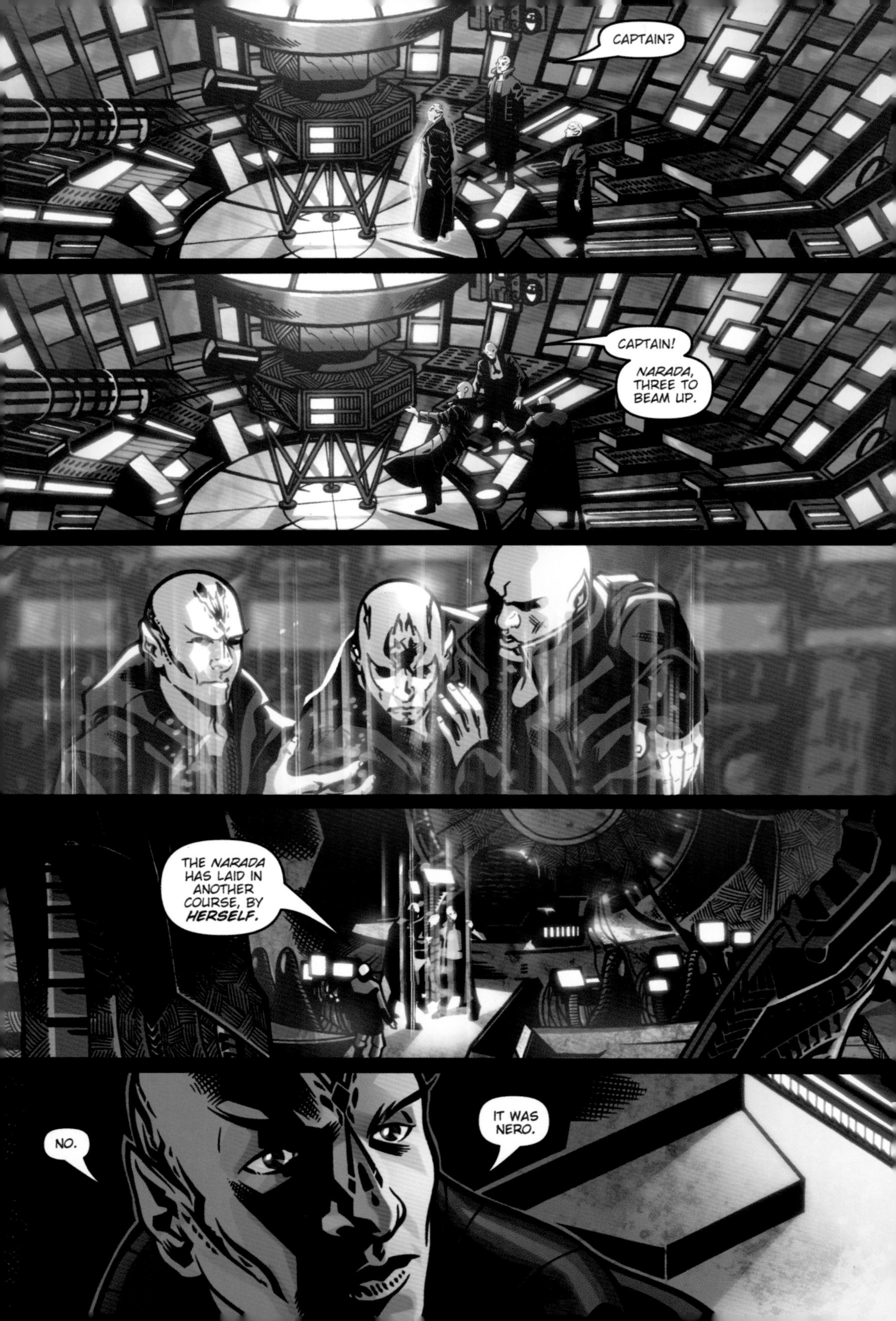
CAPTAIN?
CAPTAIN!
NARADA, THREE TO BEAM UP.
THE *NARADA* HAS LAID IN ANOTHER COURSE, BY ***HERSELF***.
NO.
IT WAS NERO.

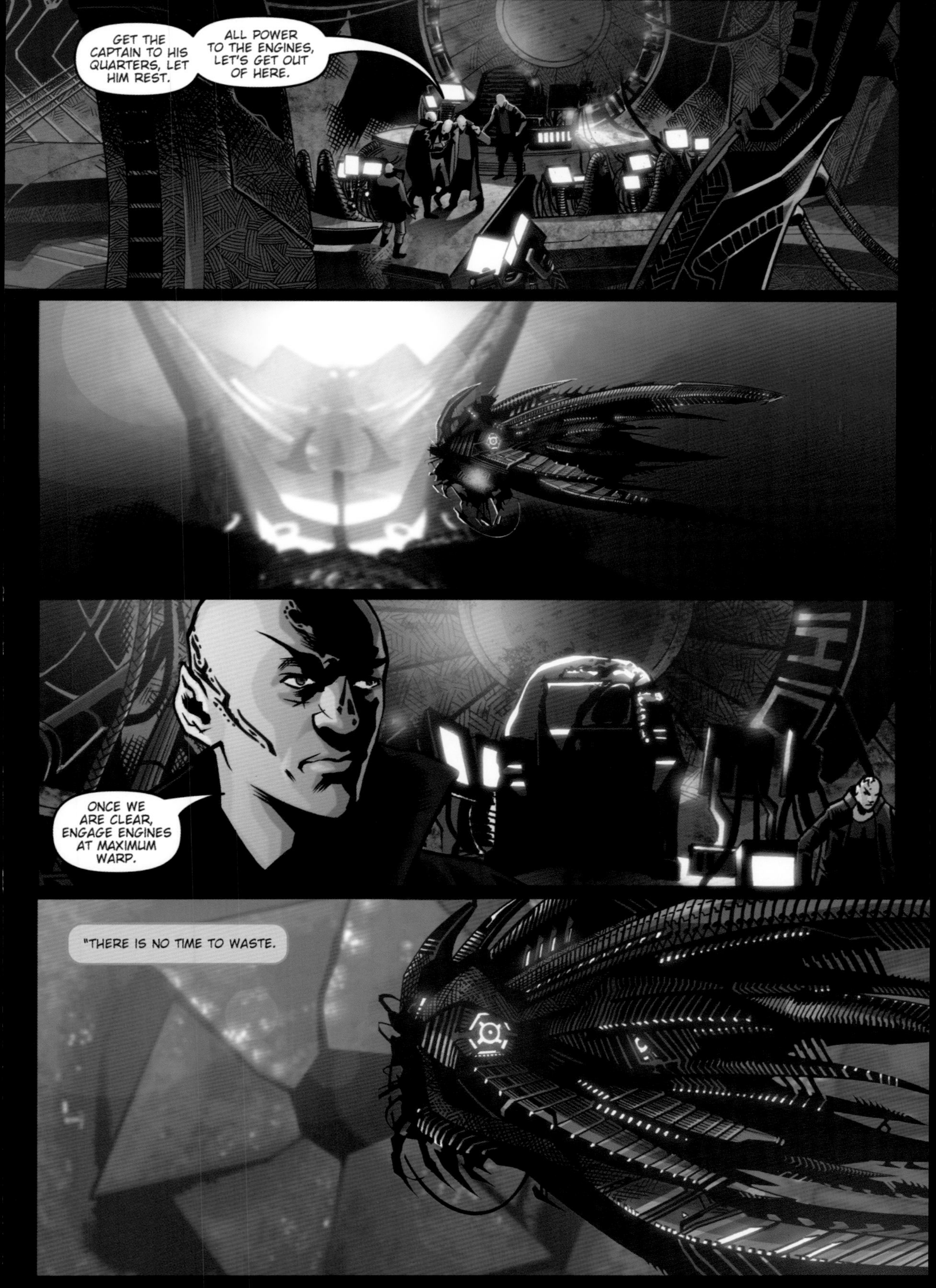
GET THE CAPTAIN TO HIS QUARTERS, LET HIM REST.
ALL POWER TO THE ENGINES, LET'S GET OUT OF HERE.
ONCE WE ARE CLEAR, ENGAGE ENGINES AT MAXIMUM WARP.
"THERE IS NO TIME TO WASTE.

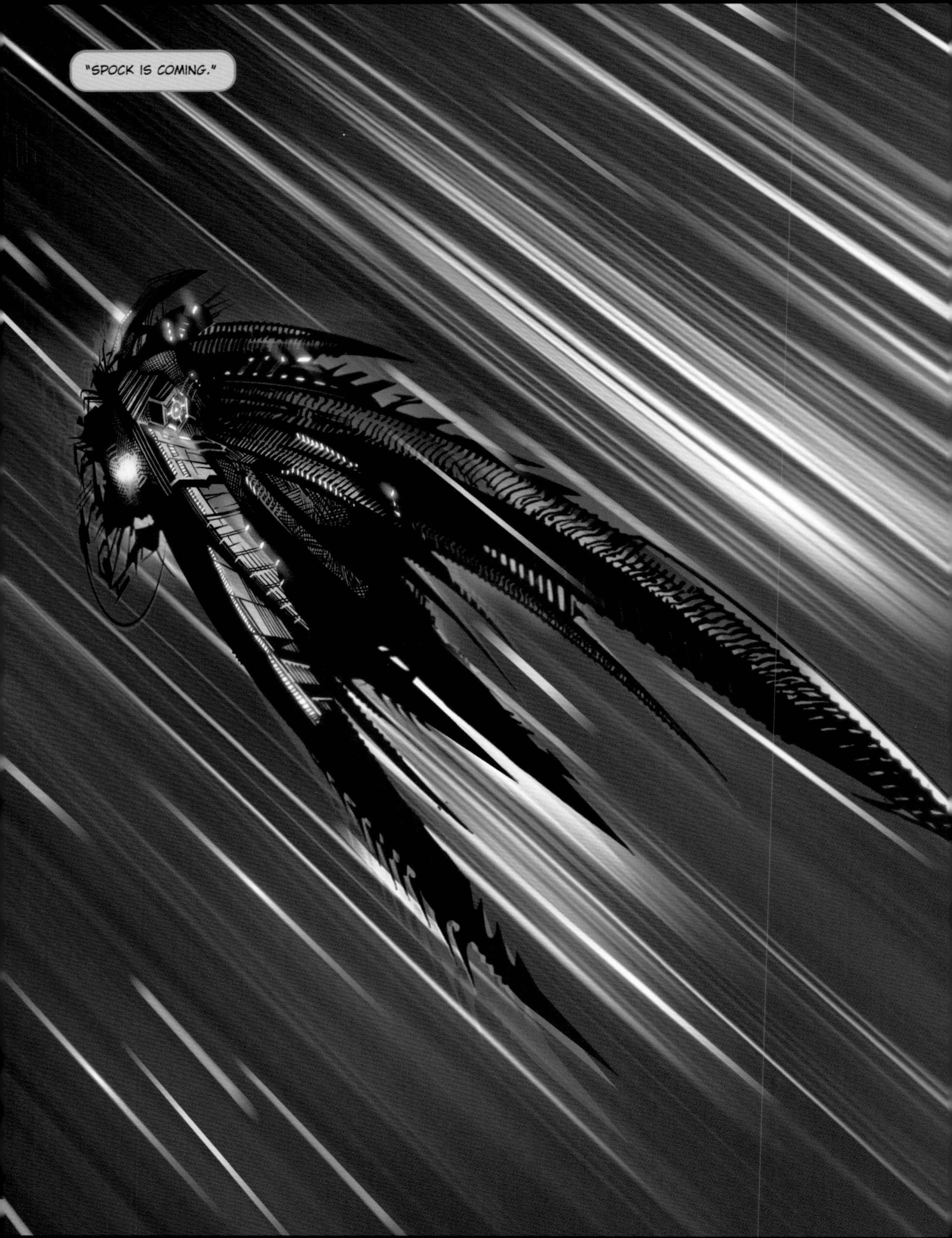
"SPOCK IS COMING."

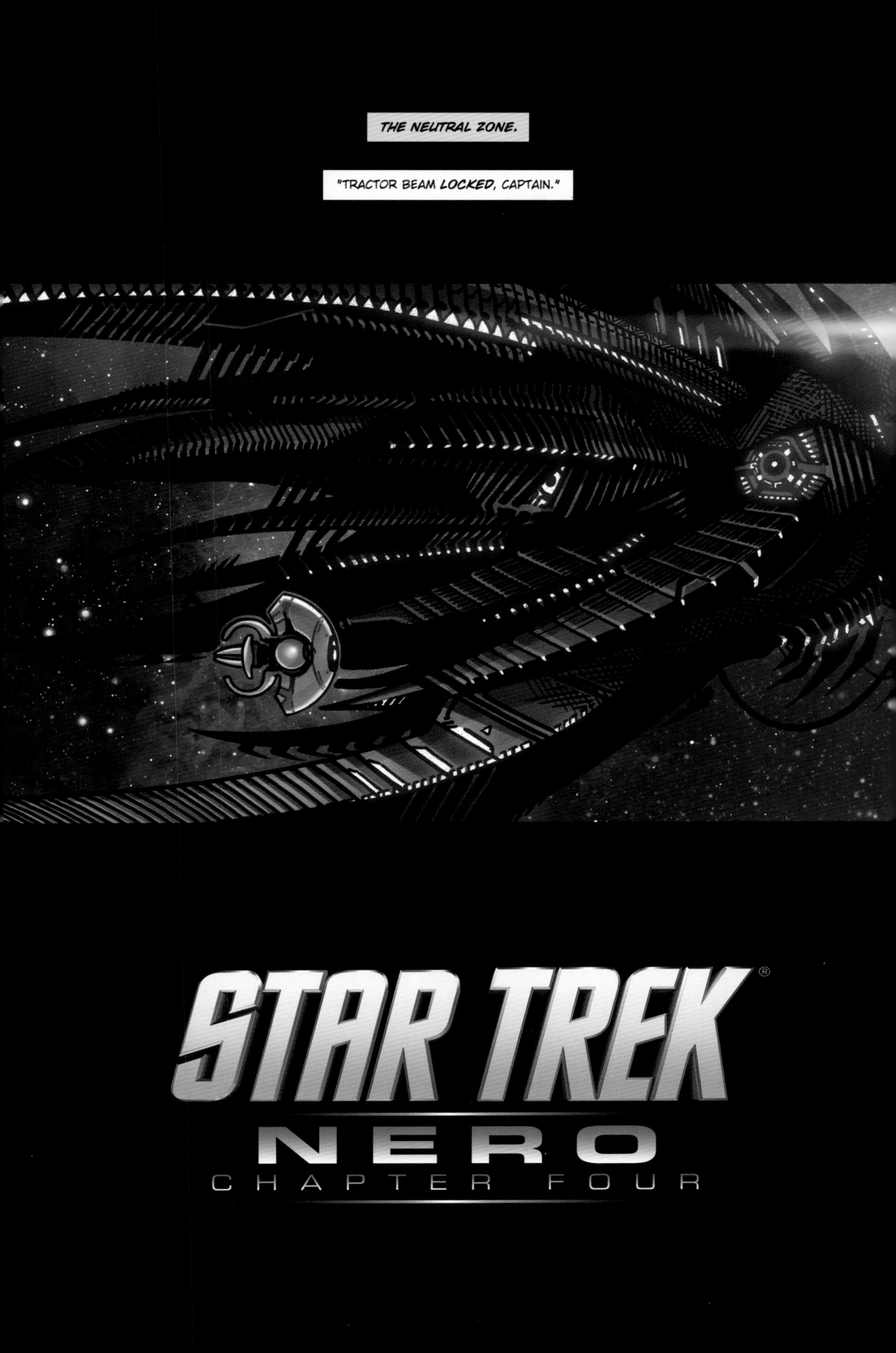
THE NEUTRAL ZONE.
"TRACTOR BEAM LOCKED, CAPTAIN."
STAR TREK®
NERO
CHAPTER FOUR

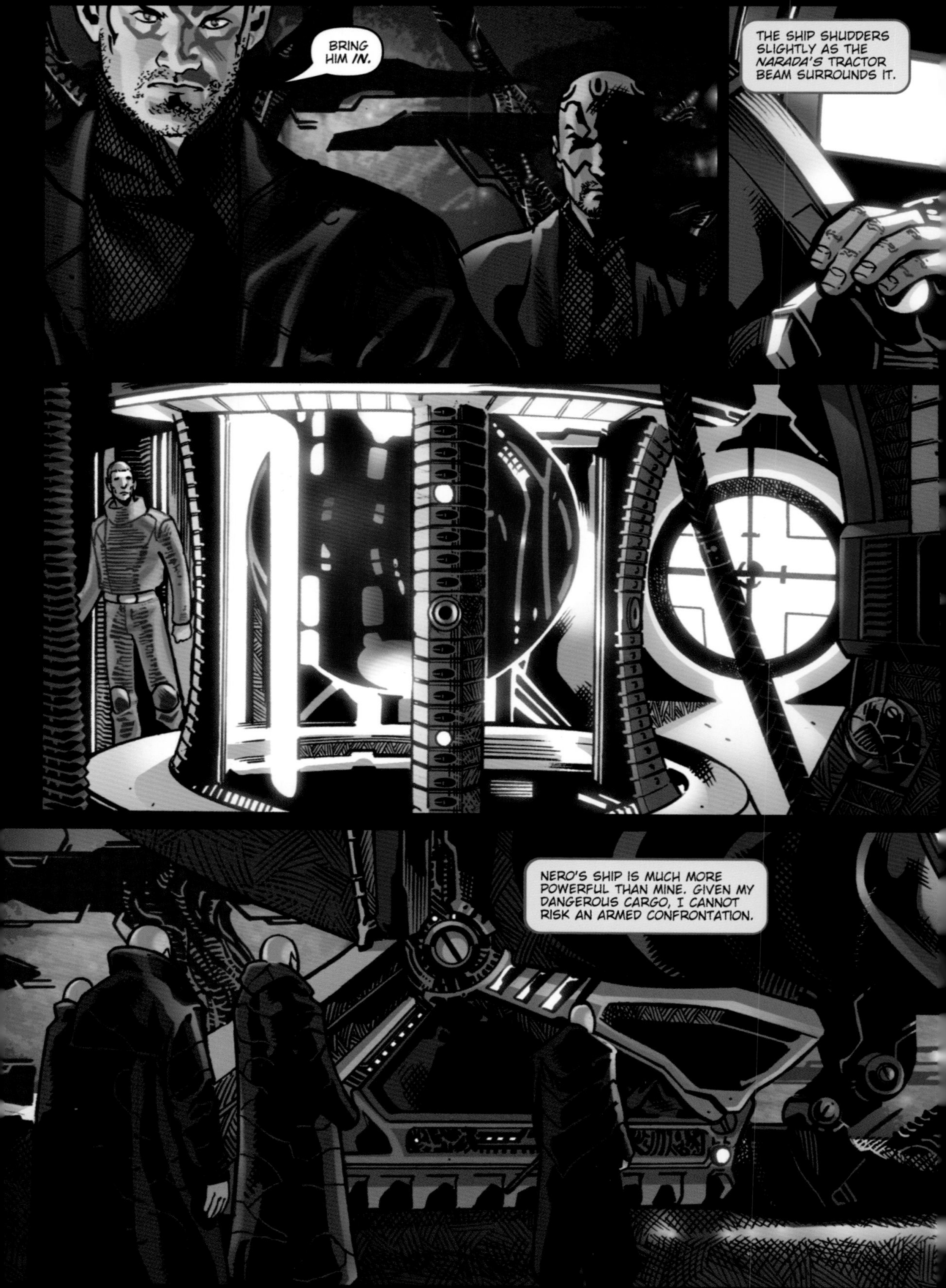

BRING HIM *IN.*
THE SHIP SHUDDERS SLIGHTLY AS THE *NARADA'S* TRACTOR BEAM SURROUNDS IT.
NERO'S SHIP IS MUCH MORE POWERFUL THAN MINE. GIVEN MY DANGEROUS CARGO, I CANNOT RISK AN ARMED CONFRONTATION.

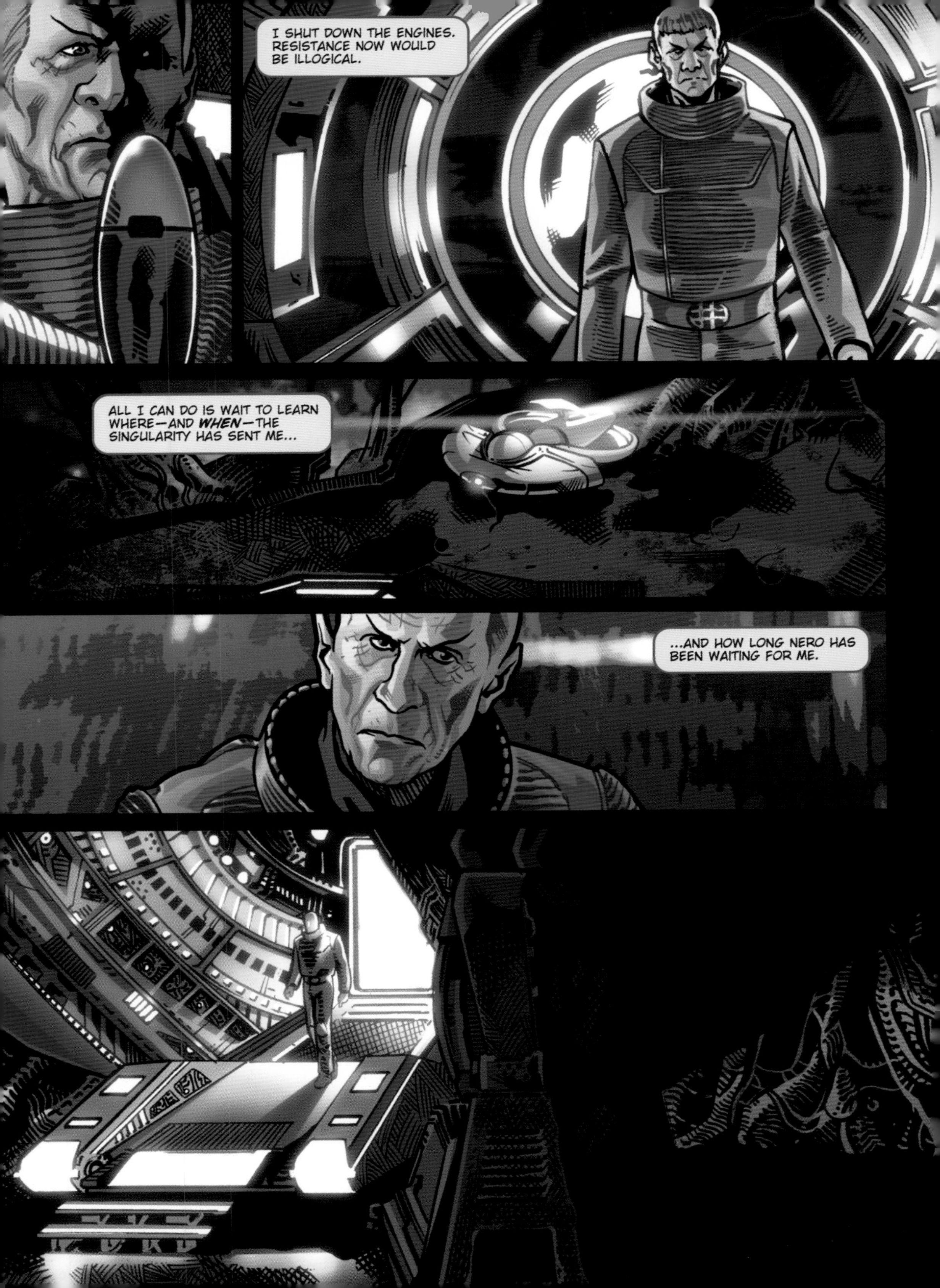
I SHUT DOWN THE ENGINES. RESISTANCE NOW WOULD BE ILLOGICAL.
ALL I CAN DO IS WAIT TO LEARN WHERE—AND ***WHEN***—THE SINGULARITY HAS SENT ME...
...AND HOW LONG NERO HAS BEEN WAITING FOR ME.

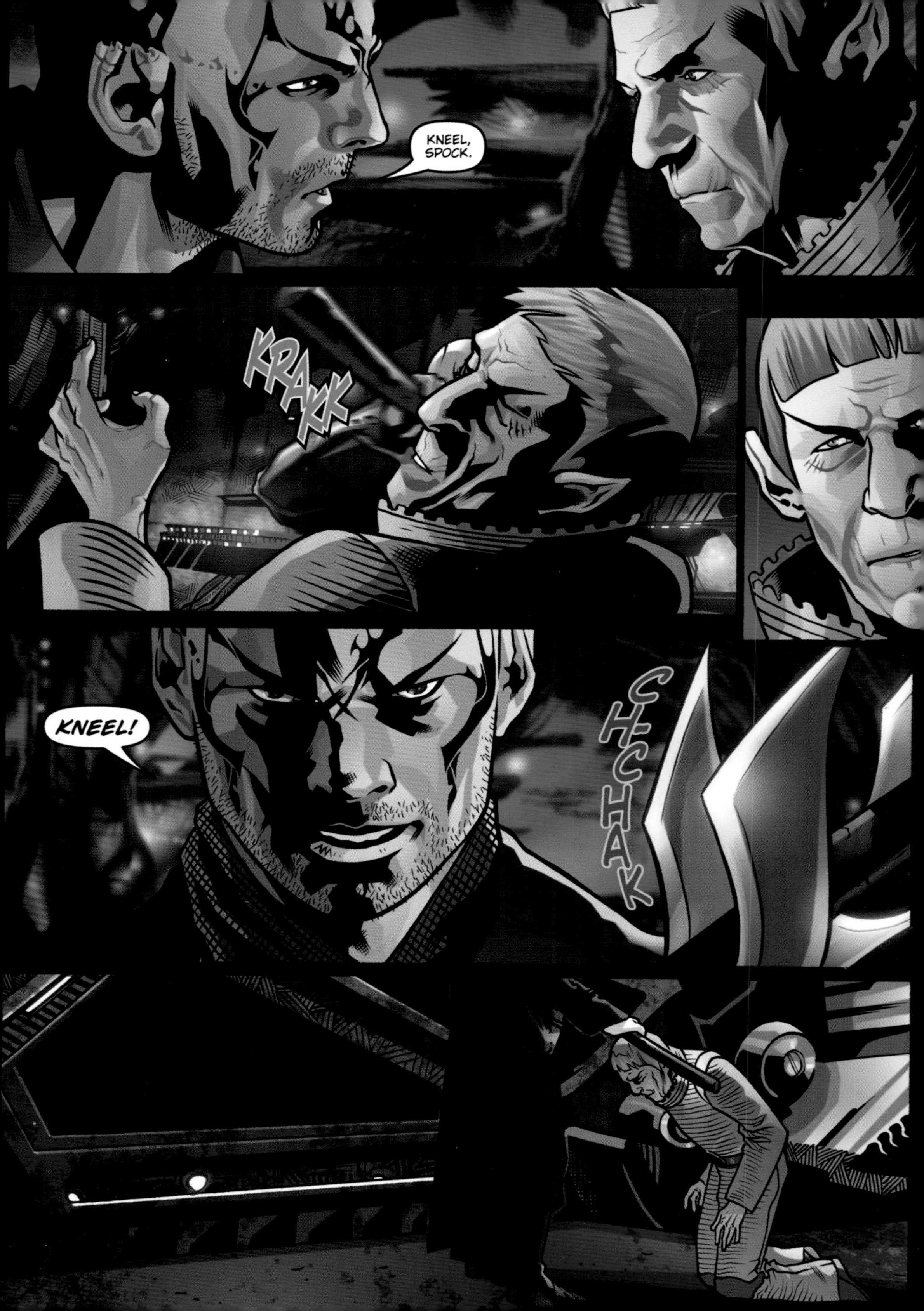
KNEEL, SPOCK.
KRAKK
KNEEL!
CHCHAK

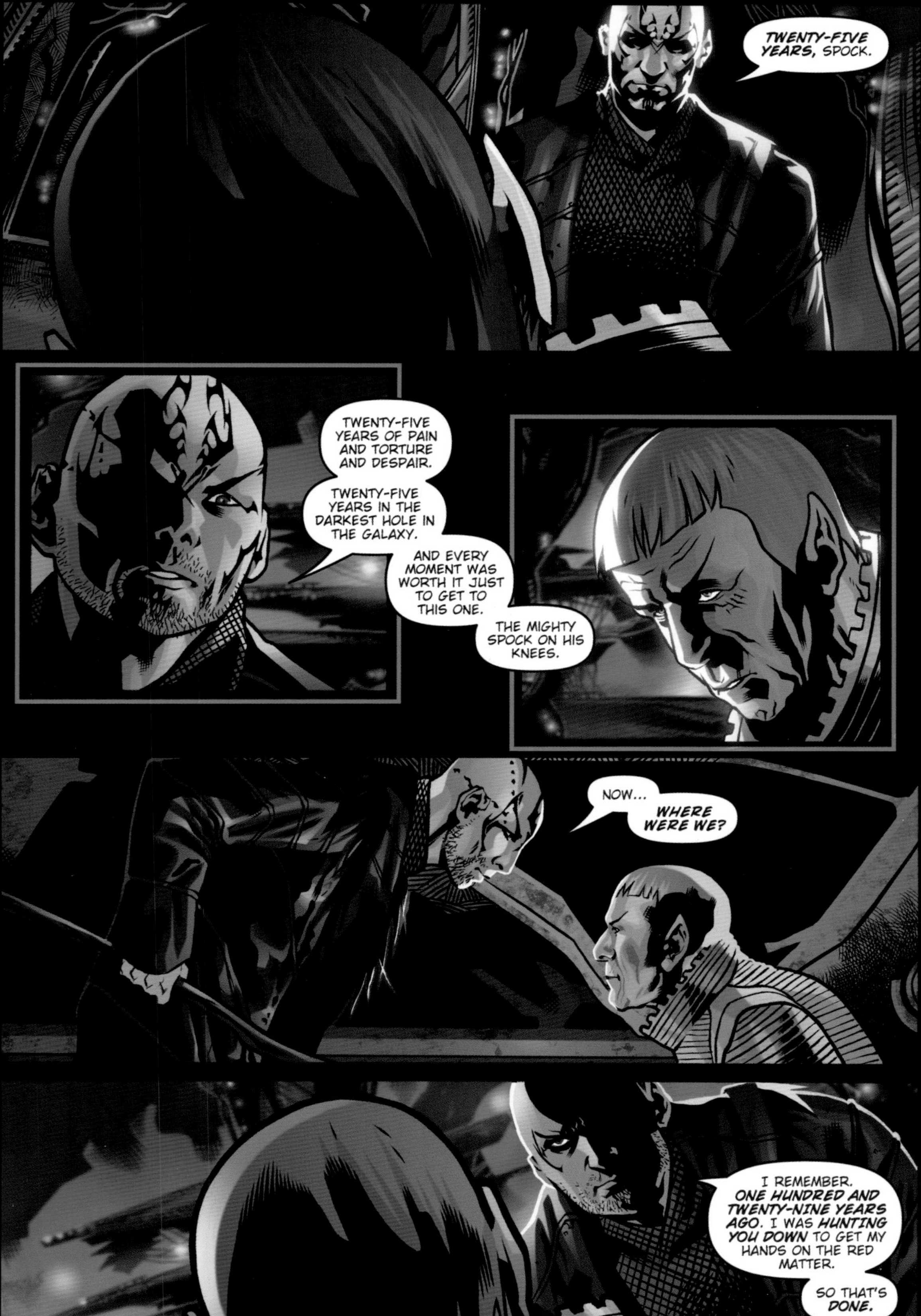
TWENTY-FIVE YEARS, SPOCK.
TWENTY-FIVE YEARS OF PAIN AND TORTURE AND DESPAIR.
TWENTY-FIVE YEARS IN THE DARKEST HOLE IN THE GALAXY.
AND EVERY MOMENT WAS WORTH IT JUST TO GET TO THIS ONE.
THE MIGHTY SPOCK ON HIS KNEES.
NOW... WHERE WERE WE?
I REMEMBER. ONE HUNDRED AND TWENTY-NINE YEARS AGO. I WAS HUNTING YOU DOWN TO GET MY HANDS ON THE RED MATTER.
SO THAT'S DONE.

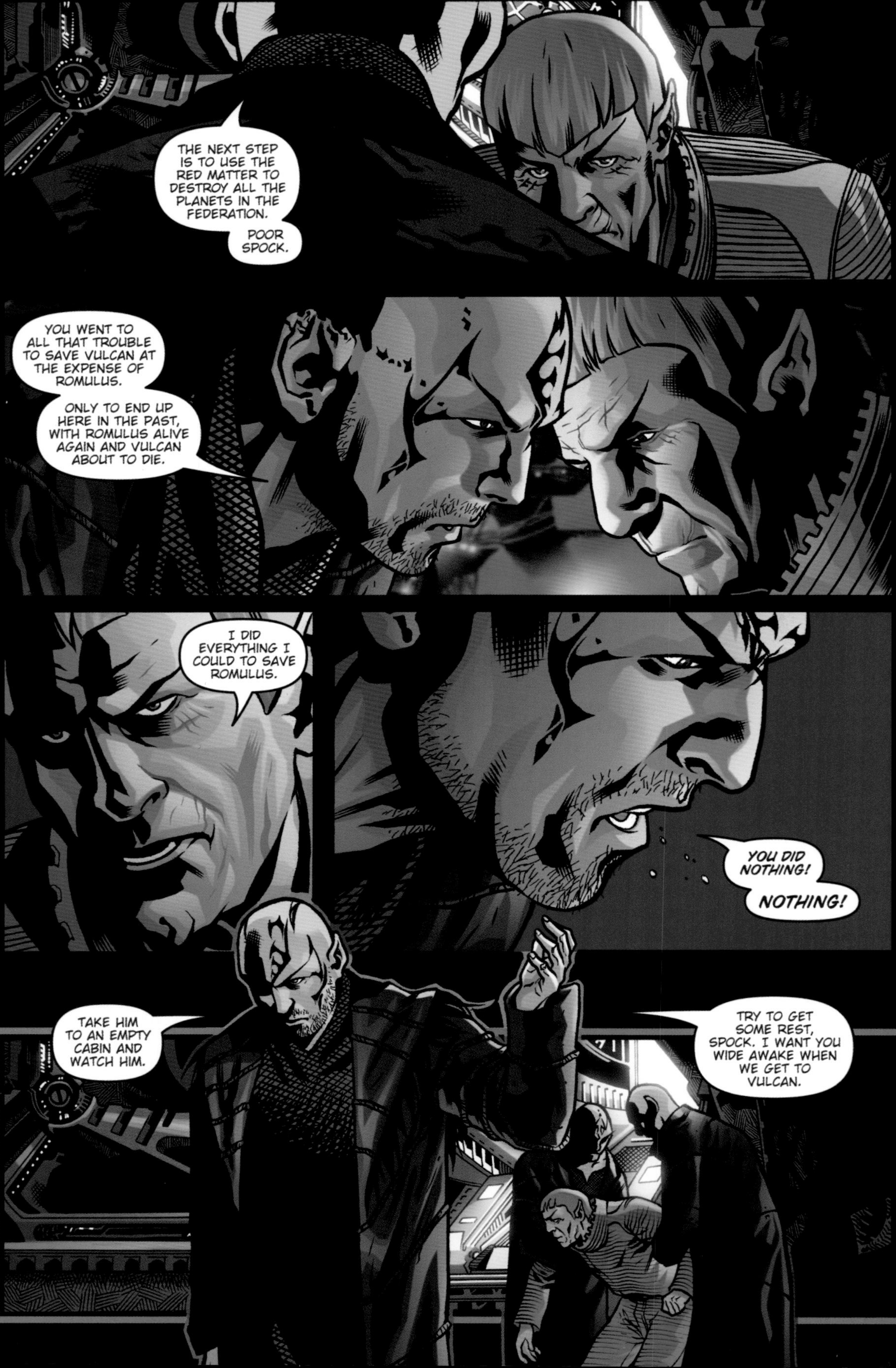
THE NEXT STEP IS TO USE THE RED MATTER TO DESTROY ALL THE PLANETS IN THE FEDERATION.
POOR SPOCK.
YOU WENT TO ALL THAT TROUBLE TO SAVE VULCAN AT THE EXPENSE OF ROMULUS.
ONLY TO END UP HERE IN THE PAST, WITH ROMULUS ALIVE AGAIN AND VULCAN ABOUT TO DIE.
I DID EVERYTHING I COULD TO SAVE ROMULUS.
YOU DID NOTHING!
NOTHING!
TAKE HIM TO AN EMPTY CABIN AND WATCH HIM.
TRY TO GET SOME REST, SPOCK. I WANT YOU WIDE AWAKE WHEN WE GET TO VULCAN.

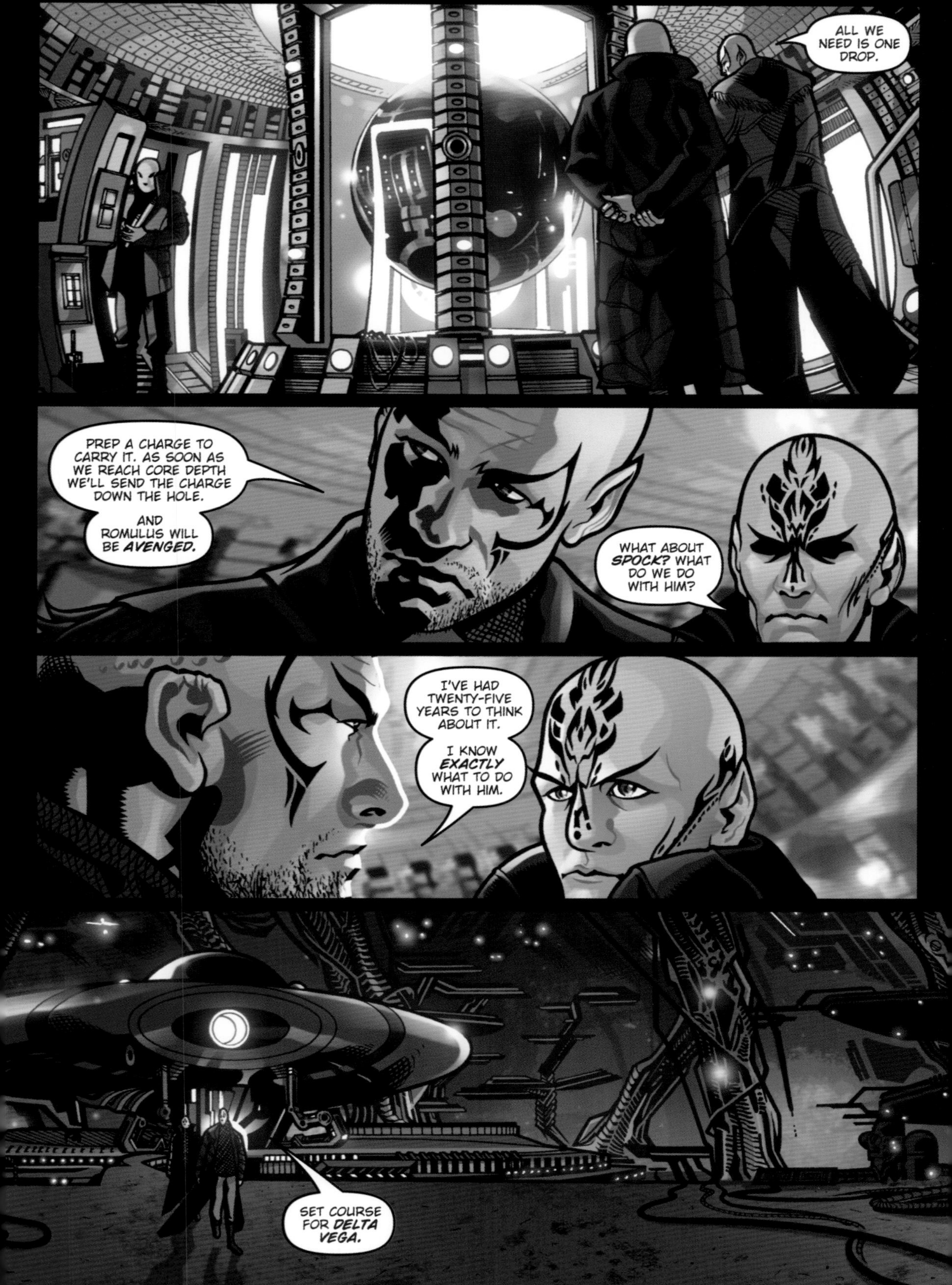
ALL WE NEED IS ONE DROP.
PREP A CHARGE TO CARRY IT. AS SOON AS WE REACH CORE DEPTH WE'LL SEND THE CHARGE DOWN THE HOLE.
AND ROMULUS WILL BE *AVENGED.*
WHAT ABOUT *SPOCK?* WHAT DO WE DO WITH HIM?
I'VE HAD TWENTY-FIVE YEARS TO THINK ABOUT IT.
I KNOW *EXACTLY* WHAT TO DO WITH HIM.
SET COURSE FOR *DELTA VEGA.*

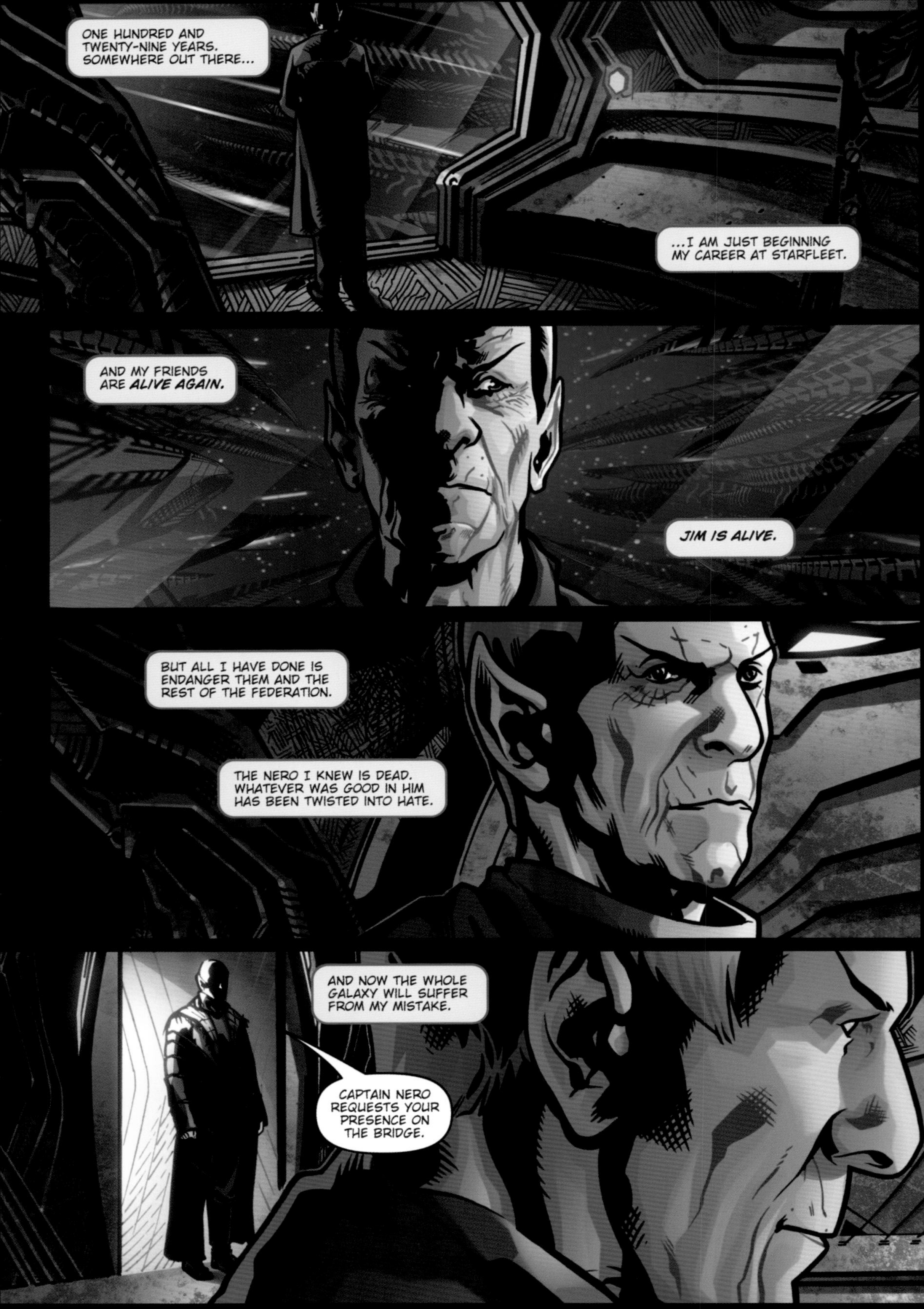

ONE HUNDRED AND TWENTY-NINE YEARS. SOMEWHERE OUT THERE...
...I AM JUST BEGINNING MY CAREER AT STARFLEET.
AND MY FRIENDS ARE *ALIVE AGAIN.*
JIM IS ALIVE.
BUT ALL I HAVE DONE IS ENDANGER THEM AND THE REST OF THE FEDERATION.
THE NERO I KNEW IS DEAD. WHATEVER WAS GOOD IN HIM HAS BEEN TWISTED INTO HATE.
AND NOW THE WHOLE GALAXY WILL SUFFER FROM MY MISTAKE.
CAPTAIN NERO REQUESTS YOUR PRESENCE ON THE BRIDGE.

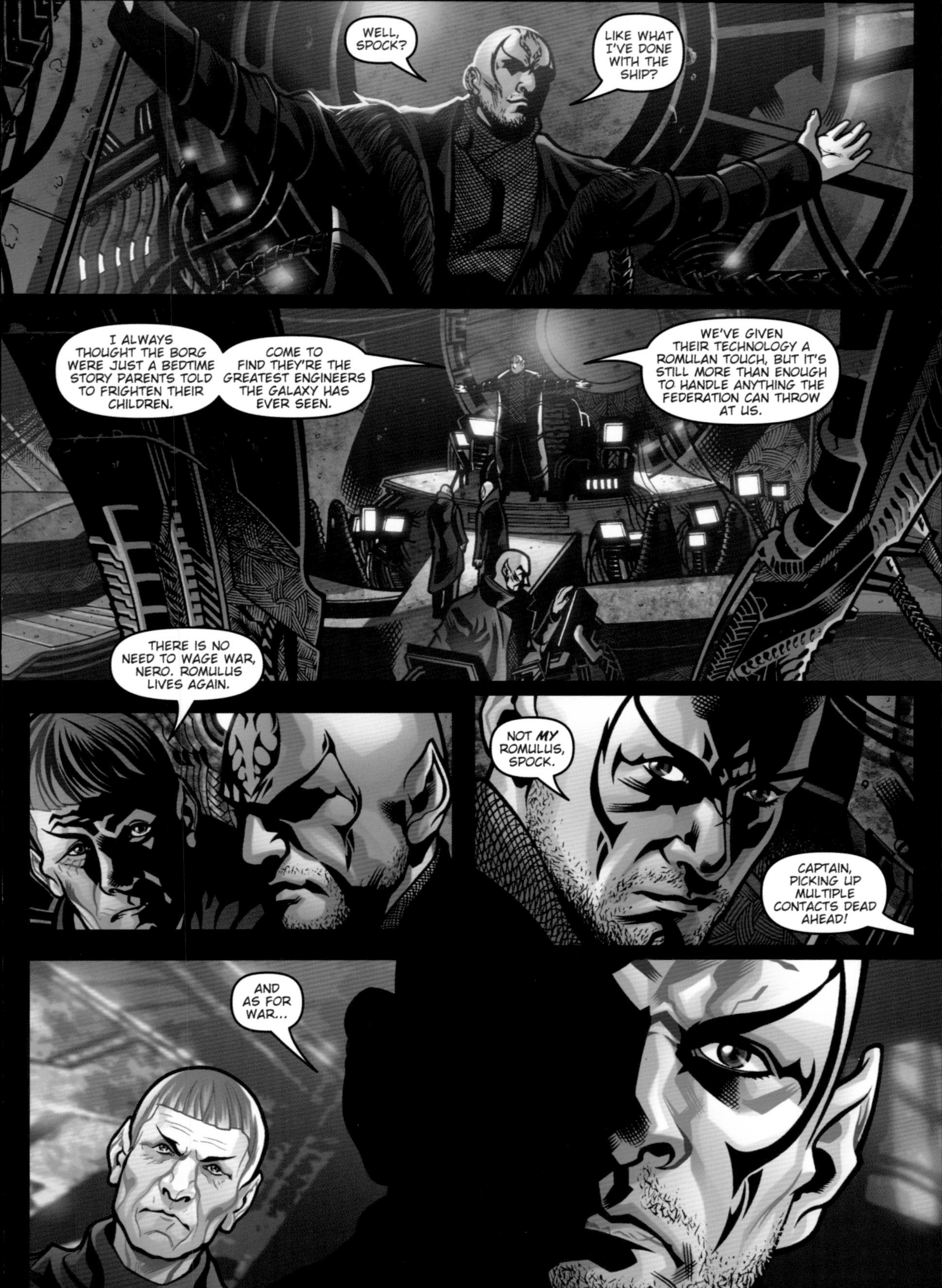
WELL, SPOCK?
LIKE WHAT I'VE DONE WITH THE SHIP?
I ALWAYS THOUGHT THE BORG WERE JUST A BEDTIME STORY PARENTS TOLD TO FRIGHTEN THEIR CHILDREN.
COME TO FIND THEY'RE THE GREATEST ENGINEERS THE GALAXY HAS EVER SEEN.
WE'VE GIVEN THEIR TECHNOLOGY A ROMULAN TOUCH, BUT IT'S STILL MORE THAN ENOUGH TO HANDLE ANYTHING THE FEDERATION CAN THROW AT US.
THERE IS NO NEED TO WAGE WAR, NERO. ROMULUS LIVES AGAIN.
NOT *MY* ROMULUS, SPOCK.
CAPTAIN, PICKING UP MULTIPLE CONTACTS DEAD AHEAD!
AND AS FOR WAR...

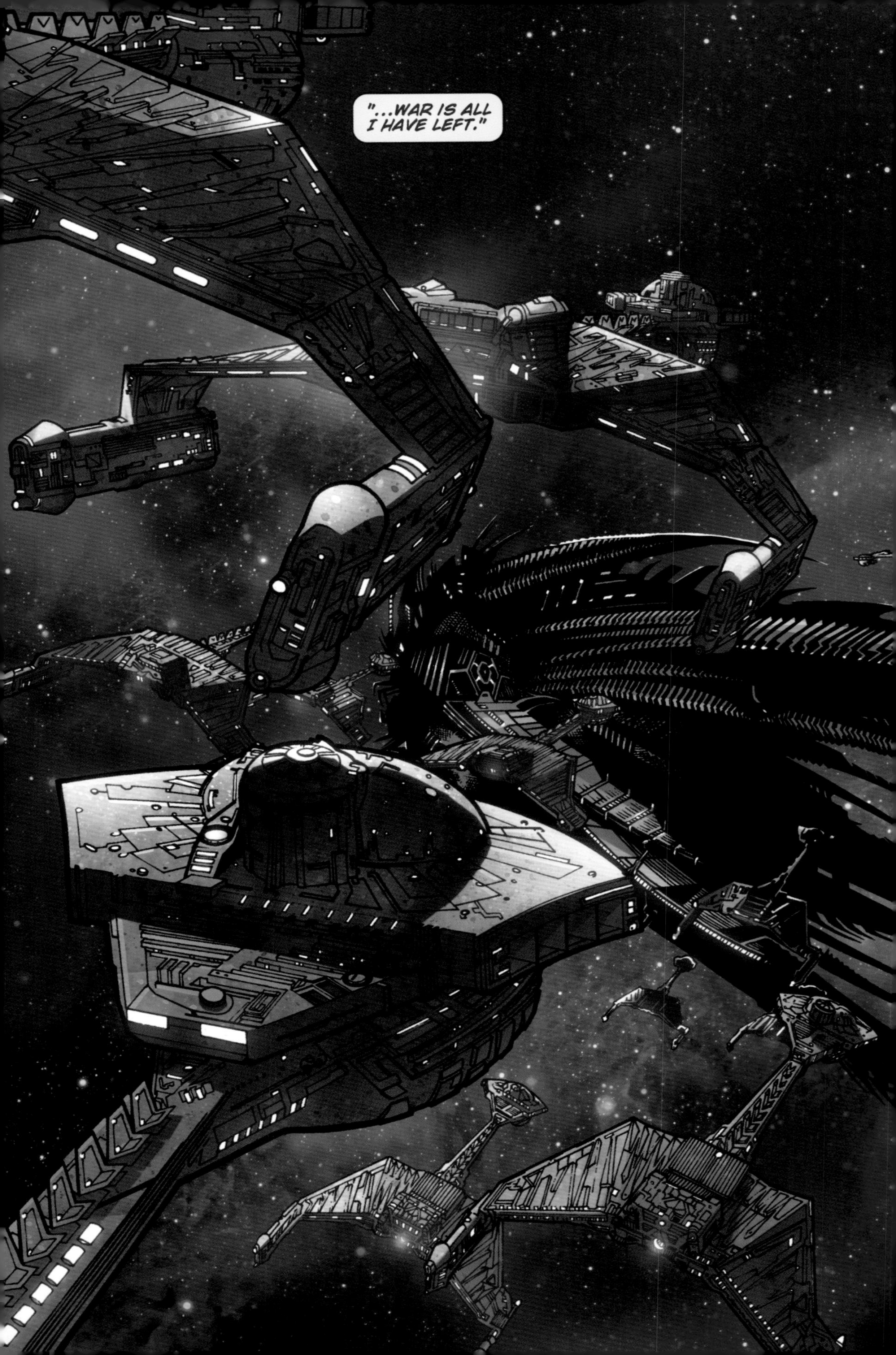
"...WAR IS ALL
I HAVE LEFT."

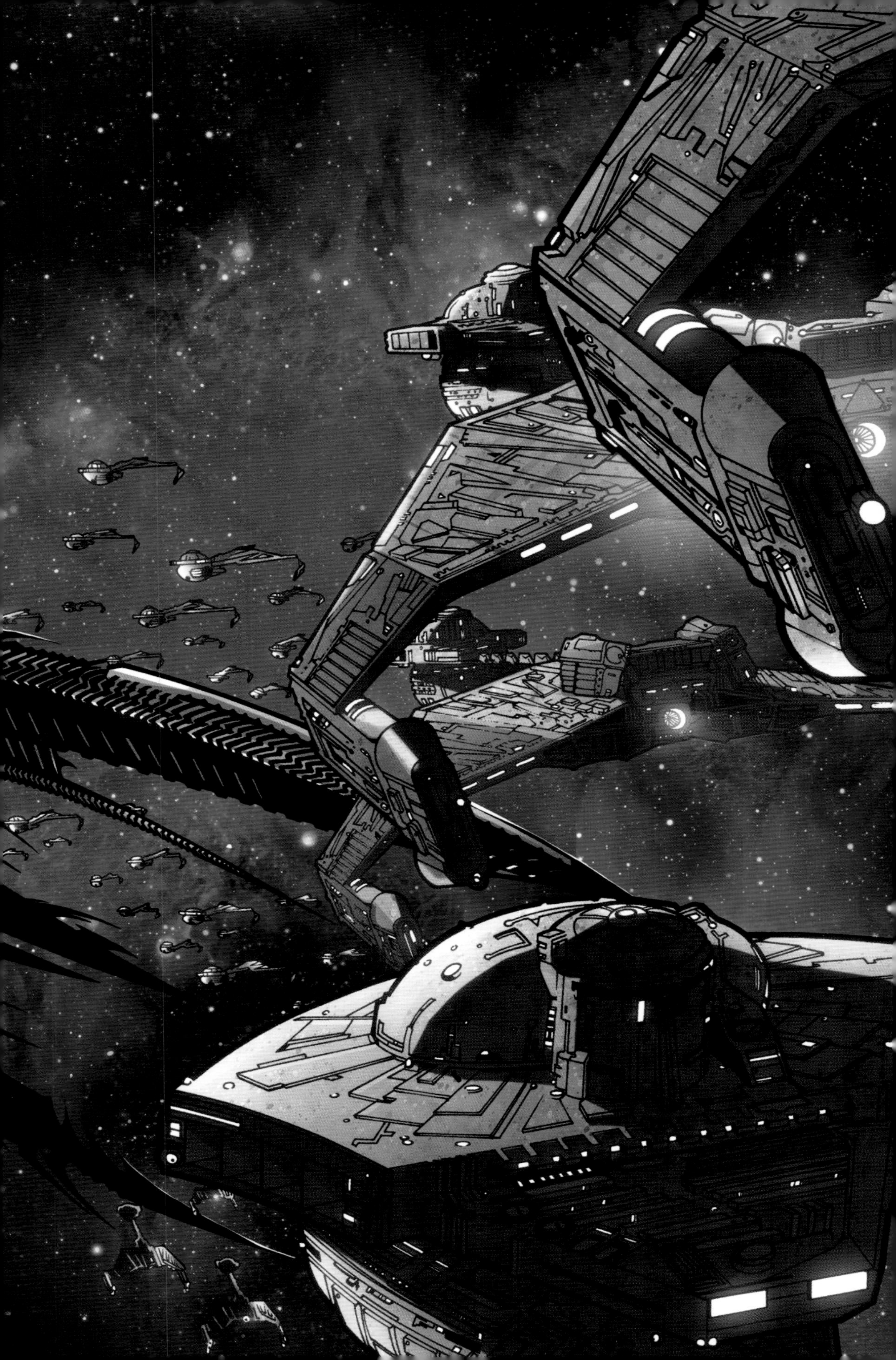

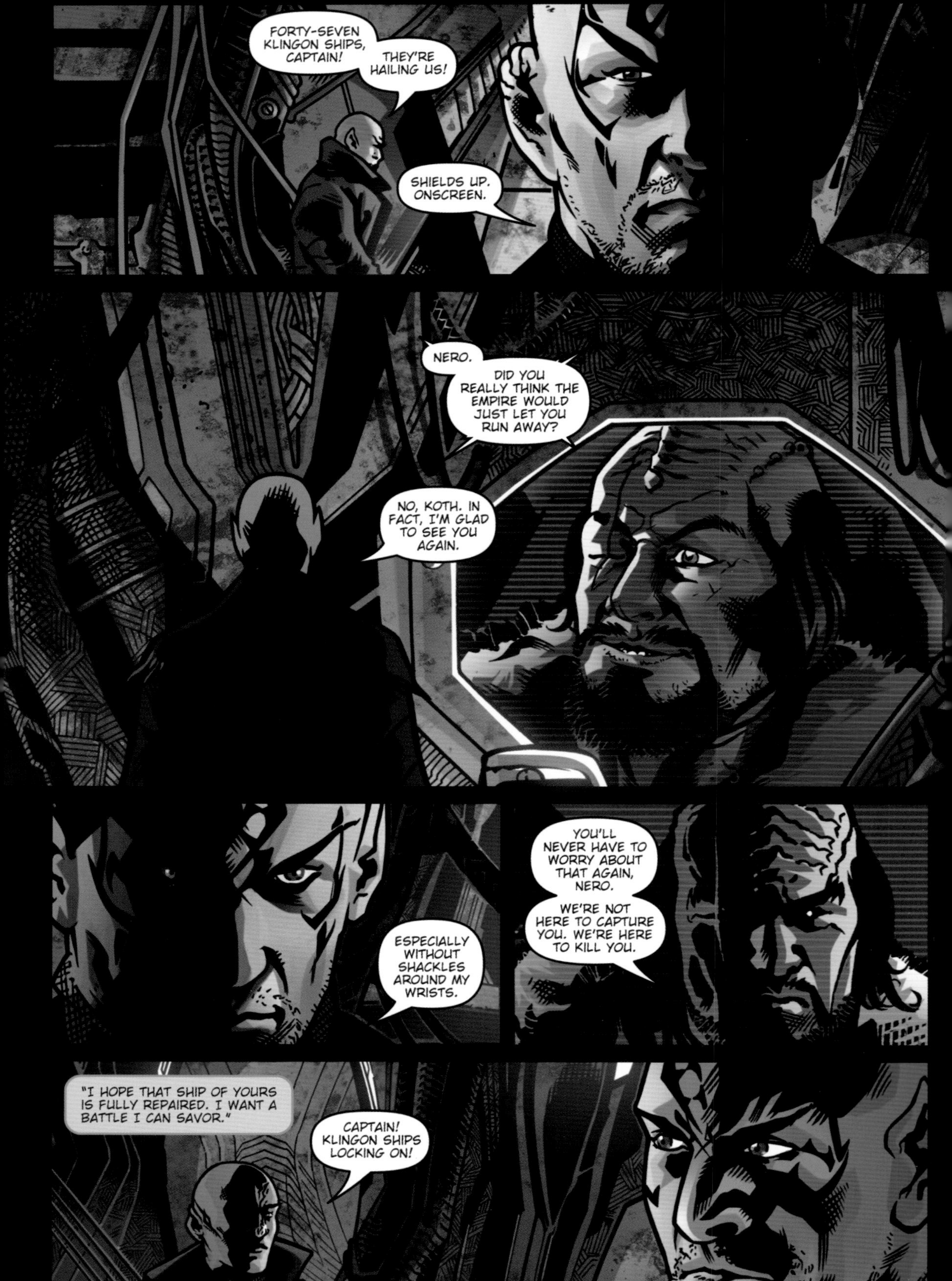
FORTY-SEVEN KLINGON SHIPS, CAPTAIN!
THEY'RE HAILING US!
SHIELDS UP. ONSCREEN.
NERO.
DID YOU REALLY THINK THE EMPIRE WOULD JUST LET YOU RUN AWAY?
NO, KOTH. IN FACT, I'M GLAD TO SEE YOU AGAIN.
ESPECIALLY WITHOUT SHACKLES AROUND MY WRISTS.
YOU'LL NEVER HAVE TO WORRY ABOUT THAT AGAIN, NERO.
WE'RE NOT HERE TO CAPTURE YOU. WE'RE HERE TO KILL YOU.
"I HOPE THAT SHIP OF YOURS IS FULLY REPAIRED. I WANT A BATTLE I CAN SAVOR."
CAPTAIN! KLINGON SHIPS LOCKING ON!

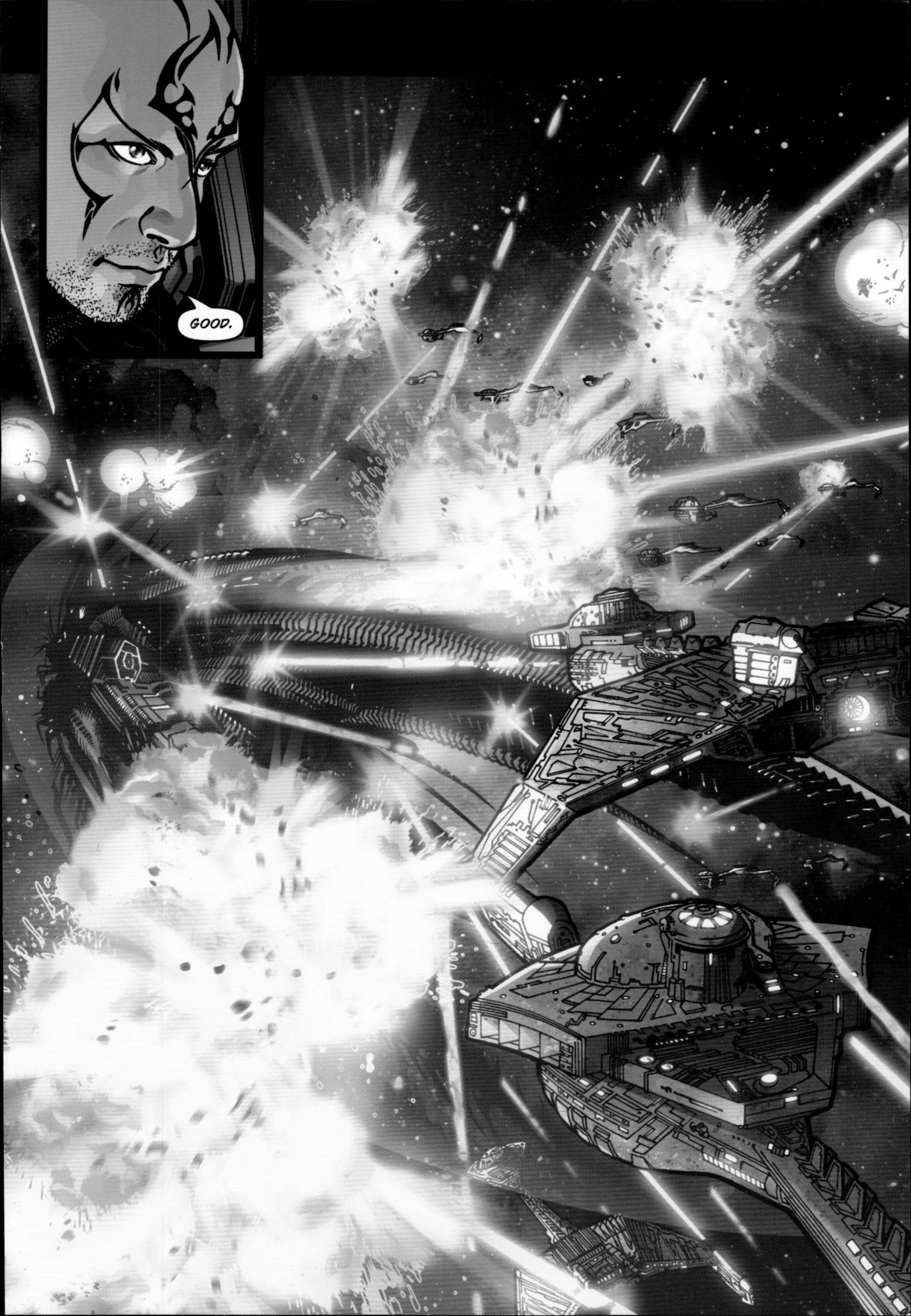
GOOD.

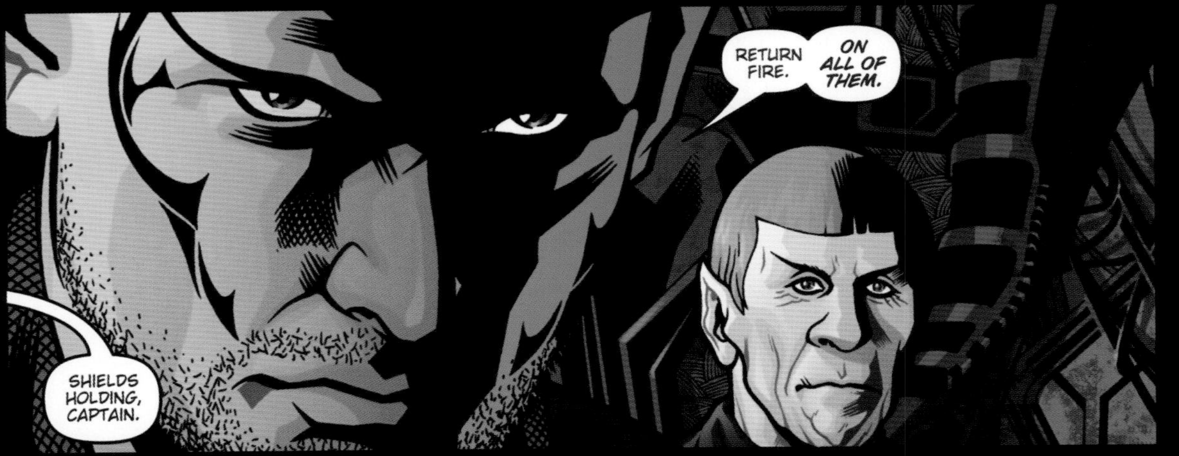
RETURN FIRE.
ON ALL OF THEM.
SHIELDS HOLDING, CAPTAIN.

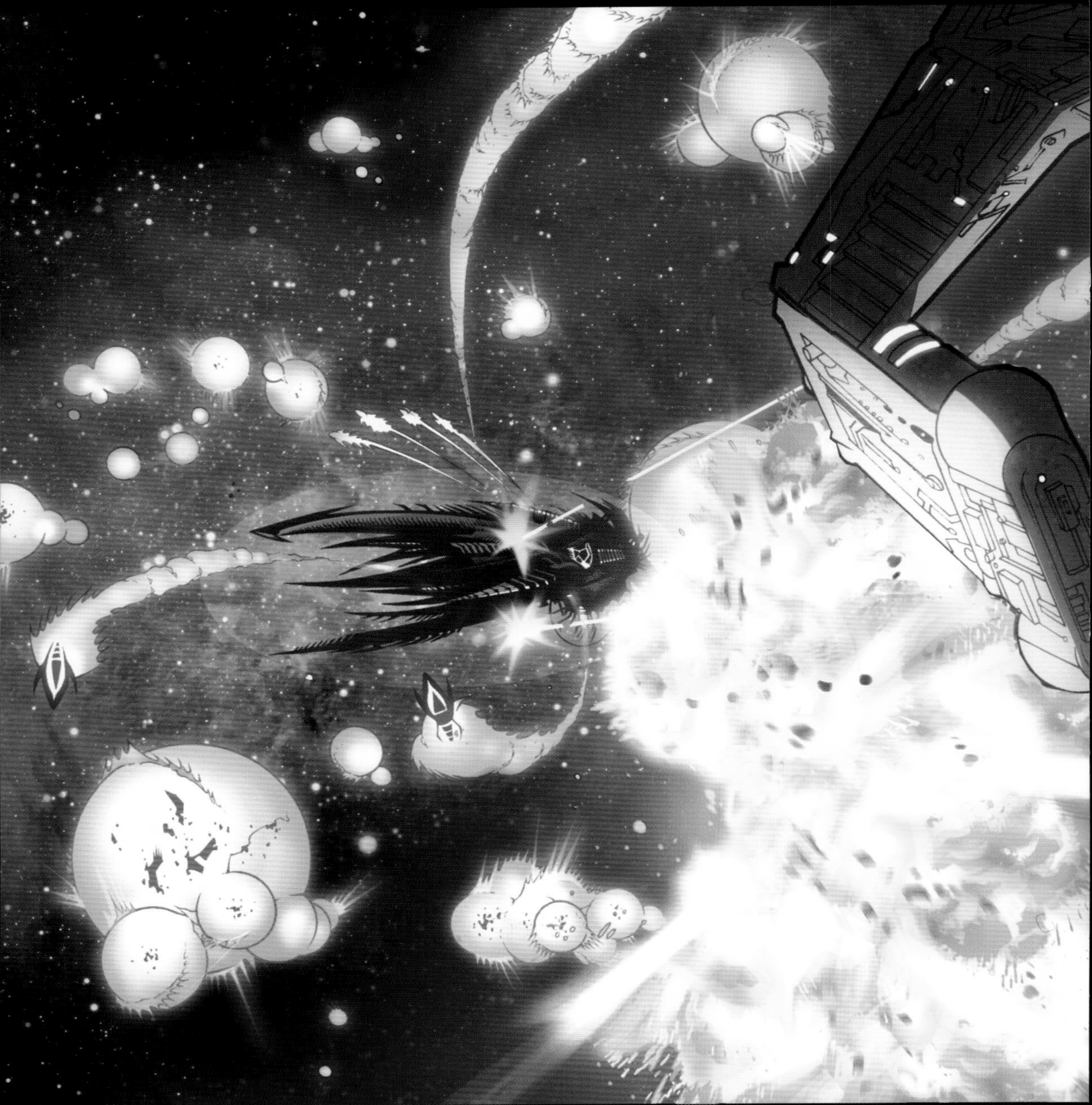

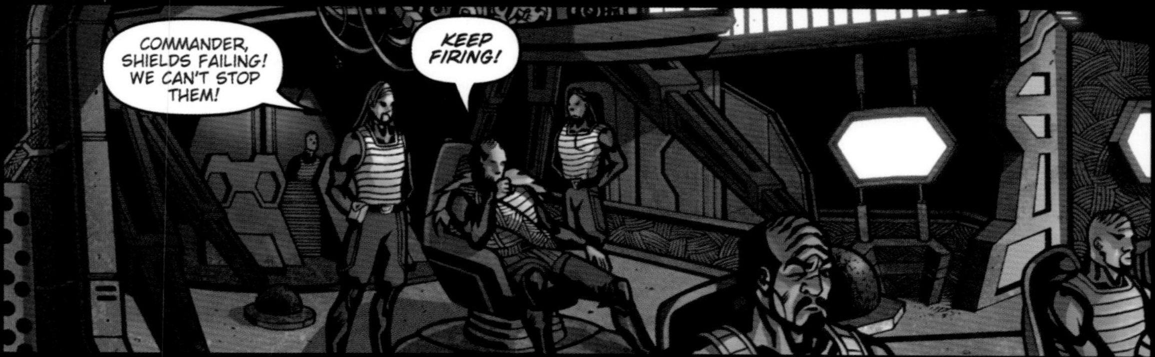
COMMANDER, SHIELDS FAILING! WE CAN'T STOP THEM!
KEEP FIRING!

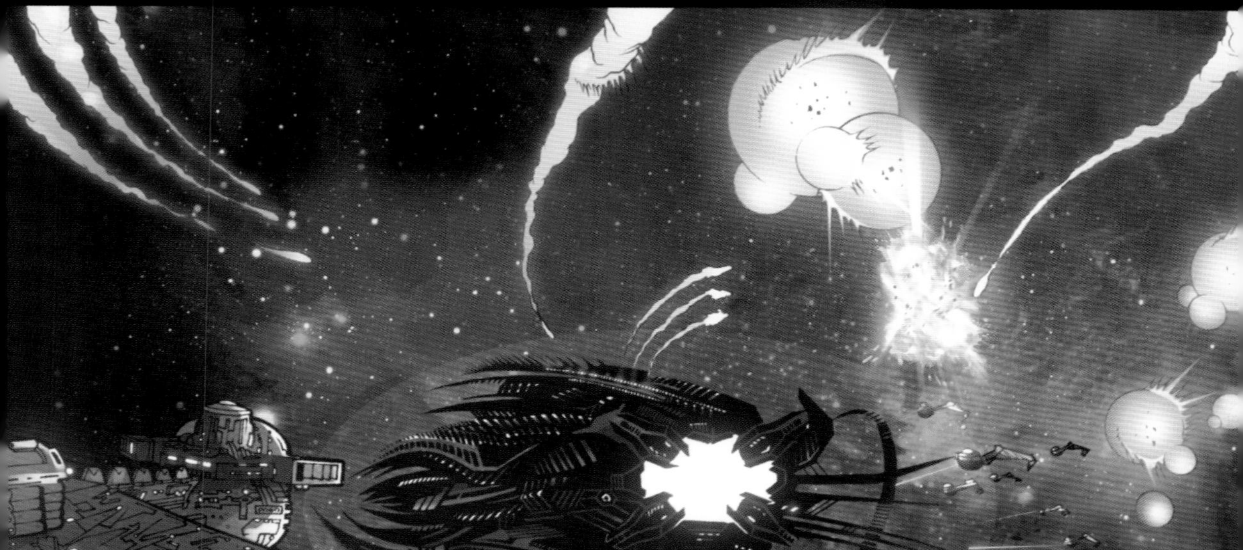

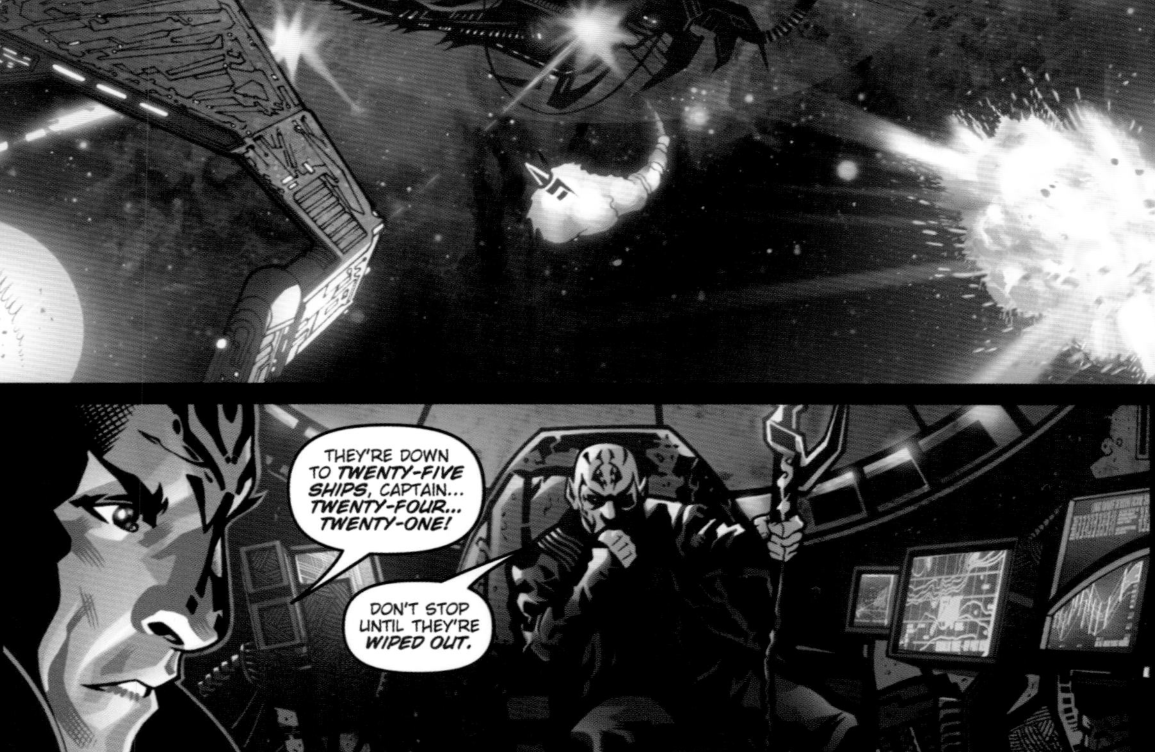
THEY'RE DOWN TO TWENTY-FIVE SHIPS, CAPTAIN... TWENTY-FOUR... TWENTY-ONE!
DON'T STOP UNTIL THEY'RE WIPED OUT.

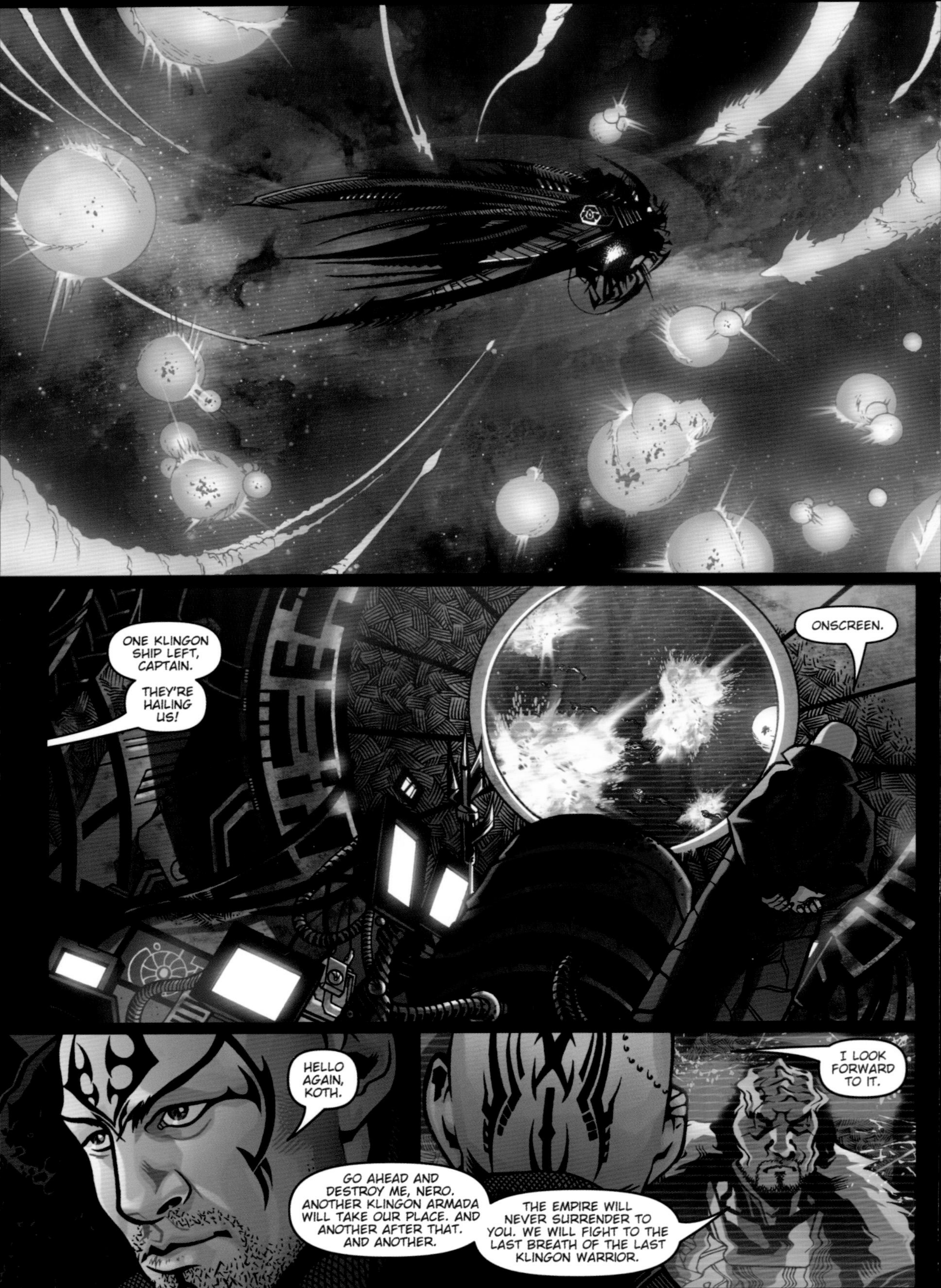
ONE KLINGON SHIP LEFT, CAPTAIN.
THEY'RE HAILING US!
ONSCREEN.
HELLO AGAIN, KOTH.
I LOOK FORWARD TO IT.
GO AHEAD AND DESTROY ME, NERO. ANOTHER KLINGON ARMADA WILL TAKE OUR PLACE. AND ANOTHER AFTER THAT. AND ANOTHER.
THE EMPIRE WILL NEVER SURRENDER TO YOU. WE WILL FIGHT TO THE LAST BREATH OF THE LAST KLINGON WARRIOR.

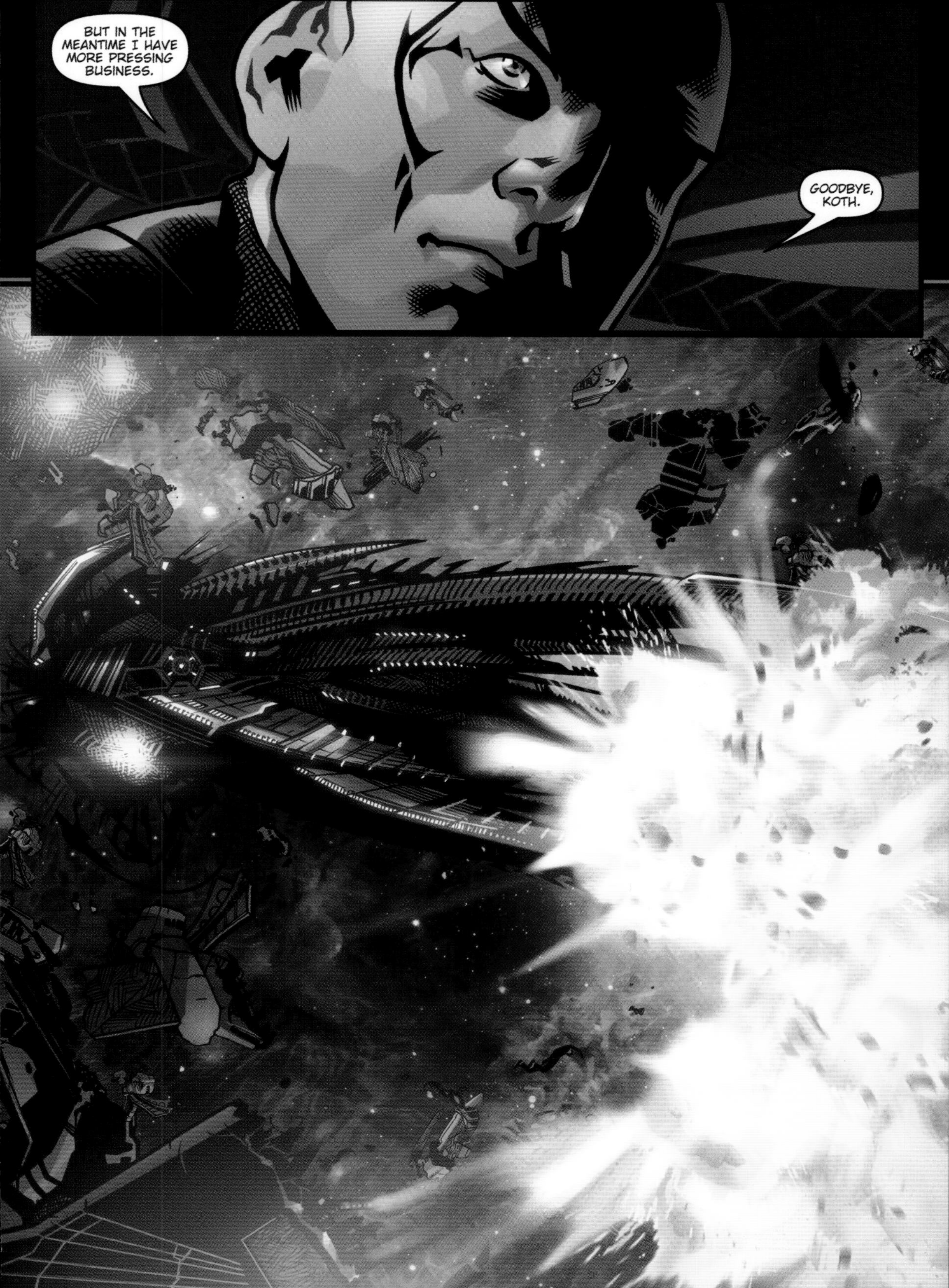
BUT IN THE MEANTIME I HAVE MORE PRESSING BUSINESS.
GOODBYE, KOTH.

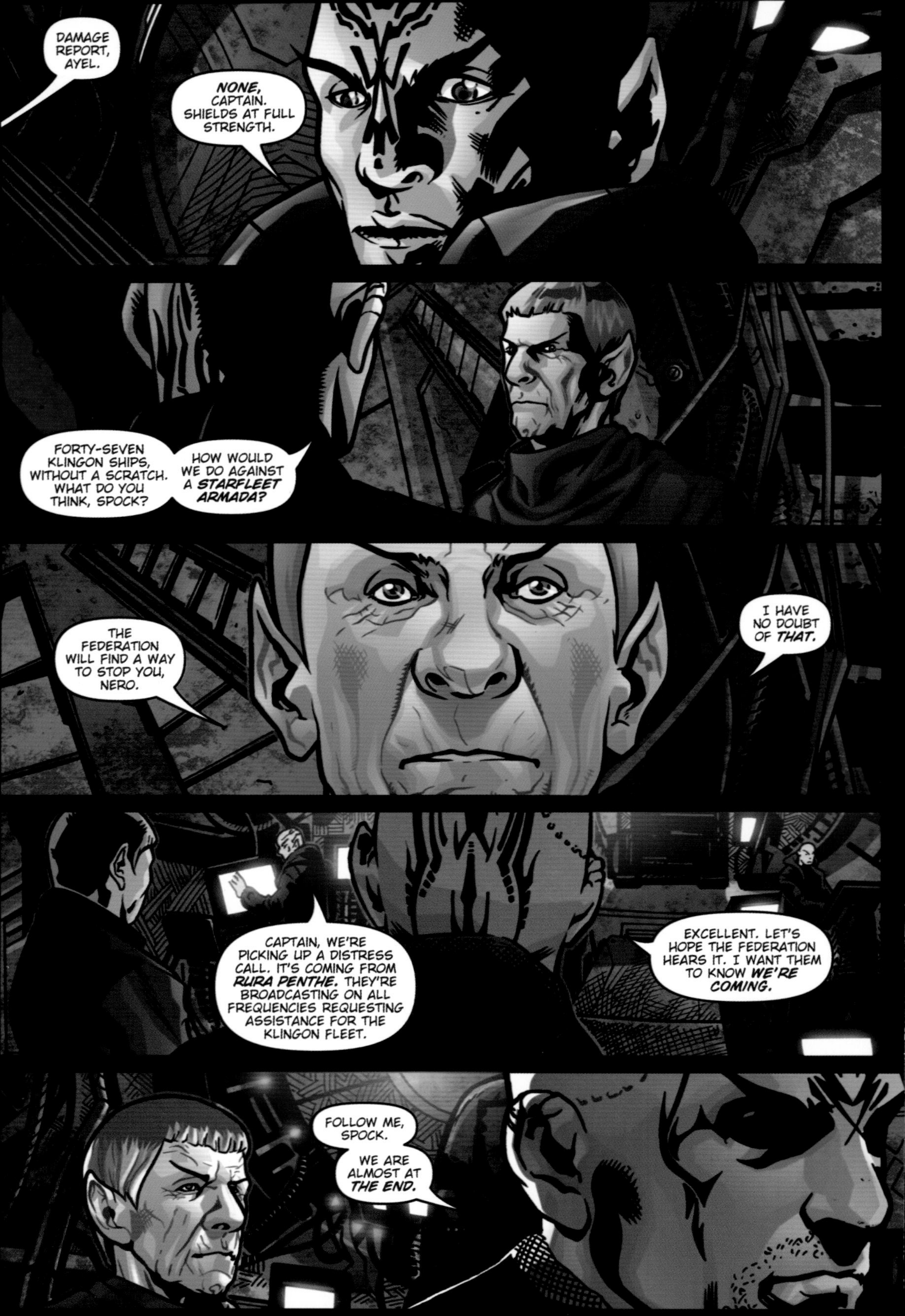
DAMAGE REPORT, AYEL.
NONE, CAPTAIN. SHIELDS AT FULL STRENGTH.
FORTY-SEVEN KLINGON SHIPS, WITHOUT A SCRATCH. WHAT DO YOU THINK, SPOCK?
HOW WOULD WE DO AGAINST A STARFLEET ARMADA?
THE FEDERATION WILL FIND A WAY TO STOP YOU, NERO.
I HAVE NO DOUBT OF THAT.
CAPTAIN, WE'RE PICKING UP A DISTRESS CALL. IT'S COMING FROM RURA PENTHE. THEY'RE BROADCASTING ON ALL FREQUENCIES REQUESTING ASSISTANCE FOR THE KLINGON FLEET.
EXCELLENT. LET'S HOPE THE FEDERATION HEARS IT. I WANT THEM TO KNOW WE'RE COMING.
FOLLOW ME, SPOCK.
WE ARE ALMOST AT THE END.

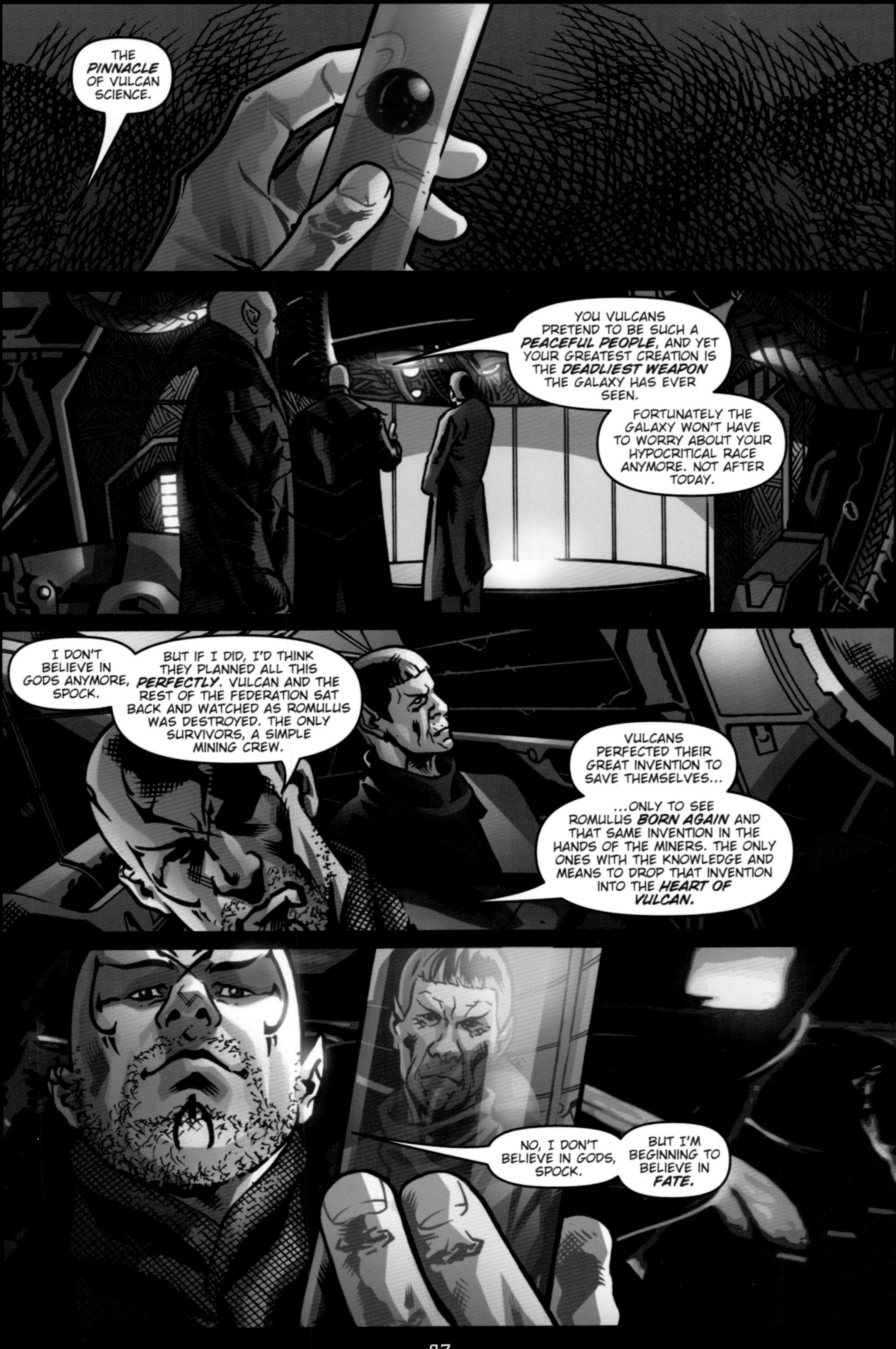
THE PINNACLE OF VULCAN SCIENCE.
YOU VULCANS PRETEND TO BE SUCH A PEACEFUL PEOPLE, AND YET YOUR GREATEST CREATION IS THE DEADLIEST WEAPON THE GALAXY HAS EVER SEEN.
FORTUNATELY THE GALAXY WON'T HAVE TO WORRY ABOUT YOUR HYPOCRITICAL RACE ANYMORE. NOT AFTER TODAY.
I DON'T BELIEVE IN GODS ANYMORE, SPOCK.
BUT IF I DID, I'D THINK THEY PLANNED ALL THIS PERFECTLY. VULCAN AND THE REST OF THE FEDERATION SAT BACK AND WATCHED AS ROMULUS WAS DESTROYED. THE ONLY SURVIVORS, A SIMPLE MINING CREW.
VULCANS PERFECTED THEIR GREAT INVENTION TO SAVE THEMSELVES...
...ONLY TO SEE ROMULUS BORN AGAIN AND THAT SAME INVENTION IN THE HANDS OF THE MINERS. THE ONLY ONES WITH THE KNOWLEDGE AND MEANS TO DROP THAT INVENTION INTO THE HEART OF VULCAN.
NO, I DON'T BELIEVE IN GODS, SPOCK.
BUT I'M BEGINNING TO BELIEVE IN FATE.

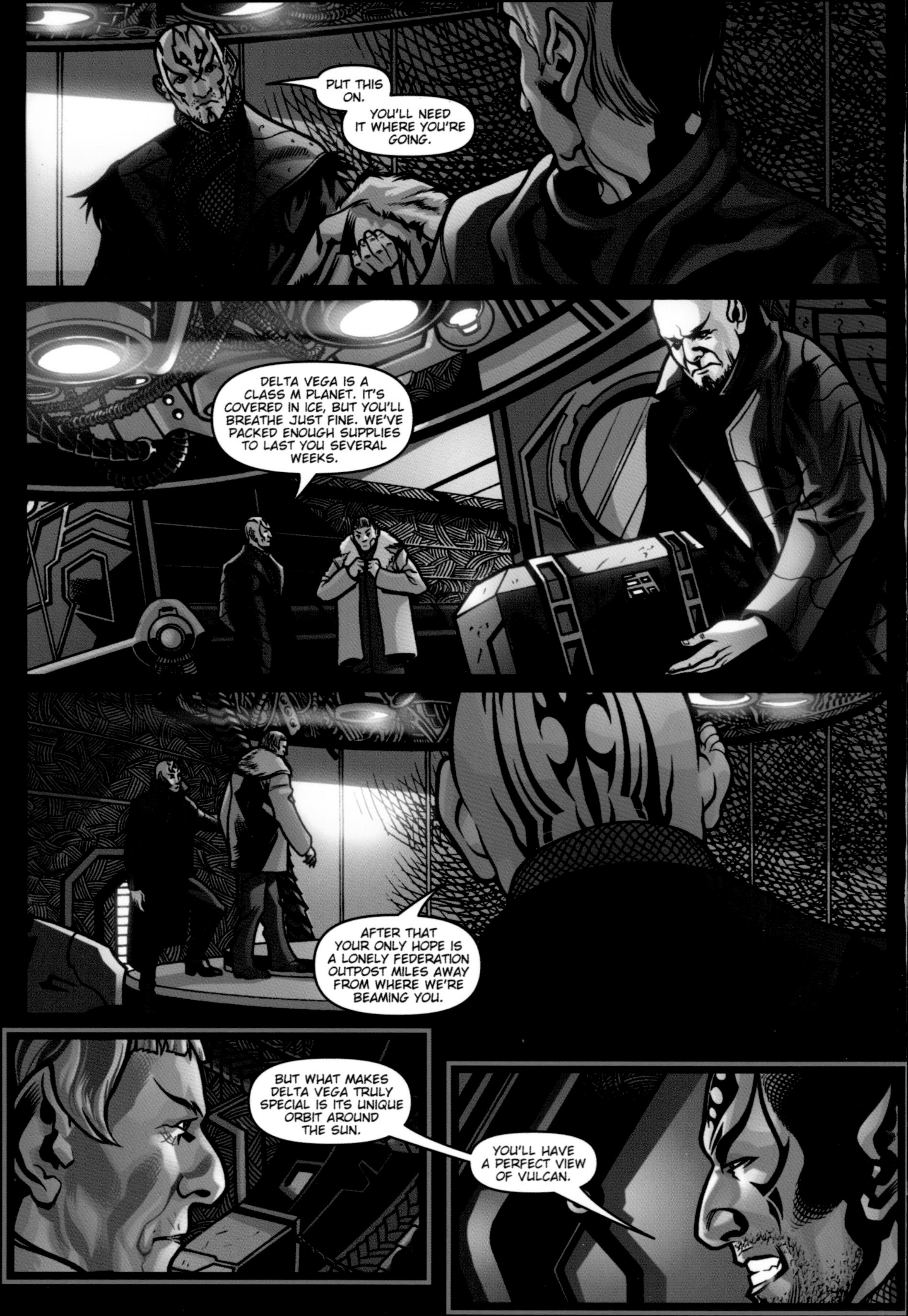
PUT THIS ON.
YOU'LL NEED IT WHERE YOU'RE GOING.
DELTA VEGA IS A CLASS M PLANET. IT'S COVERED IN ICE, BUT YOU'LL BREATHE JUST FINE. WE'VE PACKED ENOUGH SUPPLIES TO LAST YOU SEVERAL WEEKS.
AFTER THAT YOUR ONLY HOPE IS A LONELY FEDERATION OUTPOST MILES AWAY FROM WHERE WE'RE BEAMING YOU.
BUT WHAT MAKES DELTA VEGA TRULY SPECIAL IS ITS UNIQUE ORBIT AROUND THE SUN.
YOU'LL HAVE A PERFECT VIEW OF VULCAN.

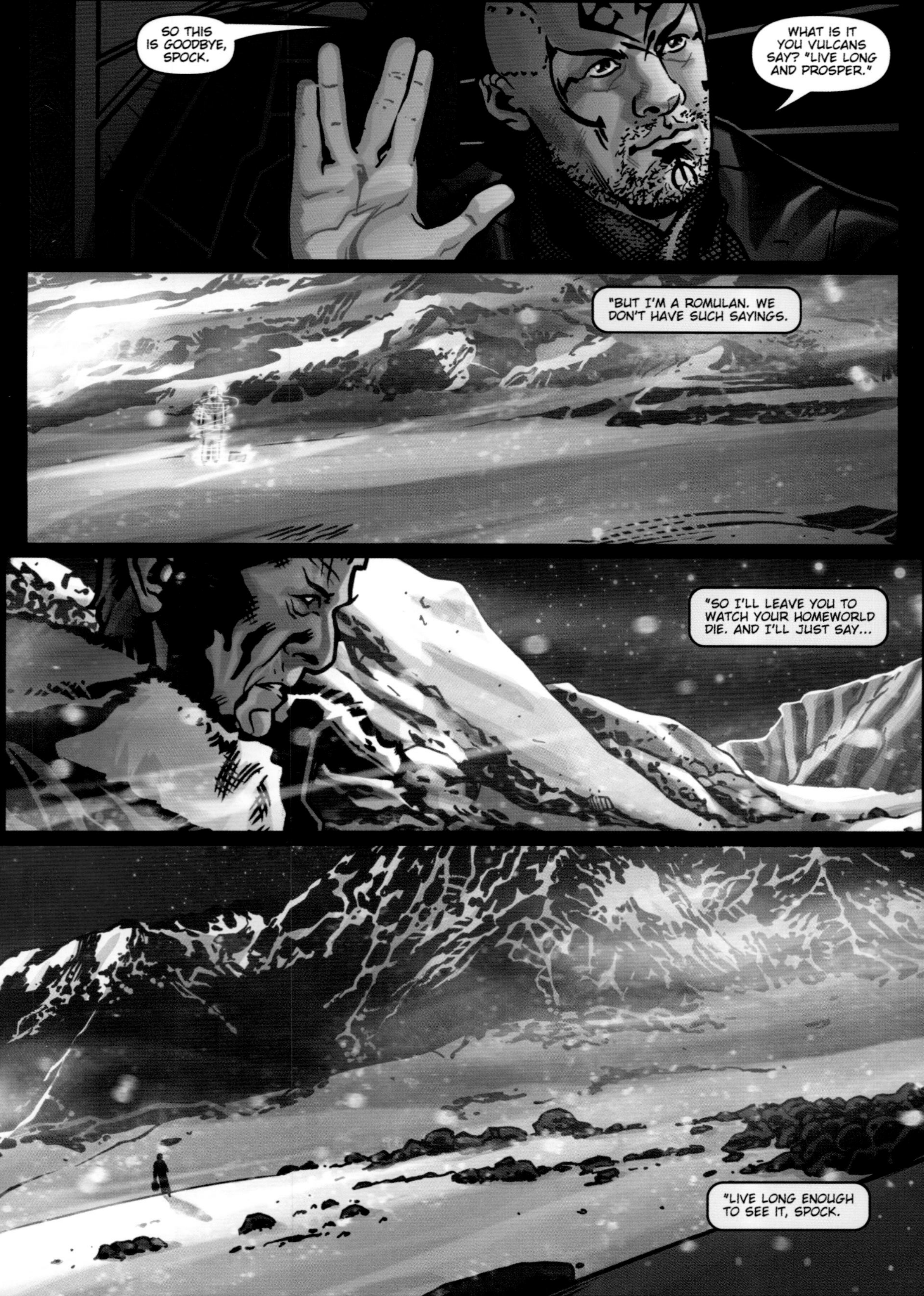
SO THIS IS GOODBYE, SPOCK.
WHAT IS IT YOU VULCANS SAY? "LIVE LONG AND PROSPER."
"BUT I'M A ROMULAN. WE DON'T HAVE SUCH SAYINGS.
"SO I'LL LEAVE YOU TO WATCH YOUR HOMEWORLD DIE. AND I'LL JUST SAY...
"LIVE LONG ENOUGH TO SEE IT, SPOCK.

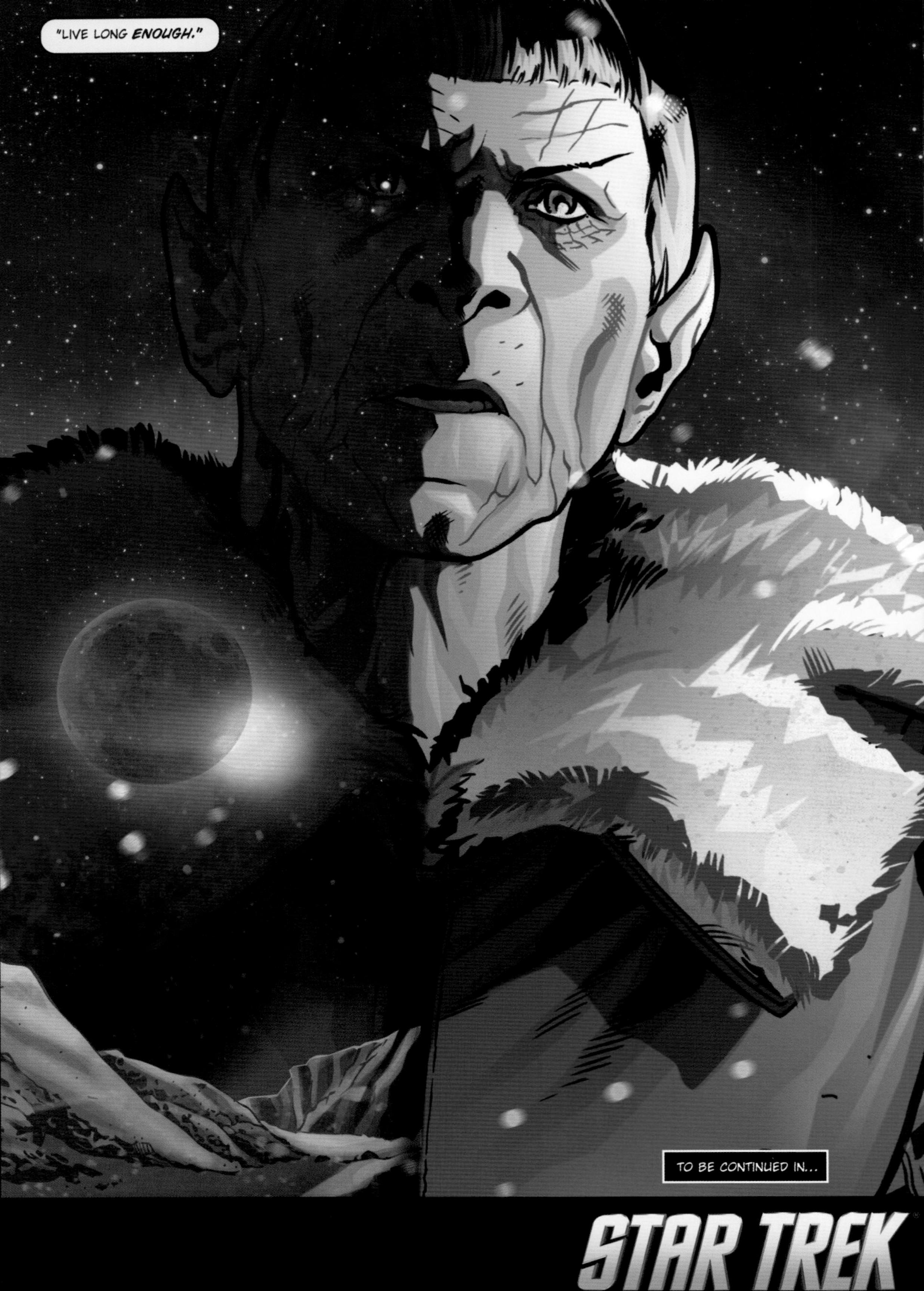
"LIVE LONG ENOUGH."
TO BE CONTINUED IN...
STAR TREK

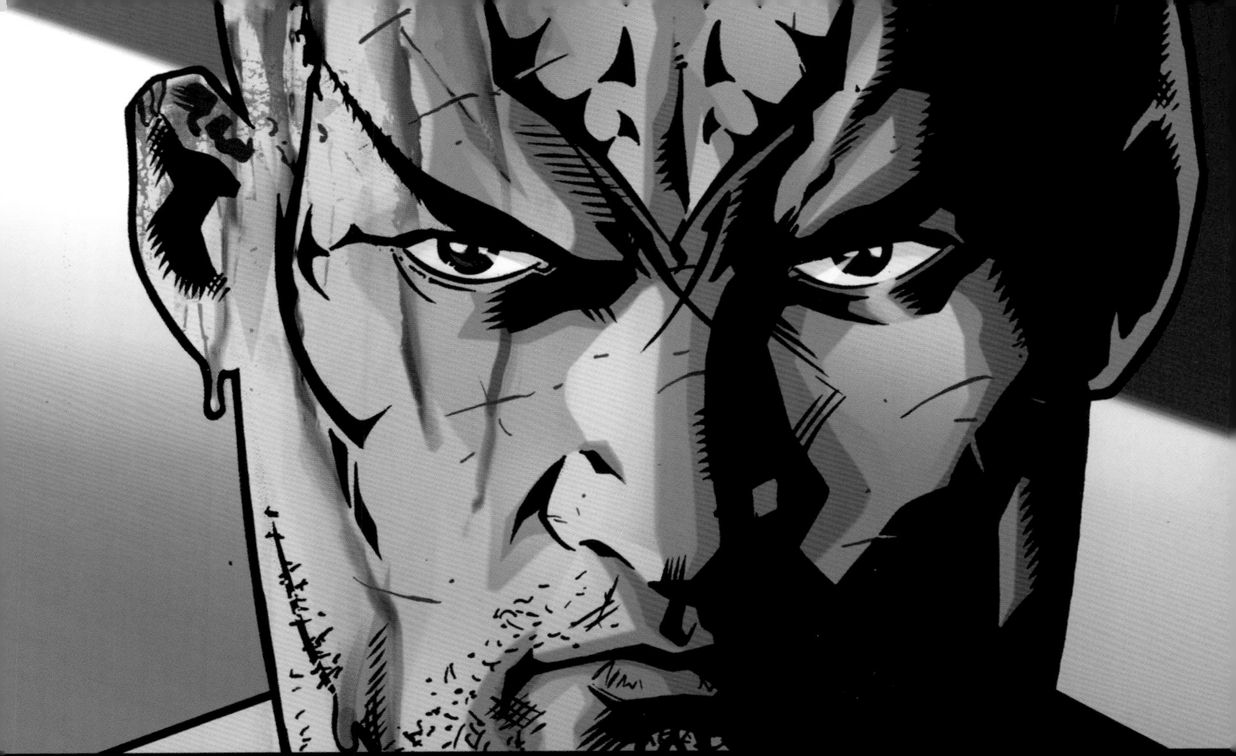

STAR TREK®
NERO
DAVID MESSINA ART GALLERY

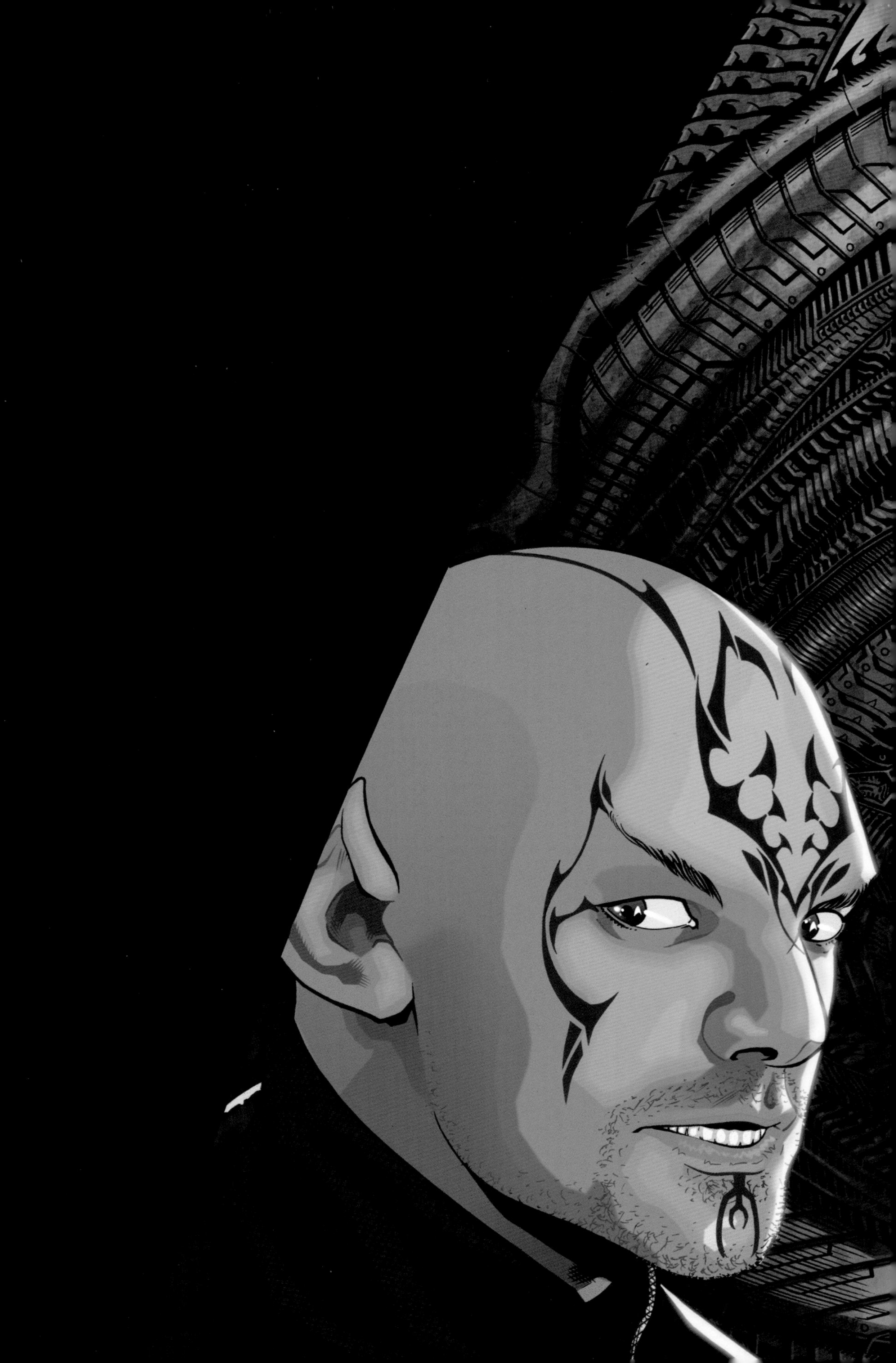

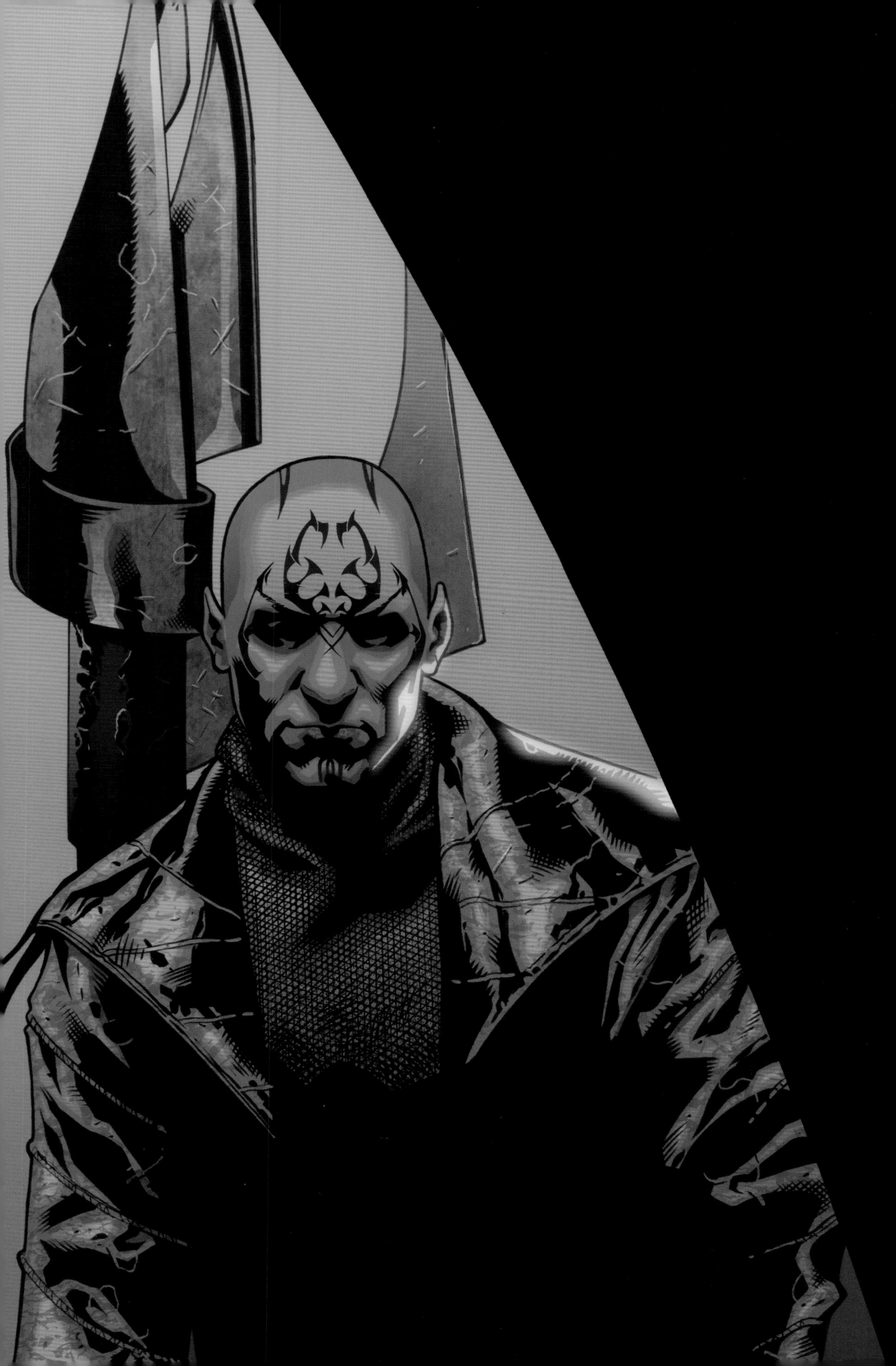

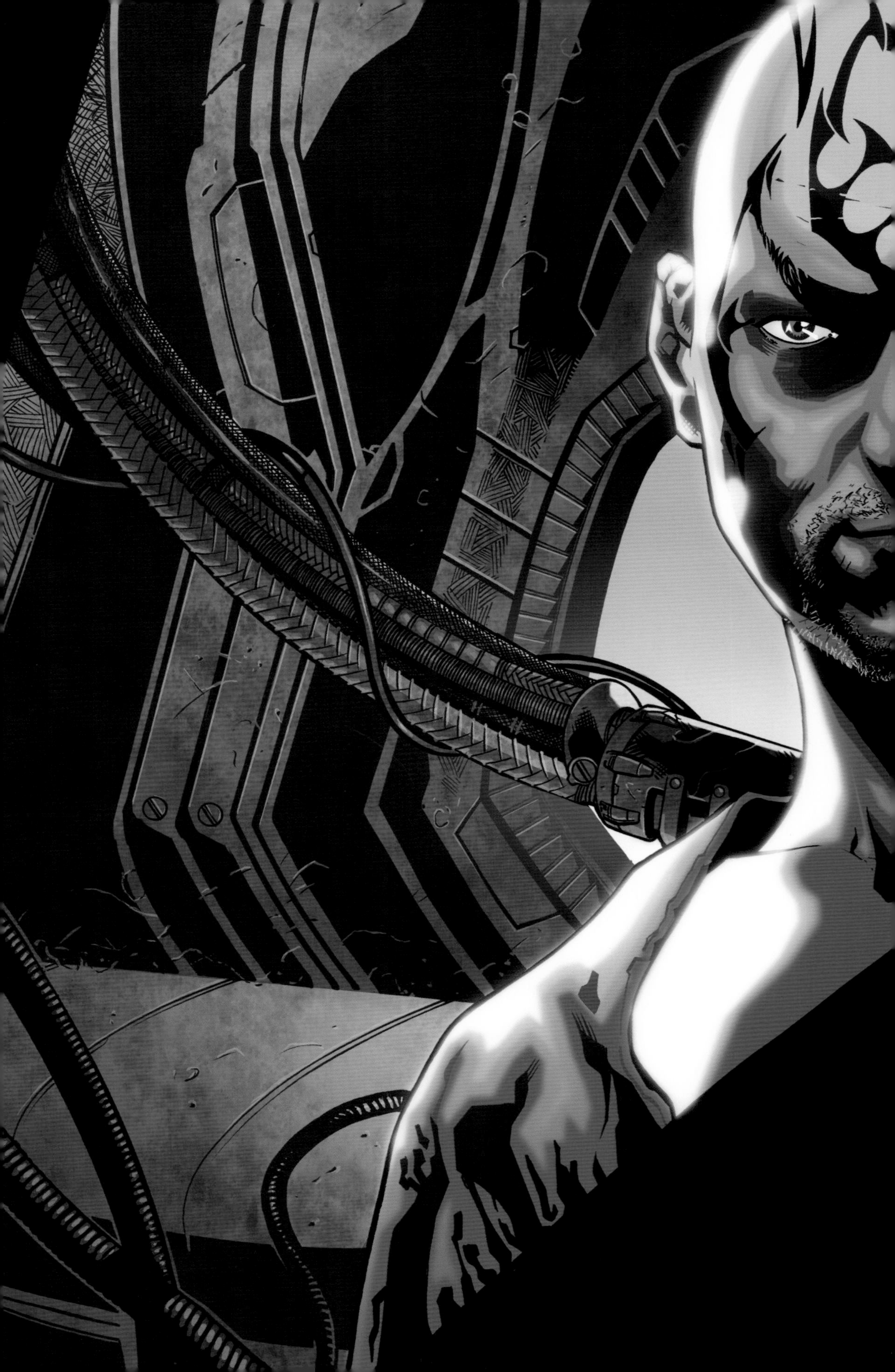

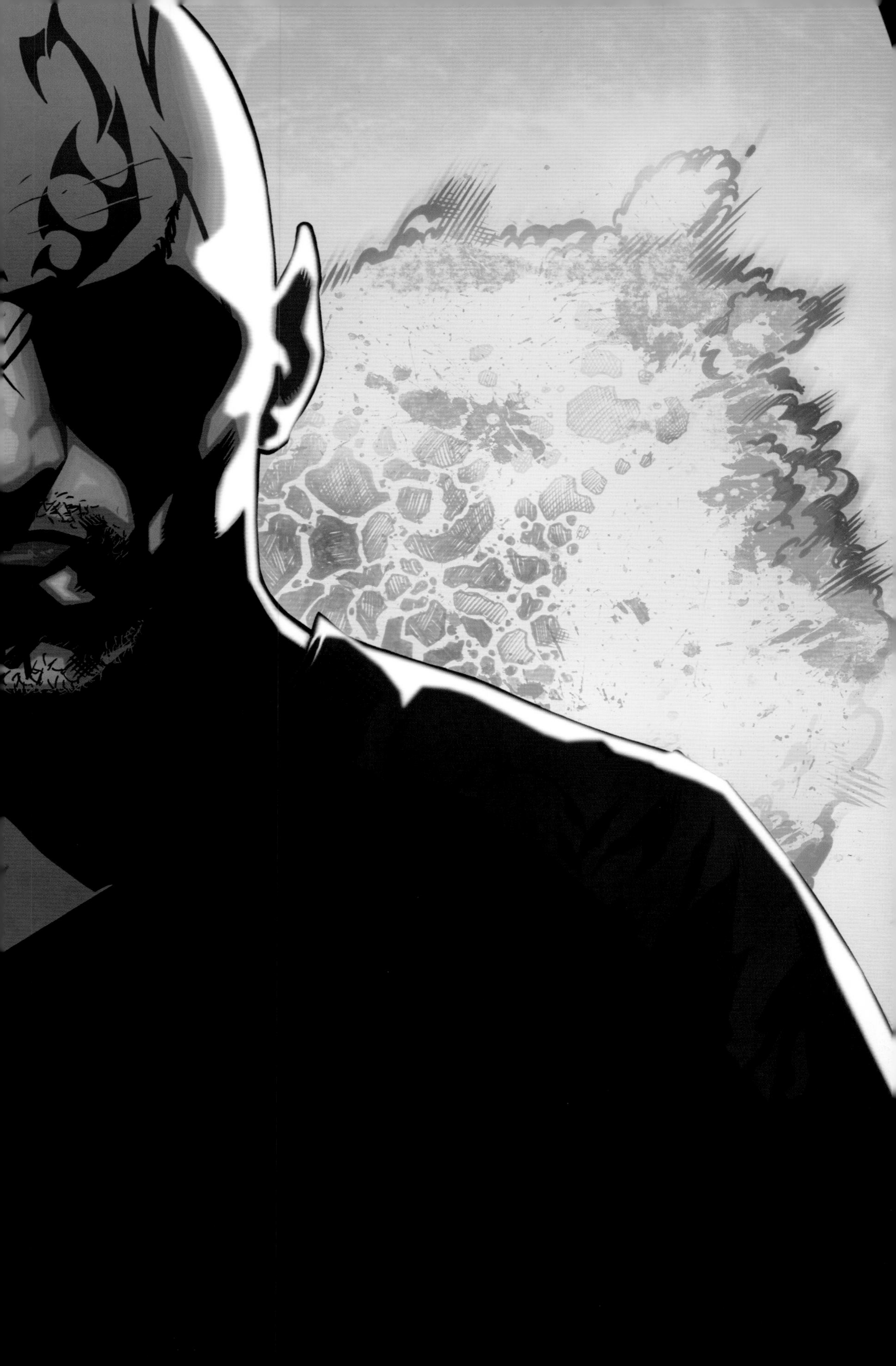

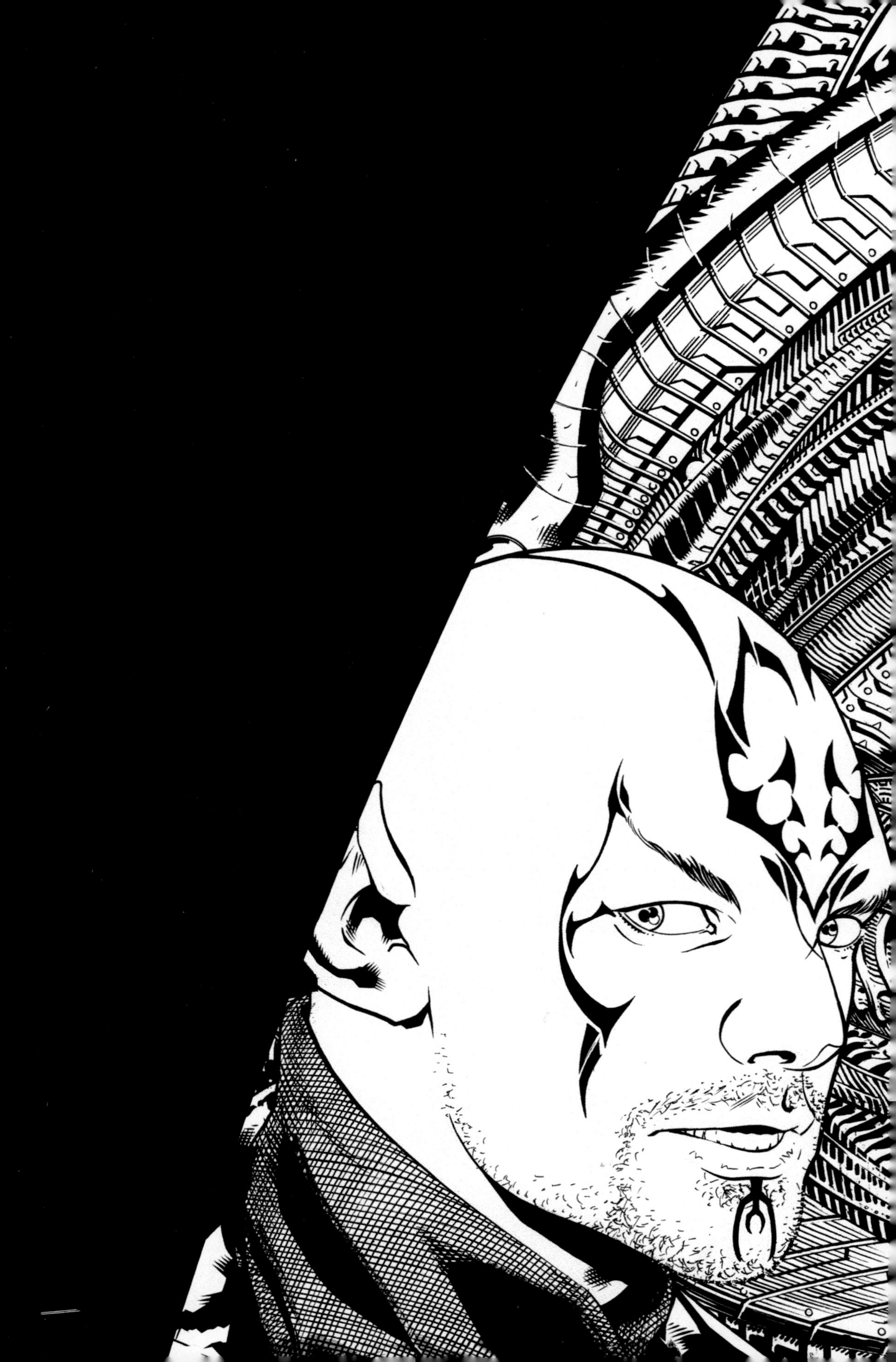

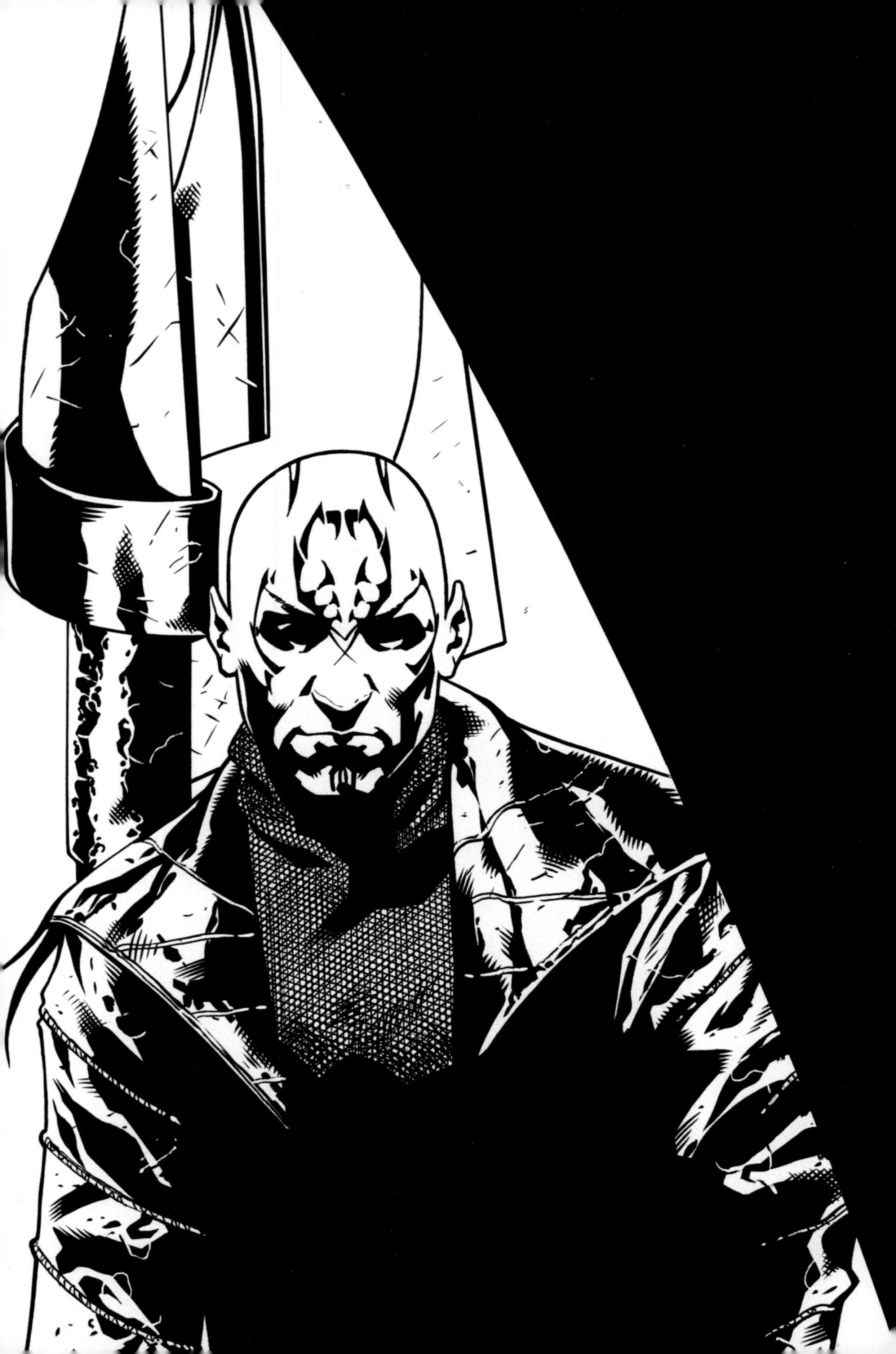

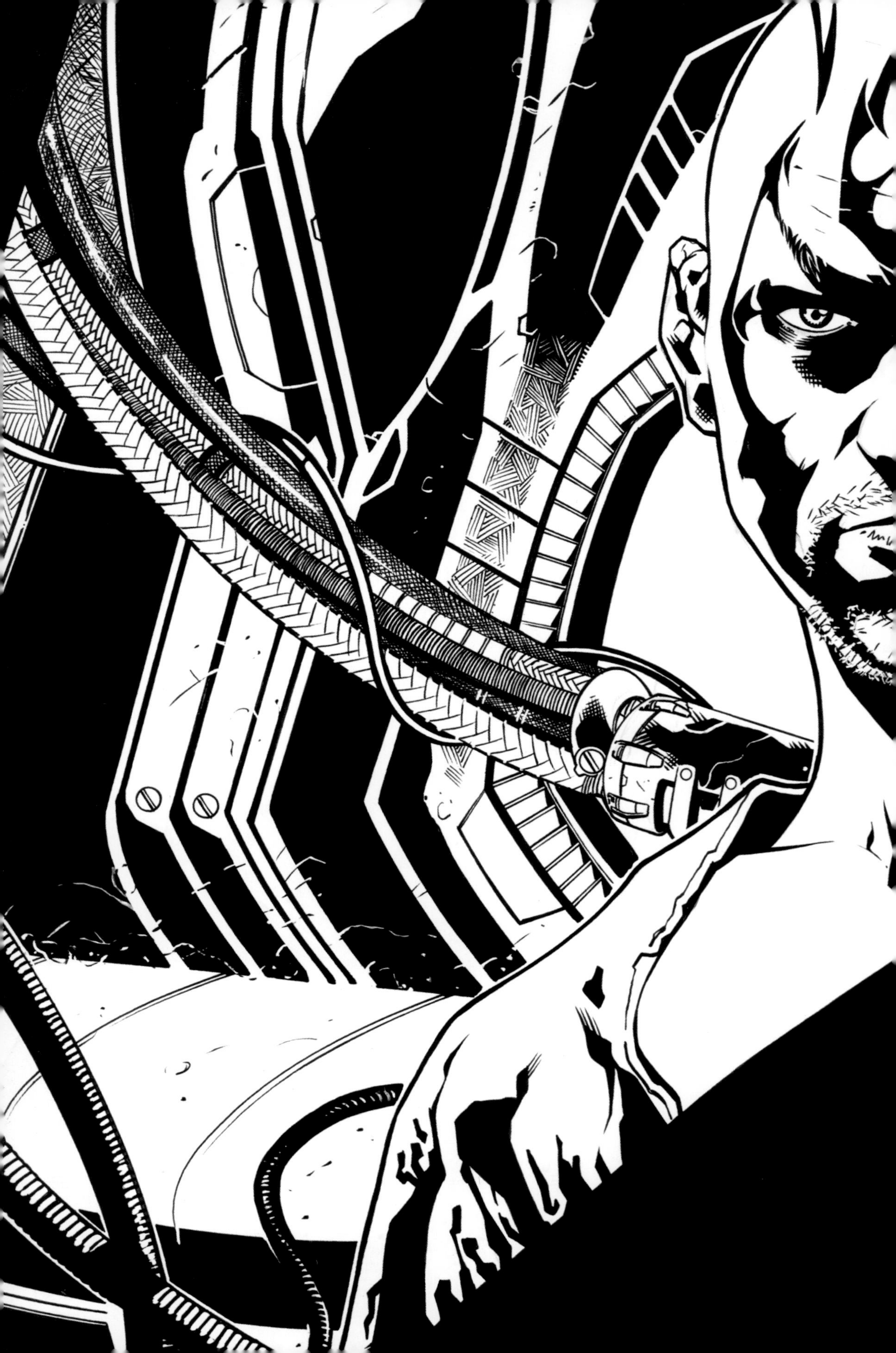

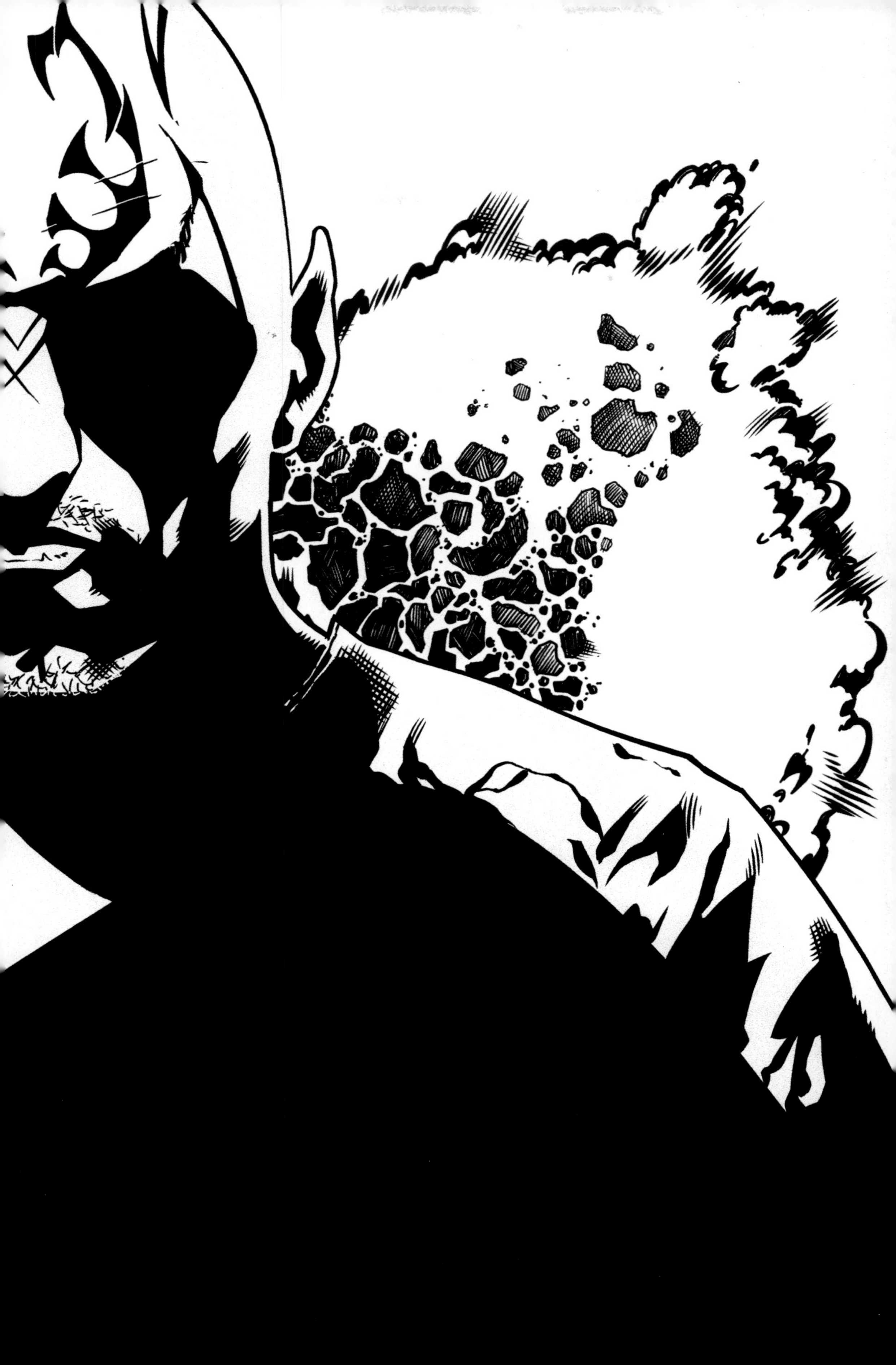

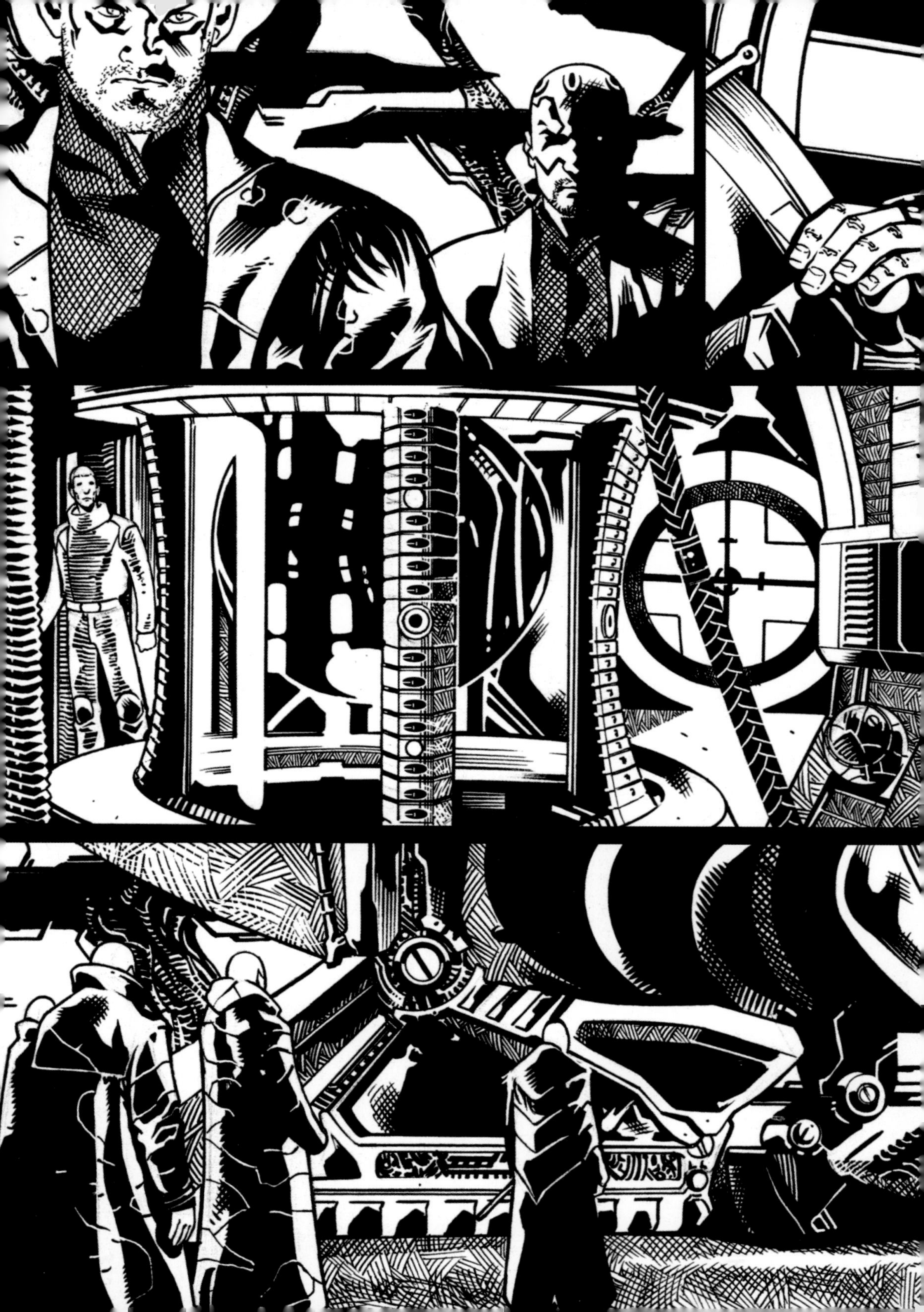

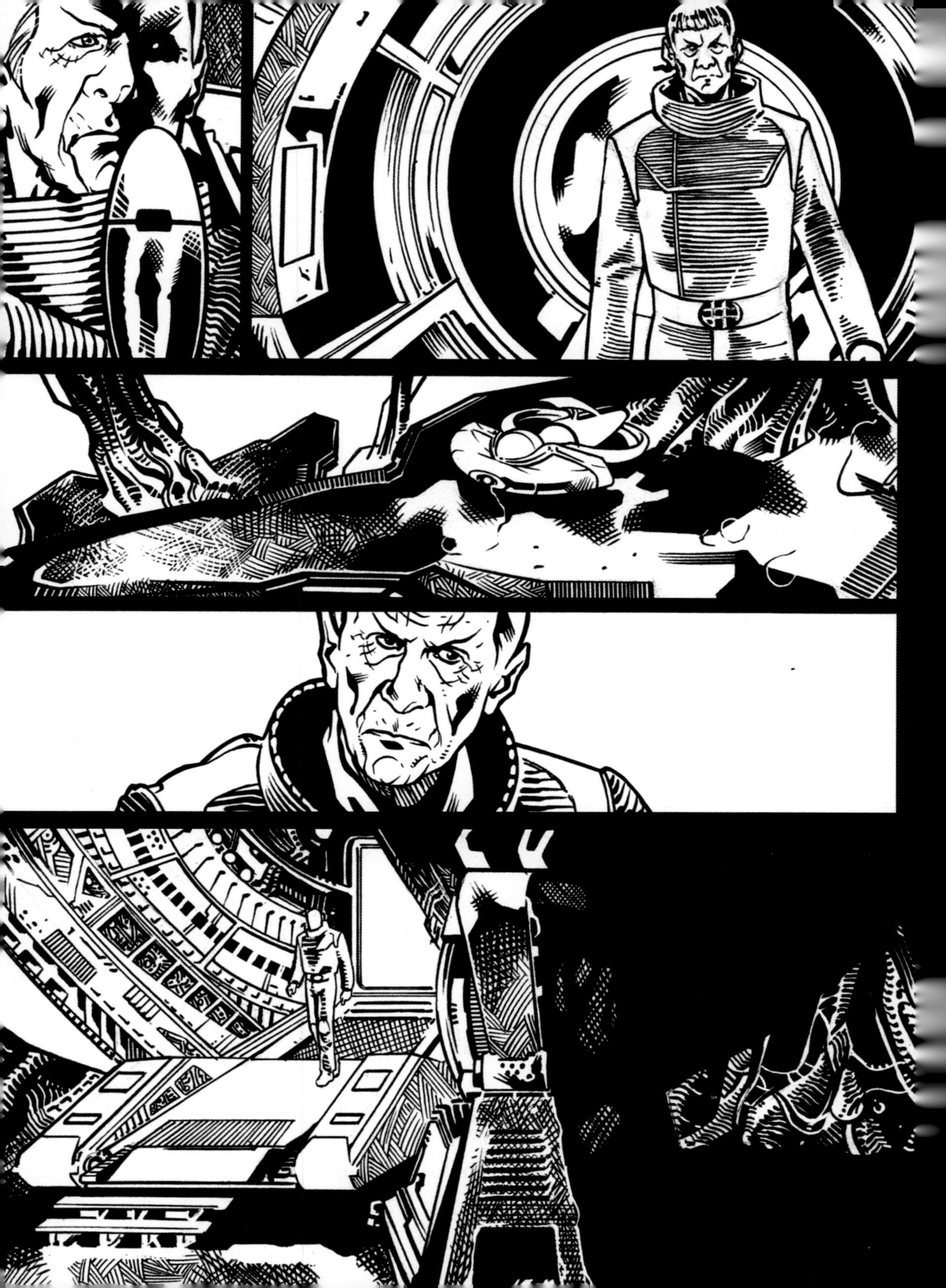

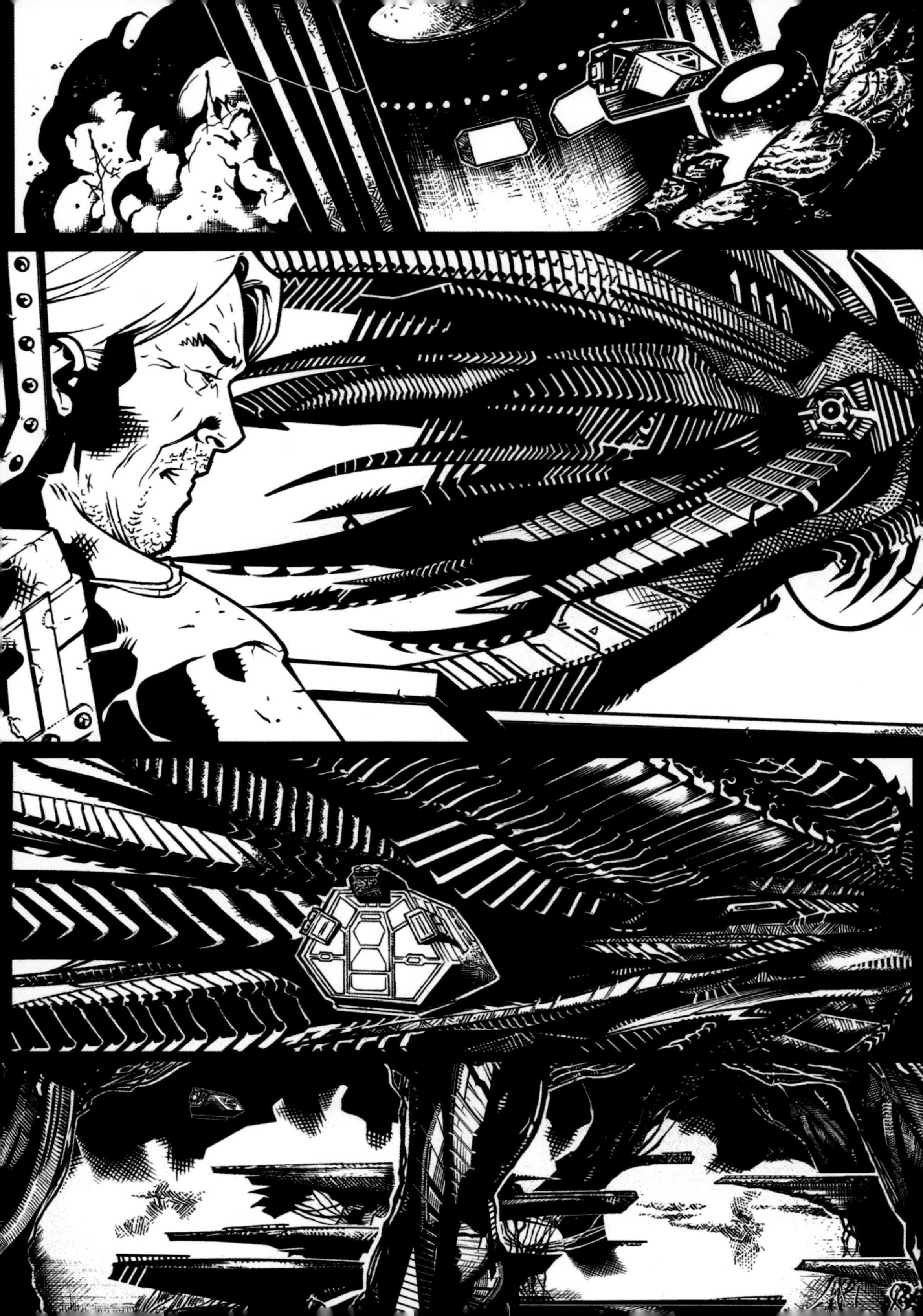

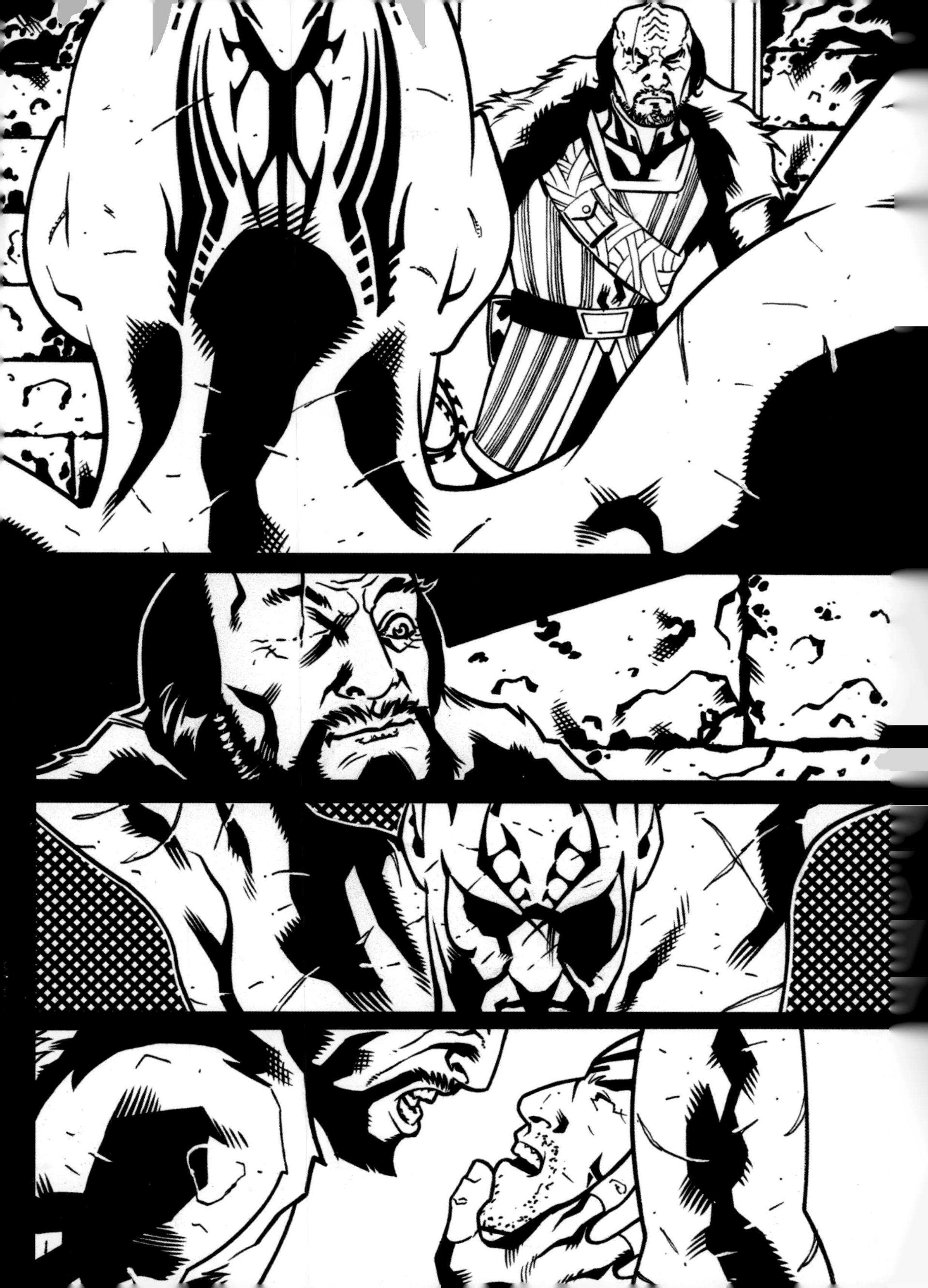

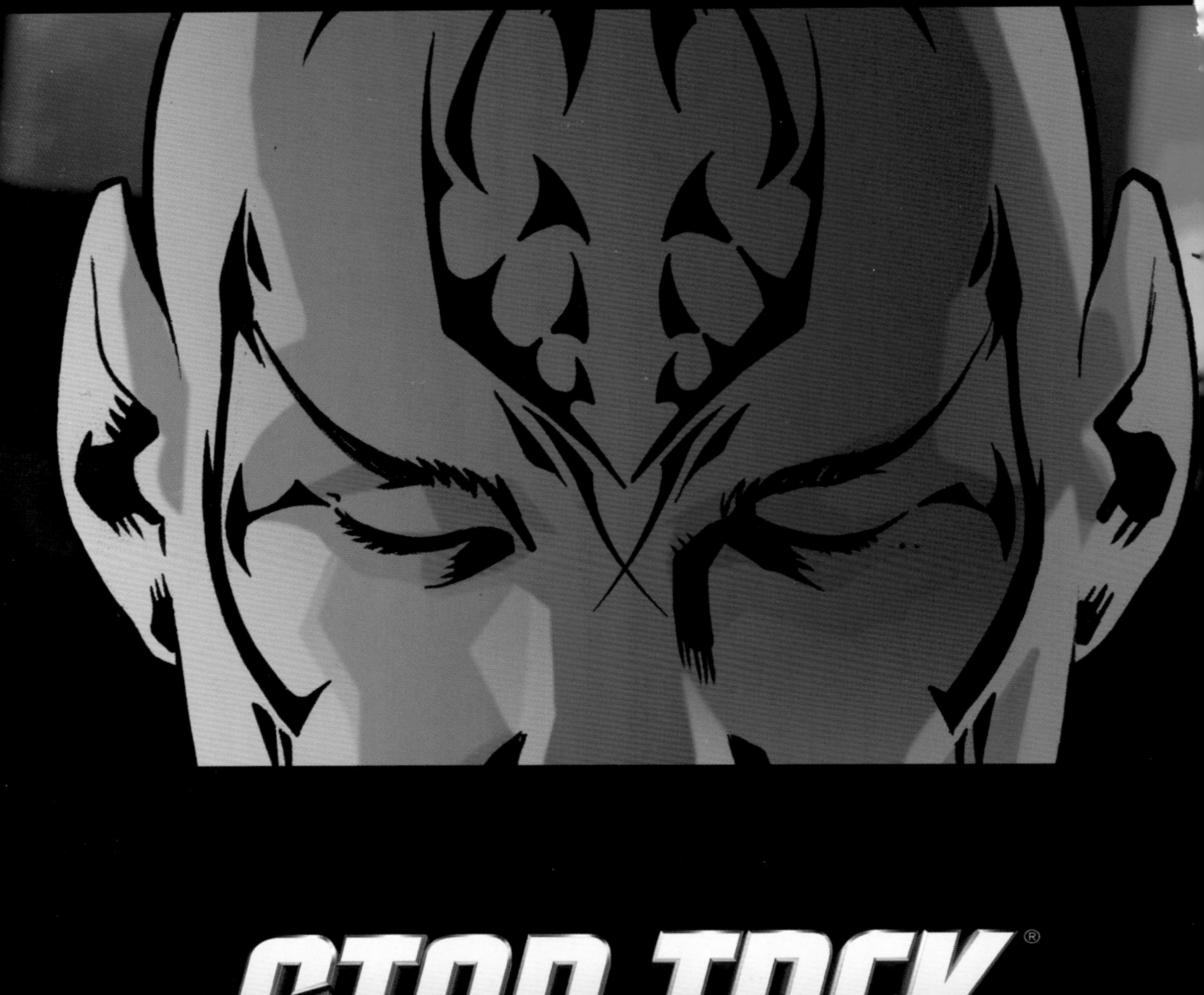

STAR TREK®

NERO